# ROGUE NEPTUNE:

## YEMEN CRISIS, BOOK 1 of 2

(Book 14 of the Rogue Submarine Series)

By John R. Monteith

## Braveship Books

D1596677

## PROLOGUE

Jake Slate considered his boss' personal bunker luxurious. With three-quarters of the building underground, Pierre Renard's hideout near Avignon, France was a mansion beneath a mansion.

In a chamber of stone walls, Jake adjusted his buttocks in the plush leather padding and rested his elbows on his chair's maple armrests. The sprawling mahogany table before him held crystal glasses and pitchers of bubbling mineral water, and familiar faces surrounded him.

Across the polished surface, the silver-haired Henri Lanier was a dichotomy of impeccable dress and invaluable knowledge of the dirtiest, greasiest systems of the *Scorpène*-class submarines, *Specter* and *Wraith*. His dark blazer outlined his torso like a second skin.

Contrasting the mechanic's appearance, the toad-headed creature to his left, Antoine Remy, wrinkled his starched white shirt by simply breathing. But since he could hear a pin drop from across the room, Jake silenced his criticisms about his appearance for fear of the sonar technician hearing his thoughts.

At Jake's right, Claude LaFontaine chewed nicotine gum in a battle to survive the gathering without lighting a cigarette. Thinner than a rail, the engineering expert could bend and twist into any corner of a propulsion plant to diagnose and fix anything.

Seated at the table's head to Jake's left, Pierre Renard epitomized grace under pressure.

Having endured the loss of his first family, imprisonment of his present loved ones, two failed nuclear weapons heists, decades of scrutiny by multiple intelligence agencies, extortion by the CIA, the theft of his flagship, and the weight of countless widows, Renard could have retired with an admirable scorecard. But his calling of this meeting and his bristling mood suggested an ongoing pursuit.

Jake faced his aging friend and listened.

Renard addressed the group in French. "We've been through much together, have we not, my friends?"

As four heads nodded, Jake commented. "Sure. And it sounds like we're about to go through some more tough challenges, by the looks of it."

Renard smirked. "You know me well. You all do. And challenges, indeed. Before I bring the others online, I wanted a private word with my inner confidants."

Henri balked. "Then shall we excuse Jake?"

Jake retorted in English. "Bite me."

After the chuckles subsided, the mansion's owner continued. "Jake may be American, but he's an honorary Frenchman in my reckoning." Renard's eyes narrowed. "And you'd better keep trusting him, for the mission I'm about to share with you will test us like never before."

The American found the announcement dramatic, even for his flamboyant boss.

The fleet's patriarch looked away in thought. "I'm getting old, and I've committed many sins..."

Fidgety without cigarettes, LaFontaine interrupted his boss. "You're not as old as Henri, and he committed enough sins for ten lifetimes during our port call to Morocco in Ninety-six. If he remembers any of it is a different matter."

Across the table, the mechanic blushed. "I won't challenge the sins. I was young and... well, I was just young."

LaFontaine countered. "You were in your mid-thirties!"

"Yes! Like I said, 'young'! And I still look better than Pierre, if I do say so myself."

Renard reigned in his team. "Enough. It's not a contest. It's a confession of sorts. Even after my latest investments in our fleet, I'm sitting on a mountain of resources that I cannot spend appropriately in my lifetime. Therefore, I believe it's time I should finance an undertaking for mankind's greater good."

Believing every mission he'd chosen to accept after the Colorado Incident had been for mankind's greater good, Jake wanted to challenge the patriarch but held his tongue.

"I've garnered matching support from several benefactors, and I've cleared a path for a humanitarian undertaking with the United Nations."

Doubting the toothless organization's power, Jake protested. "Even if anyone gave a damn about the United Nations, you don't have a seat there."

"But my network reaches the French ambassador to the UN, and fortunately, the crisis in Yemen is a perfect opportunity to supply a ravaged land with French goods while overcoming the UN's inability to deliver humanitarian aid."

Jake's head spun. "Yemen is a disaster. What good can we hope to do there?"

Renard's slow nod hinted at his answer. "This will be our Long War. There's no defined target we can destroy to claim victory. Instead, we'll create an opening for the United Nations and other humanitarian groups to bring aid safely to those in need."

"You need to let us blow something up, Pierre." Jake flipped his fingers dismissively. "Otherwise, I quit."

"There will be plenty of opportunity for creating explosions. In the first phase, we'll fight to retake the strategic island of Socotra, which the Emirates now control, and from there we'll bring aid to the mainland."

Feeling the reality of battle lurking ahead with the mention of a real adversary, Jake checked his mental catalogue of Emirati military might. "The UAE is small but serious. They've got some modern stuff in their arsenal."

"Indeed, they do. On the sea and in the air. Make no mistake about it, they will resist us credibly. Then as a second phase, we'll take Aden in the Gulf of Aden, to free its people and restage the remnants of the Yemeni Navy there. Beyond that, it's speculative."

Jake protested. "We take and free... but for how long? You called it our Long War, but we're not an occupying force."

"No. But we are capable of defending, and we'll hold these ports against a multitude of navies against a frenzy of enemies we will have created during our takings. I'll also watch what the

Saudis and Houthis do with Al Hudaydah, which is a crucial Red Sea port through which flows the bulk of humanitarian aid."

"Shit, Pierre. That sounds like we're the entire resistance." Jake caught and corrected his incomplete thought. "And from what little I know, Yemen has about two dozen resistances fighting among themselves already. Who are we shooting at, or deterring, or... stealing from?"

"Let me explain." Renard sipped water and then lowered his crystal glass. "It's an isolated Arab issue thus far, which explains the lack of international aid. The worst actors are the Houthi rebels. Beyond that, alliances become murky. I shan't bore you with the details, but suffice it to say that the land battles involve the Saudis, the Emirates, the Houthis, the proper Yemeni government under President Hadi, the secessionist group called the Southern Separatists, ISIS, and Al-Qaeda."

Jake highlighted a distinction. "We don't fight on land, and given that list of hostiles, I thank God for it. Other than sending railgun rounds into distant ground troops, we fight in the water. So, what are you leaving out?"

"The Iranians."

The American found the news incongruent. "That doesn't make sense. They're not an invading or occupying navy. They're a sneaky, lurking, mini-armada of small submarines designed to wreck your surface ships."

The challenge energized the patriarch. "True, but consider how nicely the Iranians pair up with the Emiratis if allied."

Jake conceded the point. "That would be a formidable navy, but isn't the UAE aligned with the Saudis, who hate the Iranians?"

"The Saudis and the Emirates... these so-called allies are becoming less aligned and more competitive for control as the crisis drags on. And with the Saudis backed by the United States and the Emirates backed by Iran, you can see a natural split forming."

After listening in silence, Henri spoke. "What do you intend for us to do about it?"

Renard assumed a familiar cryptic tone. "It's my most elaborate plan, and I will only divulge information only sparingly. It's for your own safety, really, as a matter of proper safeguarding."

The mechanic pressed further. "What can you tell us, then?"

"We'll begin the operation with only half our navy, assuming we can sneak the *Wraith* through the Suez Canal."

The mechanic raised an eyebrow. "Sneak?"

"Yes, I've told you about this before. In the event the Egyptians bar us from using the Suez, I've created a means to get a submarine through. However, it's just for one submarine, and it's impossible for the *Goliath*. So, we'll sneak the *Wraith* through, and it will join the *Xerses*, which is en route to the area. The *Specter* and *Goliath* will have to take the long way around Africa, I'm afraid."

Jake calculated the delays. "This will take weeks for even the first ship to show up."

"I told you, this is a long war. You remember the patience required when we moved the *Goliath* into the Black Sea. That's the sort of endurance you'll need now, only two to three times as long as that, depending what transpires and how long we dare hold the ports open against whomever should challenge us."

Shifting thoughts to his family, Jake considered their well-being during his absence. "My step-children? They've been hiding here since that thing with Olivia blew up."

"Miss McDonald is no longer a factor–for us or anyone, since she's facing possible criminal charges. So, you could send them home without harassment by the CIA. However, I advise against it since we will have new enemies. Arab nations will know of our involvement soon."

"I suppose Linda could homeschool them here."

"Or use any of the tutors I will find for you. Regardless, before approaching the other key members of the fleet, I wanted to witness your reactions."

Having immersed himself in divinity school, Jake challenged himself to embrace the philosophies he studied. Charity reigned above many of the virtues filling his mind. "I'm in."

Without hesitation, the other three Renard-loyalists agreed.

"Excellent, my friends. I thank you all, and I must say, I'm hardly surprised."

Before exploring the details with the rest of the fleet's leaders, Jake voiced his final question. "So, which of these nations, pseudo-nations, and factions will we be opposing?"

Renard chuckled. "I thought you knew me better than that, my friend. I hope to avoid as many adversaries as possible, but in my planning, I've committed us to fight all of them, of course."

## CHAPTER 1

Commander Andi Amir watched the final civilian board his warship. Desperate to evacuate the innocent victims of Yemen's violence, he turned to the lean officer standing beside him. "Executive officer?"

With his neck twisted towards a young mother holding an infant in one arm while extending her other towards a waddling toddler's hand, the warship's second-in-command was a statue.

Amir tried again. "Exec!"

Dawn's light painting his white uniform blue, the thin man showed pained eyes. "What more can we do? That's the last of them, sir. I can't help but think we have room for more."

Amir glanced at the black, rugged nonskid surface of the *Tarantul*-class corvette. Although older than its commanding officer, the *Tarantul* was respectable as a failed nation's flagship. With old but complete armament, it could attack anything on the seas, and its best attribute was speed.

Forty-five knots could outrun many threats.

"It saddens me too, but the admiral's orders were clear. Immediate family only."

"It's unfair, sir. Everyone has a right to safety."

Raising his gaze, the *Tarantul's* commander faced the thin man. "Your mistake is assuming that this ship is safe. I fear we face dangers in open waters."

The executive officer scowled. "We're only two hundred and forty kilometers from Djibouti. We should make it there unchallenged."

Movement on the pier caught Amir's eye, and he looked at the approaching group. Several captains, half a dozen staff members, and the navy's lone admiral marched towards the brow connecting the concrete landing to the *Tarantul*. After seeing his headquarters' personnel fleeing to his ship, Amir reminded his executive officer about operational security. "Don't guess where we're going. Spies are everywhere, watching and listening."

"I won't, sir. But this is unheard of. What shall I do next?"

"Do as you normally do. Make ready to get underway. Station the maneuvering team and prepare to cast off all lines."

Twenty minutes later, the portly admiral paced with nervous superiority around an annoyed Commander Amir on the *Tarantul's* bridge. Two officers of captain's rank–or formerly of captain's rank before the navy's collapse and partial resurrection under President Hadi's funding–flocked around him in the crowded space.

Amir aimed his voice at the top-ranking officer. "Do I have permission to get underway, sir?"

The thick officer waved a hand. "Do so, and make haste about it! Violate any and all maritime speed limits. You know your course."

"Understood, sir." Amir turned to a young sailor wearing a sound-powered phone tethered to a long cord. "Follow me." He led the youngster to a weatherproof window, slid it open, and stuck his head over the weather deck. The salty air was cool, given the late December date. "To the executive officer, cast off all lines."

"To the executive officer, take in all lines, aye, sir." The sailor angled the speaker towards his mouth and depressed a button. "From the captain, take in all lines."

Below him on the *Tarantul's* deck, Amir's second-in-command ordered the deck team to unravel nylon mooring ropes from their cleats and toss them back to the pier.

"Captain, the executive officer reports that all lines are cast off."

"Very well, secure the maneuvering team." Amir shut the window and yelled. "Helm, left full rudder, all-ahead one-third."

A man standing by an engine order telegraph rotated a brass lever forward.

Behind Amir, the ship created swirling water in the gap between its hull and the barnacle-covered pylons. Half a football field away, the stern churned whitewash. Satisfied with his clearance from the pier, the *Tarantul's* commander returned indoors. "Helm, all-ahead two-thirds."

Through the windows, Amir saw the ship's forecastle rise in opposing motion as the twin propellers bit into the water. Five minutes and two turns later, he pushed the warship at twenty-five knots towards its false destination of Djibouti.

With the admiral and his two captains pacing and holding anxious, whispered conversations, Amir sensed tension about his ship. He sought to reduce it with forced confidence while lifting a microphone to the ship-wide announcement circuit. "Attention everyone, this is Commander Amir, captain of the *Tarantul.*"

Trying to calm women and children, he softened his tone. "But most of you already know me, since you're the families of the crew and shore-based staff. You also know that despite our hardships, President Hadi's military budget has protected us, and we've suffered less than most. This may have been our home, but we're now temporary nomads."

He released the key, selected his next words, and then continued. "Aden will be overrun by warring factions. I don't know if it will be days or weeks, but we must evacuate the entire fleet from the city and relocate it somewhere safer. That includes you, our families, especially since you'd be considered privileged targets by whoever reaches the city first."

As Amir paused, the admiral snapped. "Don't share our destination. It's too soon."

Unsure how a spy could overhear him on his thrumming warship, Amir recognized his admiral's cowardice. A quick glance at the faces around the fleet's top-ranking officer revealed his captains as lackeys, unaware of or unwilling to challenge the weakness. Seeing the admiral pried from his desk and forced onto a ship, he believed the rumors whispered among the fleet's other commanding officers about their corrupt so-called leadership. "Aye, aye, sir. I won't mention our destination until I get your permission."

"Very well. See that you don't."

The *Tarantul's* commander keyed his microphone. "I commend you all for the courage to leave behind your homes. And I promise to show the same courage while I help your husbands, sons, and fathers escort you to safety." He tried to insert some normalcy into the desperate evacuation. "I ask you to remain in the berthing and common dining areas and out of the passageways. The ship's supply officer has rations to share with everyone, including the children. Welcome aboard, and carry on."

As he pushed the warship through the breakwater, he heard thunder rumble behind him. Then he reconsidered the noise's source.

Mortars were landing in the hills surrounding the city, and he could only guess who was firing at whom.

He uttered under his breath. "No time to play it safe." He raised his voice. "Helm, all-ahead flank."

Spray flew over the forecastle, and the ship undulated over the waves. Stepping to the side glass, he slid it open, stuck his head out, and felt wind whipping his ears. Behind him, smoke rose as the dormant volcano behind the city disappeared beyond the horizon.

He returned inside the windless bridge and yelled towards an open microphone. "Tactical center, bridge. Communications check."

From the ship's combat control room, the executive officer answered. "Bridge, tactical center. Communications check is satisfactory."

"Tactical center, bridge, report all hostile combat radar systems detected on our electronic sensor measures."

"Bridge, tactical center. I have no hostile combat radar systems."

"Very well. Report any hostile radar systems immediately. Keep our radar systems off." Amir looked to his admiral, who'd outstayed his welcome on the bridge. "May I tell everyone where we're going now, sir?"

"No! There could be listening devices on any one of these merchant or fishing vessels. I'll tell you when you can announce it."

"Understood, sir. But now that I'm beyond the Shamsan volcano's horizon, I request to change course to our true destination."

"Very well. Do it."

"Helm, left five-degrees rudder, steady on course zero-nine-zero."

After the helmsman twisted a large, polished wheel, the deck rolled away from the turn and then leveled. The risen sun brightened the bridge.

"Commander Amir."

The *Tarantul's* commander sensed haughtiness from his admiral and answered with cautious, feigned reverence. "Yes, sir."

"Escort me and my staff to a private room for a briefing. We have much to discuss."

"Aye, aye, sir. We'll meet in my dining room. I'll need five minutes to give my staff standing orders during my absence, but I'll have the chief bosuns mate escort you."

"Very well. See to it."

A short, stocky man moved into action. "I'll escort the admiral and his staff to your dining room, sir." He slipped by the handful of high-ranking riders. "Please follow me, sirs."

Freed of unwanted scrutiny and the murmured conversations among lackeys jockeying for perceived favor with the admiral, Amir sought comfort in the sounds of his ship slicing the sea.

The soothing waves pressing his trembling hull reminded him of his ship's awesome speed. He'd employed the *Tarantul's* powerful combination of diesel engines and gas turbines to chase down and thwart countless Somali pirates. But today's sprint harkened dangers beyond bands of robbers.

It signaled the crumbling of his world.

Although raised in Southern Yemen's Aden, the port city from which he'd just fled, he considered himself a citizen of the grander nation. Like President Hadi, a fellow Aden native, Amir favored the strength of national unity. After watching the civil war unfold during his childhood, he'd welcomed the unification of the northern and southern states.

For him, the bloodshed needed to have meaning, and for two decades it did. When the southern and northern navies had combined, Amir had signed up to protect the fisheries and merchant traffic that fed and clothed his people. Then five years ago, multiple factors cracked his country into a fractured mess of famine, warfare, and shifting alliances.

Mistrusting of politicians, he'd dedicated his attention to learning seamanship, leadership, and naval combat while his countrymen watched Hadi's rise to power, his ousting, and his subsequent Saudi-backed return. Clueless about his president's true character beyond rumors and biased news sources, the *Tarantul's* commander saw only one path forward to stability—backing a legitimate ruler.

Although deprived of action against blue-water navies, Amir had studied the strategies his fleet's smaller missile boats had used against the Saudis, the Egyptians, the Emirates, and the Americans. Yemeni engineers had proven competent in reacting to challenges with their aging inventories, and the military leaders had learned to employ their available technologies in combat.

He expected to test his engineers, his fleet's latest tactics, and himself before returning to a stable homeland.

Addressing the lieutenant who scanned the waters ahead of the racing warship, Amir barked an order. "Officer of the deck, you have the deck and the conn."

Turning to his commander, the junior officer revealed a homely visage. "I have the deck and the conn, sir."

"Keep this base course of zero-nine-zero, but maneuver as necessary to keep a distance of five nautical miles from any ship."

"Aye, sir. A base course of zero-nine-zero and five miles from any ship, sir."

"Inform me immediately if you detect any military craft or if any vessel challenges your five-mile buffer."

"Aye, sir."

Before catching up to the admiral's entourage, Amir sought

a conversation with his second-in-command. He grabbed a sound-powered phone from its cradle on the bulkhead, dialed the tactical center, and waited.

"Tactical center, executive officer."

"It's the captain. Set up phone talkers throughout the ship in all but the least frequented compartments."

"Aye, sir. I'll see to it."

"You know why I'm doing this, don't you?"

"Uh… to send word throughout the ship if necessary without terrifying our families over the annunciation circuit?"

"Correct. And more." Amir lowered his voice. "I don't like what I'm seeing in the admiral's behavior. He's shaken. I'm not sure he can handle the pressure."

"What are you saying, sir?"

"I'm saying that I don't know the admiral's plans, but he's going to reveal them soon. I'm wary of him, and I'll be wary of his plans."

"I admit that he seemed shaken to me."

Encouraged, Amir shared perilous thoughts. "There's something amiss with this exodus. I agree with us fleeing to… well, I can't say where yet per his orders. But it's a logical destination. What I don't like is not knowing what his plans are once we get there."

"You doubt him, then?"

Having known his executive officer for more than a decade, the *Tarantul's* commander risked vulnerability. "I'm asking you if the admiral or any of his minions commit to a blunder, and I need to counter him, would you give me the benefit of the doubt?"

The pause spiked Amir's adrenaline, but his second-in-command's response was ideal. "You know I'm behind you, as are the navigator, weapons officer, and engineer. We believe in your abilities and are aligned to your cause."

"I appreciate it." Amir reconsidered the urgency and downshifted his intensity. "It's probably nothing. I might be paranoid."

The executive officer's tone relaxed in lockstep with that of his commander. "I hope so, but paranoia is expected in this environment. Regardless, you can count on me and the department heads. I'm sure the rest of the crew would fall in line, too. I overhear them talking."

Amir hung up and darted through passageways and up ladders to his dining room. Entering his private space, he saw the admiral sitting in his commanding officer's personal chair. Without acknowledging the seizing of privilege, the top officer ordered Amir to take a lesser seat.

Hiding his displeasure, the *Tarantul's* commander sat beside an underling captain and swallowed his emotions.

The admiral drew a dramatic breath and then launched his explanation. "I've spoken to President Hadi himself." Pausing for effect, the portly man let his lackeys nod their feigned awe. "And the president approved my plan to relocate our forces from Aden to the island of Socotra."

Having known his ship's destination, Amir found the declaration useless but found the patience to listen for the stocky man's intent.

"When I spoke with President Hadi, he was receptive." Again, the admiral paused to let the name linger. "And he approved my plan to bring the families with us. Of course, it would have been a tragedy to trust our retreating ground forces to protect them in Aden."

*We know this. Get on with it,* Amir thought.

"I've arranged for armaments, fuel, food, and all necessary supplies for all our remaining loyal ships and support staff to be available in Socotra. The resistance leader, who, as you know, is loyal to President Hadi, reports that half the supplies have arrived already."

*Obvious. Necessary. Continue.*

"And to defend our interests, I've ordered all available warships to establish a perimeter around the island to prevent maritime interference or enemy troop landings."

Before he could restrain himself, Amir protested. "No!"

Displaying his haughtiness, the admiral released an indignant smile of disbelief. "No? What can that possibly mean?"

Recognizing the admiral's strategic blunder he'd feared, Amir voiced his displeasure. "That would alert the Emirates and give them easy targets. That would undermine our efforts. I'm sure the mercenaries would disagree with it if–"

Reddening with anger, the admiral countered. "The mercenaries work for me, commander, with President Hadi's full confidence. Perhaps you weren't listening when I said that President Hadi approved my plan personally."

Missing the political cue, Amir continued. "We need to deliver our families to Socotra but keep our ships on the move. We're outnumbered and outgunned by even a fraction of the Emirati military. We don't even know who controls our own air force at the moment. We need divert Emirati attention from the island–from our families–and make them seek our ships on the seas."

Wagging his finger, the admiral snapped. "You're out of line, commander. I suggest you find your bearing before I'm forced to discipline you."

Growing wary of the man's narcissism, Amir altered his tactics, recalling from experience that confronting arrogance was pointless. Instead, he retreated and planned to counter from the flanks. "My apologies, sir. I was out of line."

"That's better. Watch yourself." The admiral kept his smug glare centered on his victim to reinforce his positional authority. He then shifted his attention to his minions. "After I release you all from this brief, you may announce our destination of Socotra to the crew and families. Now, as for the details of our new fleet. With our forces in Al Hudaydah compromised by the Houthis, I'll be in charge of the new and regrouped fleet, with President Hadi's approval, of course. I've selected you, my captains, to lead very important functions..."

Amir watched the eager underlings accept power beyond their abilities while he listened to the incompetent flag officer talk for half an hour. After being dismissed from his own dining table, he scurried up ladders to the highest deck.

His senior radio operator led a small team in listening for wireless transmissions. "Sir? What can I do for you?"

Amir was curt. "I need a global satellite phone. Now."

"Aye, aye, sir." The senior operator gestured to an underling who disappeared behind a console. After slamming a locker shut, the younger man returned cradling six phones in his arms. "You get your choice, sir."

"Are these aligned with the fleet's daily encryption?"

The senior man smiled. "Yes, sir. I make sure of it every day at midnight. You can call anyone else in the fleet in security, as long as it's a secure number to a phone in our network."

"Good." He grabbed the thick device and extended its antenna. "Give me the list of fleet phone numbers. Then clear out."

"Aye, sir." The radio supervisor handed his captain a laminated list and ushered his team from the room. "Everyone out! The captain has the radio room!"

With the door clicked shut, Amir looked through the window at the swells rushing by his ship and dialed a number. He lifted the phone, heard the dialing, and waited.

And he waited.

After dozens of rings, the voice he sought issued from the speaker. "Commander Gulla."

Relieved to hear his friend, Amir recruited his first ally. "Najib, it's Andi. We need to talk. Are you alone?"

"No, I'm on the bridge. Hold on. I'll start walking while you tell me what you can."

"We need to take action. The admiral just revealed his plan, and it's dangerous. He wants to park the fleet at Socotra and invite a bloodbath. He hasn't thought this out any further than that, and it's showing. He's afraid and making things up foolishly."

His footsteps echoing through the receiver from his distant *Osa*-class missile boat, Gulla confirmed Amir's fears. "I know." The echoes subsided. "I can talk freely now. Damn it, Andi, I'm with the other missile boats, and we're all in sight of Socotra, but we don't have orders to make landfall. We don't have orders for anything, and he sent us ahead before you."

The news compounded Amir's evidence against his admiral. "He should have been on the first ship to arrive."

"Agree, but it's a fool's errand anyway. Any idiot knows our safest location is hidden at sea. He's weakening our position and turning our families into targets."

"Then you understand."

"Yeah, but what can we do? The admiral is Hadi's cousin's brother-in-law, and that's his best quality. The man's a dunce, but I know that most of the other *Osa* commanders are aligned with him. It's simple nepotism."

The *Tarantul's* commander knew the misaligned commanders and doubted they'd join him. They were talentless politicians per his reckoning. "Where are they?"

"They've broken formation, such as it was. They're grouping together already and creating a faction, unless I'm being paranoid."

Reflecting upon the incompetence and fear of the politicized leadership, Amir saw an opening for division. "You're not being paranoid."

"We're going to lose three or four *Osas*, Andi."

Amir lamented aloud. "Half our fleet."

"Yeah. I'm watching it happen. They're all within sight of each other, and they're not talking to me. I don't know if they're planning to support whatever the admiral orders next, or if they're preparing to run for their lives."

"They may join the separatists out of fear, just to save their hides. Let them run like the cowards they are. At least that will keep them out of our way."

"Good idea. What else can we do?"

Amir considered the other missile boat commander, a man as talented and dedicated as Gulla. "What about Sharki?"

"He's with us. We'll have *Osa-2*. I'm not sure about *Osa-5*. Hussein's gathered with the others, but he may come back to us."

"He's competent but too procedural. He's with us in spirit but slow to act when presented with chaos."

"Right. Good assessment. We may get him back when he sees a plan working, if there's a plan to be worked."

"What about Gharsi?"

Gulla perked up. "We'll have his refueling tanker. He'll carry spare stores and ammunition for us, too."

"Good. We can arrange that later. Our present concern is... I hesitate to say it."

Silence suggested shared trepidation. "As do I. But one of us must. We're talking about a coup."

Encouraged his companion agreed, Amir pressed. "A hostile takeover. I have the admiral and his staff on my ship, with no reason to suspect anything. I could arrest them under the justification of no confidence, but we need someone to answer to the president."

Gulla's tone was hopeful. "Is Captain Damari with them?"

Amir perked up. "No. I haven't seen him since we deployed."

"He planned the attack in the Red Sea against the Saudis. He knows how to manage a fleet."

"Yeah, but would Hadi accept him?"

"You'll have to ask Damari himself, but I expect so. He's married to Hadi's third or fourth cousin."

Butterflies swarmed Amir's stomach. "I need to have a very dangerous conversation with the highest-ranking competent man in this navy."

"I don't envy you. But I'll handle the talks with the other unit commanders."

"Not until I confront Damari."

"Of course, not. But hurry. We're following orders that are making us easy targets."

Amir snorted. "No pressure. I just need to overthrow what's left of our navy and convince a man to risk his neck leading us against at least three larger fleets."

## CHAPTER 2

In the soft light of the tactical center, Amir sought his champion. He stepped to the central chair where his executive officer oversaw a dozen warriors in the *Tarantul's* old but updated technical brain. Leaning into his second-in-command's ear, he whispered. "Don't look towards him, but is Captain Damari in here?"

The seated man nodded.

"Good. I expected him to be more interested in our status than in kowtowing to the admiral. Now, I assume you remember our most recent conversation about loyalty, do you not?"

Again, the silent second-in-command nodded.

"Good. I'm going to have an important conversation with Captain Damari. Depending how it goes... I'm not sure how it might go, to be honest. But if you start hearing orders from the admiral or his other captains, I trust you to ignore them unless I confirm them."

"Of course, sir."

"Now, tell me where Damari is."

"By the electronic sensory measures suite."

Amir snorted. "I might have known. That's a sign he knows what he's doing." The *Tarantul's* commander traversed the deck until reaching earshot of the reddish ghoul bent over a seated technician.

Stiffening his back, he began his recruitment. "Captain Damari?"

A tall, lean man with a spine curved forward to avoid bumping shipboard objects, Damari exposed hawkish features and a long nose. "Yes, commander?"

"A word please, sir. In private."

After a final glance at the electronic sensor display, the tall man agreed. "Very well. The passageway?"

"Yes, sir." Amir strode behind sailors seated at consoles, stopped at a door, and then clicked open the latch. In the passageway, bright lights made him squint. His stomach knotted as he tested the captain. "May I ask your opinion about the admiral's decision to concentrate our ships around Socotra?"

The tall officer's voice was deep. "You just asked, and it's a dangerous question."

Crestfallen, Amir resigned himself to his potential champion's reluctance. "You're right, sir. Desperate times require obedience. I'm sorry for wasting your time. Excuse me." He turned and took three steps.

Damari appended his answer. "Dangerous questions lead to dangerous actions."

Amir stopped.

The fleet's potential leader turned the inquiry on the *Tarantul's* commander. "And if you're considering action, it's best that I hear you out before you would act."

Pivoting, Amir pled his case. "Any fool can see he's creating our own demise. He'll have us surrounded at Socotra, and the fleet's presence will invite the Emirates, the Saudis, or even the Iranians to crush our entire fleet with one offensive."

"You're challenging your leader's authority. Get to your point."

"Yes, sir. We need to drop off the families and let them hide among the Socotran populace. We'll keep two missile boats operating in local waters to suggest a nominal defense without attracting attention, but the rest of the fleet must be deployed."

Damari grunted. "What do you hope to gain by telling me this?"

"We need someone to lead the fleet, and it has to be you."

"Yet the fleet has leadership."

Amir chanced his solution. "That leadership is captive on my ship with a loyal crew. I could have them escorted and held anywhere you'd wish, as the new commodore."

The potential champion raised an eyebrow. "You assume much."

"I see little choice."

Damari reached for the door. "I'm going to return to observing your tactical team. I recommend strongly that you keep such thoughts to yourself. Good day, commander."

Amir's hope disappeared into the tactical center.

Mentally cursing Damari and himself, the *Tarantul's* commander tended to the next item on his harried agenda.

After a slow walk to deflate his lingering tension, he heard children's voices coming from the crew's dining hall. Two hundred souls stuffed a space designed to feed fifty.

He approached a sailor wearing a headset. "Phone-talker, inform the bridge that I'm in the crew's dining hall."

"Aye, sir." The sailor spoke into his sound-powered microphone and then looked to his captain. "The bridge acknowledges."

"Very well." Feeling hundreds of eyes upon him, Amir scanned the space for his supply officer. Seeing the hefty man, the *Tarantul's* commander yelled over the din. "Supply officer! Supply officer! Damn it... Lieutenant Naser!"

An elderly woman in a green hijab noticed Amir's efforts and yelled for Naser's attention.

The supply officer twisted, saw his captain, and swiveled his portly belly through the obstacle course of misplaced folk who rocked with the heaving deck. Reaching his superior, he wiggled his mustache while talking. "This is an overcrowded disaster, sir. One of my cooks had to help with a diaper change!"

Unable to enjoy the anecdote, Amir stuck to business. "You're keeping them calm, though? Hydrated and fed?"

"Modest rations, sir. Luckily, half of them are seasick and can't eat. There's enough to keep people from complaining."

"Good. Get their attention and then introduce me."

The overweight man waved his arms and shouted. "Everyone! Everyone, please, may I have your attention?"

After the din faded, the supply officer continued. "This is Commander Amir, the commanding officer. Go ahead, sir."

Unsure about any future, Amir fibbed. "The first thing I want to do is assure you that you're all perfectly safe."

Worry and doubt covered his audience's disbelieving faces, and he shared the truths he knew. "I can finally tell you our destination."

All human noise ceased, leaving the whir of ventilation fans and swishing of waves against the hull. "We're going to Socotra."

Half the audience seemed in disbelief while others nodded in confirmation of their suspicions.

"The resistance leader in Socotra is looking for housing in the homes of volunteers. This will be a challenge to accommodate everyone's needs, and I ask for your patience. Once you leave this dining area, you'll need to move together and keep moving since there's so many of you."

An elderly man raised his hand and shouted. "What about people who can't move well?"

Amir retorted. "Please withhold all questions until I finish." He softened his attitude. "But please address that with Lieutenant Naser. I see enough strong men here, brothers of our crew, I assume. The strong ones will help those in need."

The supply officer leaned towards his commander. "You want me to essentially assign the families into platoons?"

"Actually, that's a good idea. Assign them numbers and have them line up before they leave the compartment. Draw lots for determining who gets off the ship first. But plan ahead for special accommodations to avoid a panic. Oh, and officer families go last. The exec's family second to last, and then mine."

From a nearby table, Amir's silent wife gave her husband an understanding nod while reaching for one of his stirring children.

"I can handle that, sir. This group's surprisingly better behaved than some new recruits I've dealt with."

"Good. Do it when I leave. This is going to be a chaotic day."

"It is already, sir."

A middle-aged woman with a teenage boy by her side posed the next unsolicited question. "My oldest son and the families of several of your crewmen are following us in their fishing boats. But I'm sure they've fallen behind. Can you tell them about Socotra?"

Wondering if this ad hoc fishing fleet had seen his turn from Djibouti towards the Yemeni-held governate, Amir agreed. "If you'll give Lieutenant Naser your son's name and his phone number, I'll have word sent to him."

Relief washed over the mother's face. "Bless you, sir."

Amir instructed his supply officer. "Have the radio supervisor contact Commander Gulla on *Osa-1* over the secure satellite phone and speak to him in person only. Then have Commander Gulla relay Socotra as our destination to that woman's son."

"I'll see to it, sir."

The *Tarantul's* commander faced his civilian audience and shouted. "As for anyone who needs special–"

"Captain!"

Amir swiveled his head towards his phone-talker. "Yes?"

"From the executive officer in the tactical center, he says–"

Raising his index finger, the *Tarantul's* commander hushed the sailor and strode to him. "Quietly, lad."

"The executive officer says we've been detected by a Terma I-band navigation radar, used by Emirati *Baynunah*-class corvettes."

Amir faced the hushed families and raised his voice. "Excuse me, everyone. Duty calls." He marched away and pondered his options while walking to the bridge.

Flanked by lackeys, the admiral was shouting into the overhead speaker. "... don't care where he is. Find him!"

Assuming himself the topic of angst, Amir cleared his throat. "I'm here, sir."

"Where have you been?"

"Comforting the families."

"You're lax in your duties. Do I have to manage you?"

Amir sprang into action. "No, sir. I know what to do."

The portly admiral protested. "Hold on! State your intentions."

"I'm energizing my ship into a full alert status. All radar and sonar systems, except fire control radar."

The admiral glared. "And invite a war? Are you mad?"

"No, sir. I'm lighting off our systems to behave like the warship that we are, since we've revealed ourselves by moving at forty-five knots. Now that we've been seen, it's time to act like we're patrolling, or else they'll suspect otherwise."

His face shifting from sanguine anger to a pallor, the admiral tried to hide his fear with a scowl. "No. We... we need to hail them."

Amir's jaw tightened as he bantered with the idiot. "What would you like me to say, sir?"

"Find out their intentions, of course!"

"Sir, I'll do that, but they're probably in international waters. Since they've already found us, I think–"

"I don't care what you think. Tell them we have women and children aboard and that we're on a humanitarian mission."

Stunned, Amir hesitated.

"Did you forget how to follow orders?

"No, sir. But that could be inviting disaster. It's informing our adversary of our vulnerability."

"Do you really think they'd risk the political damage?"

Unwilling to let a politician's misconception threaten civilians, Amir narrowed his eyes. "Politicians talk. The Emirati Navy acts, as do I." He glared at a stocky sailor. "Chief bosuns mate, escort the admiral and his staff to my dining space and have them held there under guard."

The admiral barked. "Don't you dare, sailor!"

Uncaring what the families heard, Amir walked to the ship-wide announcing circuit and keyed the microphone. "This is the captain. Security reaction team, lay to the bridge to escort the admiral and his staff, with the exception of Captain Damari, to my private dining."

While paleness painted the underlings' faces, the admiral raged. "What's the meaning of this? I'll have you destroyed, Amir!"

The *Tarantul's* commander feared the man's threat would materialize, but he'd committed. "Do you wish to resist, sir?"

"Why should I? I relieve you of command." He faced a minion. "Captain Walid, take command of this vessel."

His voice filling the bridge like an angel from loudspeakers, the *Tarantul's* executive officer rescued his captain. "That won't be necessary, admiral. The tactical center supports Commander Amir."

The portly officer shouted towards an overhead microphone. "I don't care! I'll have you replaced, too!"

"All of us, sir? We've been listening down here, and the security team will ignore you and your staff, except for Captain Damari. He's heading up there to replace you."

Before the admiral could finish his brewing temper tantrum, six armed guards burst into the bridge and eyed their proper captain.

Amir pointed to the admiral. "Arrest him and the two captains. Detain them in my private dining." He faced his husky bosuns mate. "See that they're treated with the respect of their ranks. See that they have no phones, and disable the phones in the dining space."

Amid a verbal tirade, the senior officers departed without physical resistance.

Unfettered to command his ship, Amir yelled while marching to a radio stowed in the overhead. "Radio, line me up to speak to the Emirati warship over high-frequency voice."

The answer arose from the speakers. "You're lined up on high-frequency voice, sir."

Amir grabbed a handset and keyed it. "Emirati warship to my northwest, this is Yemeni warship making forty-five knots. Communications check. Over."

Nothing.

The *Tarantul's* commander tried again. "Emirati warship to my northwest, this is Yemeni warship making forty-five knots. Communications check. Over."

Nothing.

Amir raised his voice into the overhead speakers. "Tactical center, bridge, light up all search and navigation radar systems. Bring up sonar in active search mode. Keep fire control dark."

His executive officer responded. "Bridge, bringing up search and navigation radars... bringing up sonar... we're radiating on all radar systems except fire control. Sonar is warming up."

"Very well." Amir keyed his handset. "Emirati warship to my northwest, this is Yemeni warship making forty-five knots. Communications check. Over."

This time, he earned a response. "Yemeni warship to my southeast, this is Emirati warship. State your intent. Over."

The executive officer interrupted the radio dialogue. "Sir, you've got three contacts plotted correlating to the Terma I-band navigation radar. They're on the same bearing, distance thirty-two miles."

"Very well. Transmit this data to all our fleet assets. Confirm identification as one Emirati *Baynunah*-class corvette and two unconfirmed escorts." As complexities threatened to overwhelm Amir, he felt his world became more complex.

All eyes facing him upon entrance, Captain Damari reached the bridge. "You have quite a way about you, Commander Amir. I overheard the admiral's incompetent planning, and I agree with your actions. Annotate in your deck log that I have replaced him as the commodore."

"Aye, sir." Amir nodded to the sailor who strode towards the log. "You heard your new commodore."

Juxtaposed against his predecessor's nervous and interfering presence, Damari was quiet. "Keep doing what you're doing. I'll stop you if I must." He slid to unoccupied deck plates behind the bridge team.

Amir side-stepped to a sailor's flank and glanced over his shoulder. With the console showing the Emiratis moving at twenty-two knots, he surmised his adversary was in no hurry. The realization comforted him with hopes of his nation's ground troops holding invading forces beyond the range of naval gunfire.

A harsher tone came from the Emirati. "Yemeni warship to my southeast, this is Emirati warship. State your intent. Over."

Again, the executive officer interrupted. "Sir, the *Baynunah* just lit off its Sea Giraffe air and surface surveillance radar."

"Very well, tactical center. I lit off ours first. That's an ex-pected response." He lifted the radio handset and gambled on a ruse. "Emirati warship to my northwest, this is Yemeni warship. My intent is to prevent uninvited warships from entering my home waters. State your intent. Over."

"Yemeni warship to my southeast, this is Emirati warship. My intent is to transit international waters without harassment. I recommend that you stay twelve nautical miles from me. Over."

Uninterested in harassing his adversary, Amir conceded. "I will honor that distance excepting when I'm within my nation's waters. Be advised, I will cross in front of your track en route to my national waters. Acknowledge. Over."

"Acknowledged. Emirati warship, out."

As Amir's head spun with the gamesmanship inside and out-side his ship, he called out. "Radio operator, send a global satel-lite phone to the bridge immediately."

"A global satellite phone is on its way, sir."

Checking the waves, Amir stepped from the tactical console and reached for the ship-wide circuit's handset. "Attention, this is the captain. We've discovered Emirati warships a safe dis-tance away, but to hide our purpose of evacuating our families, I'm going to chase them. However, before doing so, I want all ci-vilians off the ship."

He let the drama settle upon his audience before lifting their spirits with a plan. "I'll have *Osa-1* turn back from its trek to Socotra. Once it's here, you will board it. It won't hold you all comfortably, but you can find safe places on the deck."

Again, he let the intrigue weigh upon his listeners. "I need all civilians on the weather deck immediately. Don't move ahead of your assigned positions, or my crew will move you to the back of the line. I'm not here to break apart families. I'm here to save them. Behave like the strong people you've become under our harsh living conditions. I know you can do it. Deck division, prepare to offload all civilian personnel onto *Osa-1*. That is all."

A phone-talker called out. "Sir, the executive officer concurs with your plan and has assigned the navigator officer and his staff to assist the supply officer and deck division with the task."

"Very well."

Heaving from running, a sailor strode onto the bridge and extended a satellite phone.

Amir grabbed it and dialed *Osa-1*.

His friend's voice was a welcomed sound. "Commander Gulla."

"Najib, it's Andi. I just arrested the admiral and his staff. Captain Damari agreed to be our new commodore."

"That's fantastic. How'd you–"

"No time for that. I need you to double back at twenty knots and pick up my cargo."

"Why? I can't... damn it. Hold on." After ten seconds, Gulla spoke again. "I just turned around to come back to you. I assume this is related to the data you're broadcasting about the Emiratis?"

"Yes. I need you take station on me and pick up the cargo. Did my radio operator mention the small fishing fleet behind us?"

"Yeah. You're thinking I could use them for overflow?"

"Yes. Then escort the civilians and fishermen to Socotra."

"You want me limited to twenty knots now to avoid revealing myself as a warship?"

"Correct."

"I'm checking my chart... if we use emergency backing bells when we meet and tie up bow-to-stern, we'll be mated in twenty-five, maybe thirty minutes."

"Agreed."

Twenty minutes later, Amir saw deck hands standing on the old approaching *Osa* warship. "Helm, mark your speed."

"Three knots and slowing, sir."

"Very well. All-stop."

"Engineering answers all-stop, sir."

"Very well." Amir lifted his phone. "I'm at all stop. I'll drift from here. You should have an easier time handling the smaller ship."

Gulla snorted. "Make me do the hard work while you take the credit, huh?"

Forty minutes later, Amir watched through his side window as the last civilian ambled by the oversized Styx-missile launchers on the *Osa's* bobbing deck. The *Tarantul's* crew pulled back the gangplank, threw nylon ropes to the *Osa's* waiting sailors, and then yanked aboard the come-alongs that had prevented the warships from sharing paint.

Unable to see the *Osa's* bridge, Amir lifted his phone and addressed his unseen friend. "Stay put while I sprint out of here."

"Done. Good luck, Andi."

"You too, Najib." After pocketing the phone, Amir barked. "Helm, right five-degrees rudder, no course given. All-ahead one-third." With the sun overhead, he watched water churn behind the *Tarantul* and waves slosh between the separating hulls. With clearance, Amir accelerated towards his flank speed and turned to an intercept course for the slower Emiratis.

Four hours of hard forging through the seas placed Amir closer to his home waters than the adversarial combatants. When he had the proximal advantage, he cut towards the Yemeni coast, paralleled the Emiratis' courses, and slowed to let them catch him.

Within an hour, they did.

Without communicating, the two Emirati *Lurssen* patrol craft remained in international waters while the *Baynunah*-class corvette angled towards Yemen's twelve-mile national boundary.

Amir reached for his radio handset. "Emirati warship off my port beam, this is Yemeni warship. You are one mile from Yemeni national waters. Turn back. Over."

Nothing.

The *Tarantul's* commander felt Captain Damari appear by his side. "What will you do if there's no answer?"

"If they meant to sink us, they would have already, sir. The three of them outgun us ridiculously. This isn't a battle–it's a test of wills. My ship is bigger, older, and faster. I'll nudge the *Baynunah* until its commander gets the point."

The commodore crossed his arms. "I assumed you would. Why not instead feign cowardice? Give the illusion of a challenge, and then back off. Let him think you're weak, in case you meet again."

Amir embraced the idea. "It would avoid any collision damage, which would hurt us more than them, since we have no place to make repairs."

"Correct."

"I'll keep warning him while I maneuver." The *Tarantul's* commander keyed the handset. "Emirati warship off my port beam, this is Yemeni warship. You are half a mile from national waters. Turn back or I will use nonlethal force. Over."

The new commodore proved his acumen. "Come in too steeply, more like you're ramming than pushing. Make it look like a frightened man's bluff."

Pleased with his choice of leadership, Amir smirked. "Yes, sir."

The *Tarantul's* commander gave the wayward corvette repeated, unanswered warnings while barreling down on it. One minute from a collision, the Emirati ship energized its fire control radar.

As a hedge against dying for naught, Amir prepared his anti-ship missiles for a second-strike retaliation. "Tactical center, bridge. Warm up all Styx missiles. Assign missiles one and three to the corvette. Assign missiles two and four to each of the patrol craft."

"Styx missiles are warming up, sir."

Thirty seconds from the Emirati, he watched his adversary's cannon swivel in his direction.

He half-asked, half-announced his intention. "Time to play coward?"

Damari snapped. "Yes."

"Helm, right ten-degrees rudder, steady course one-eight-zero."

"My rudder is right ten-degrees, sir. That's the long way around."

"I know that. Better to turn away from the angry ship with the big gun that's rotating its barrel towards us."

"Aye, sir."

Satisfied with a long day's efforts, Amir sighed. "Cowardly enough for you, sir?"

His demeanor unreadable, the commodore issued his first opinion. "Well done, Commander Amir. Aim us towards Socotra and then let's discuss our new fleet over dinner."

# CHAPTER 3

Terry Cahill thought he might never give back the *Xerses*.

Though technically belonging to the fleet's latest addition, Danielle Sutton, the *Xerses* was his for the Yemeni mission. Since the British commander was new, they'd traded ships so she could learn the *Goliath's* abilities. Taking the ship around Africa with Jake Slate and the *Specter* as its cargo was great training for Danielle.

While she trained on his ship, the *Xerses'* interim commander sought action aboard the fleet's newest hardware.

With his Australian crew, Cahill had navigated from Taiwan, around Singapore, and to within fifteen nautical miles of Socotra, the Yemeni island of sixty-thousand inhabitants situated at strategic maritime crossroads between the Red Sea, the Gulf of Aden, and the Indian Ocean.

He considered the *Xerses* an exact replica of the *Goliath* in handling and gunnery. When he'd tested it before the voyage, its railguns behaved per his expectations, as did the Goalkeeper close-in-weapon-system stowed in the port bow.

But his childlike wonderment came with two new toys.

Where he remembered a backup control room on the *Goliath's* port hull, he'd found the fruits of Pierre Renard's investments aboard the new ship.

Two quad launchers housed eight French MICA surface-to-air missiles, fed by guidance from the *Xerses'* phased-array radar and providing a defense against inbound missiles and aircraft to a range of twelve nautical miles. For training, Renard had allowed Cahill's crew to expend one new weapon against an unmanned aerial vehicle, and it had impressed as advertised.

As the *Xerses'* commander surfaced into the early dusk, he anticipated using his other favorite new asset. While translucent moonlit sheets cascaded down the bridge dome, he announced his intentions over the ship-wide circuit. "Standby to open the UAV hatch."

Having loaned several senior sailors to Danielle Sutton and

her new recruits on the *Goliath*, he heard his second-most sea-
soned port-hull sailor's voice. In a shrill tenor, Darren Smythe
affirmed the absence of humans from danger. "The UAV compartment is empty, sir. Standing by."

"Opening the drone hatch." Cahill tapped an icon, and then
metallic clunks echoed.

Beside him, Liam Walker lamented. "That's a dead giveaway
to any submarine that's listening."

The *Xerses'* commander countered. "If there's an enemy submarine within in torpedo range of us, it's our day to die."

"Right. You're in rare form this evening."

Taking a calming breath, the *Xerses'* commander gazed at the
stars. With the dome allowing a full vertical view, he stretched
his jaw upward and spied the zenith. Then he lowered his eyes
to his panels. "Sorry. I don't like all the complexities. Too many
things need to line up just right..."

"You mean for this evolution or this entire mission?"

"I was thinking about the mission." Cahill reconsidered his fatigued crew, after averaging twenty-two knots with them while
dodging possible spies over nine long days. With hundreds of
lives in the evening's balance, he guarded his optimism. "But I
hesitate to jinx our rendezvous. It seems like an easy task, but
no need to get sloppy. After this long trip, I can only wonder
how alert we are."

"We'll make it work. We always do."

Appreciating his colleague's positivity, Cahill raised his voice
upward towards a microphone. "Launching the UAV." After tapping an icon, he watched through the dome's windows as a
teardrop-shaped silhouette blacked out stars on the horizon.
The automated Schiebel Camcopter climbed, banked across the
*Xerses'* bow, and then shrank into the night.

Walker announced the link. "I have control of the UAV. Data
feed is nominal. Coordinates are set for its hovering station."

"Very well."

When the camcopter reached ten miles from its host ship, its
surface-search radar energized.

Walker shared updated information. "The UAV has turned on its radar. That's us, right there." He pointed to a screen. "That contact looks like a vessel transiting in the proper shipping lane, based upon its location and speed vector, and that one there's another vessel in the lane going the other way. And finally, in the middle of nowhere, we see our four new friends."

Cahill translated 'four new friends' as three Yemeni combatants and their supply ship loitering over his visual horizon. From its heights, the rotary-wing unmanned aerial vehicle gave the *Xerses'* commander battlespace information. "What's it got on infrared?"

Walker tapped icons and invoked the greenish-blue thermal renditions of four hulls drifting atop Arabian Sea. "Looks like the heat signatures of three warships and one supply ship trying to look like they're not there. They're not even trying to make bare steerageway."

The *Xerses'* commander agreed. "Yeah. Cautious, for sure. Won't even light up their propulsion plants to give off heat."

"What they lack in equipment, they make up for in paranoia."

Cahill glanced at an overhead view of the camcopter's view. "We know where they are now. Shut down the UAV's active radar."

"Shutting it down... the UAV's back in stealth mode."

"I love that thing already, mate. Don't you?"

"Makes me wonder what we ever did without it. Pierre had better damned well give us one of those and the MICAs on the *Goliath*."

"He will. Eventually. But that's Danielle's problem for now."

Walker gave his commander a sideways glance.

Cahill defended his comment. "Hey, she's still the new kid. Why should she get the good toys first?"

"I'm not arguing. We need them right now anyway."

"Alright then. Let's visit our new comrades-in-arms." Cahill sent the *Xerses* in a gentle turn towards the Yemeni group.

"I'll get the translators ready." The executive officer lifted a microphone but then reconsidered. "I think I'll make it a walkabout. I'll be stuck up here with you for a while. Need to stretch me legs a bit."

"Hurry. I don't want to be stuck behind a language barrier."

As Walker descended the stairway, the *Xerses'* commander tapped the first menu graphic to send his camcopter to the largest of the Yemeni warships. More taps merged the *Tarantul's* coordinates with the UAV's destination, and then the autonomous helicopter affirmed its new trajectory towards the corvette.

Minutes later, the infrared view showed five sailors standing on the Yemeni corvette's undersized fantail. As a Cold War Russian design, the ship left little room for anything but exposed weapon systems on its weather decks. Where the common *Tarantul*-class corvette held twin thirty-millimeter guns upon a magazine that crowded the ship's aft section, Amir's vessel sported a single homemade Kashtan close-in weapon system, demonstrating one of many impressive efforts by Yemeni military engineers.

Over the dome's loudspeaker, Walker's voice caught Cahill's attention. "I request to bring a translator to the bridge."

The *Xerses'* commander pressed a button, and the latch below him clicked. Two pairs of footsteps echoed behind him, and then his executive officer and a doctor of languages stepped to his side.

"Just in time, gents. Check out the UAV."

As the Yemeni sailors' body heat signatures grew, they extended and waved their arms. One of them exposed a strobe light and lowered it to the center of the makeshift landing pad.

Watching as the three-meter-long helicopter slowed its approach and descent, Cahill trusted the camcopter to land itself over the blinking light.

The Yemeni sailors darted from view, and then the corvette's port railing plummeted below the camera's field as the helicopter hopped faster than human reactions as it dodged the fantail's pitch. The camcopter recovered, landed, and idled its rotors.

Tempted to swivel a camera or attempt communications through the UAV's loudspeaker and microphone, Cahill waited while the Yemeni sailors muscled the two-hundred-kilogram helicopter steady under straps.

He gave his thirty-something-year-old translator a sideways glance. "Grab the microphone and get ready."

The doctor's accent was mild but enough to hint at the Jordanian dialect of Arabic as his native tongue. "I'm ready."

Minutes passed, testing Cahill's patience. "We don't have all bloody day."

Walker comforted him. "Easy, mate. They're doing this for the first time."

After another minute, a screen showed a new video source's availability over the UAV's wireless connection. Walker stabbed his finger into the touchscreen, allowing the communication, and then a man with hawkish features and a long nose appeared.

Excited, Cahill nodded at the doctor of languages. "Say 'hello' or something friendly."

Before the translator could obey, the Yemeni man's yelling over a gust on the corvette filled the dome.

"He asks if we can hear him. I'll respond affirmatively." The doctor replied and then entered a short back-and-forth verbal exchange with the sailor.

As the *Tarantul's* representative angled his phone towards the UAV, Cahill saw the USB tether to an access port on the idled camcompter and then a wider view of his automated helicopter as the Yemeni man stepped back.

"He says he's the senior officer in charge. He assumed the position of commodore within their restructured fleet and calls himself Captain Damari."

The *Xerses'* commander ran through his mental checklist and then reaffirmed the sequence of events. "Tell him we intend to submerge, approach to fifty meters off his starboard beam, contact him from periscope depth, and then await his divers."

The translator relayed the message and then interpreted the Yemeni officer's response. "He agrees and expects you to deliver his divers to two prescribed infiltration release points. He requests your intent with the submarine drone."

The *Xerses'* commander looked over his left shoulder at the Israeli hardware. Large enough to get pinched between his ship's hydraulic arms but small enough to have arrived in Taiwan aboard a C-5 Galaxy aircraft, the automated vessel rested in the cargo bed.

Cahill considered the Caesaron submarine drone the best un-manned undersea vehicle available to him, thanks to Pierre Renard's willingness to pay, the Israeli Navy's desire to gather field testing data against Arab adversaries.

There was also the added advantage of goodwill, thanks to his marriage to an Israeli Aman intelligence officer.

He considered the vessel a weak shadow of the *Wraith* and *Specter*, but with his fleet's submarines in transit, the Caesaron offered him his best short-range detection against enemy sub-marines, and–if needed–mines.

"I'll release the Caesaron before I ask his divers to approach. The Caesaron will then follow a prescribed search pattern ahead of me, and I'll follow it to each successive infiltration point."

The translator underwent another exchange with the long-nosed Yemeni officer. "He acknowledges and wishes to confirm your intent after his divers are delivered."

"I'll remain submerged and undetected and will scan for enemy submerged threats along with the Caesaron. Remind him not to call for me directly. Communicate only through the UAV if needed. And I hope it's not needed."

The translator had another verbal exchange. "Captain Damari says he'll establish a radio link with the UAV while you ap-proach his starboard quarter. He'll top off the UAV's fuel tank, too."

"Very well. Tell him I'll need two hours to reach him. I'll be moving slowly and listening for threats."

After receiving the Yemeni officer's acknowledgment, Cahill submerged the *Xerses* and aimed it towards the *Tarantul*. At seven and a half knots, he had his sonar team listen for hos-tile adversaries the best the disadvantaged hydrophones would allow.

Jagged edges begat flow noise over the transport ship, reducing its hull-mounted hydrophone's effectiveness, and the *Xerses* lacked the bow-mounted sonar system that warriors considered a necessity on combat submarines. But the array towed behind the starboard hull, being free of the ship's machinery and flow noise, heard the quiet seas.

As hoped, his ship's arrays heard safe seas, and two hours of transit placed him within a stone's throw of the drifting *Tarantul*.

He tapped icons to energize the *Xerses'* exterior lights, illuminating the Caesaron. "Prepare to launch the drone."

Beside him, Walker tapped his touchscreen. "I've queued up our present coordinates and final commands for the drone. I request permission to transmit acoustically over the underwater phone."

"Transmit acoustically."

Sharp clicks and beeps from the communications sonar flowed through the domed windows.

"The drone acknowledges receipt of the order. The drone is pumping water to achieve one ton of positive buoyancy. It's light enough now."

"Very well. Release the drone."

The unmanned submarine rose and cleared its host ship. As it slid from the exterior lighting's luminous cones, it started its propeller and pushed itself towards Socotra.

"Liam, bring us to periscope depth and raise the starboard scope."

"I'm bringing us to periscope depth." A minute later, the heavy ship rocked in the shallows. "Raising the starboard scope."

After tapping icons to employ the limited antenna atop his periscope, Cahill extended a handset to his translator. "Use high-frequency voice at low power. Hail the *Tarantul*."

"I'm hailing." The doctor greeted the fleet's new clients in Arabic, and the Yemenis responded. "It's a sailor on the radio.

He's getting an officer." Moments passed, and a new voice filled the *Xerses'* bridge. "It's the ship's commanding officer, Commander Andi Amir. He requests our status."

"Tell him we've launched the submarine drone and... wait. Liam, the induction unit?"

His executive officer snapped to action. "Right. Sorry." He stooped to a cubby and then stood, holding a black box. Speaking to the translator, he pressed the unit's suction cups against a window. "Plug that into a USB port."

"Done."

From the corner of his eye, Cahill saw a green light glow from the box. "Tell Commander Amir that we await his divers."

Another exchange happened between the interpreter and the *Tarantul's* commander. "His divers are ready. He requests that you secure any active sonar systems, and then he'll order them to you on your mark."

With his sidescan system already deenergized, Cahill snorted. "Cautious and thorough. I like that. Okay, then. Mark!"

"He's sent over all twenty-four divers."

"Alright, then. We wait." The *Xerses'* commander considered the greater scenario. "In the meantime, tell him to launch the UAV." After the Arabic exchange, Cahill swiveled his periscope to witness the moonlit camcopter rising from the corvette's fantail into the starry sky.

Moments later, the first pairs of Yemeni frogmen appeared in external camera views, and then they landed over Cahill's shoulder on the starboard hull's back. Seconds later, more arrived.

With his buddy, one of them landed on the dome and then pressed an induction unit against a window. Behind his mask, the human limpet's lips moved.

Cahill heard nothing. "Is that thing working?"

Walker eyed the box and cord. "Yeah. It should be. I'm not sure what's wrong." He looked at the frowning diver and pointed to his ear.

To no avail, the diver uttered his silent greeting again.

The *Xerses'* commander improvised. "Grab the whiteboard and markers. We'll do it old-school style." He eyed the translator. "You can write in Arabic, right?"

While Walker bent again towards a locker, the doctor nodded. "Of course. What shall I say?"

"Unit malfunction. Use the board to communicate."

"I'll do what I can. I'm not known for penmanship."

Requiring extra gestures, the exchange succeeded.

"Tell Commander Amir we'll be descending now, with a floor of twenty meters. Then write that for the divers."

After multiple two-way messages, Cahill made the *Xerses* lower its periscope and sink below radar detection. He then warned the divers before sending this ship ahead at five knots.

When the divers indicated their acceptance of the acceleration, the *Xerses'* commander increased his ship's speed to seven and a half knots.

Then Cahill's next order brought the vessel to ten nautical miles per hour to trail and match the speed of his escort Caesaron drone.

The slow voyage required six hours to reach the first drop point, three hundred meters off the coast of the island's seaport. After checking his precise location, Cahill secured the propellers. He then had the translator write the coordinates, the bearing to the pier, and instructions to leave.

From his port hull, half the dive team swam away.

An hour later, he reached the next insertion point off the coast of the airport. After a final visual exchange of information, he set the second insertion team free.

With the divers departed, Cahill addressed his two companions. "We're three hours from sunrise. This ingress will be over soon, one way or another. Liam, have the sonar team focus their search on Iranian submarines and undersea drones. The mission now is to hide. Nobody can know we were here."

## CHAPTER 4

Twelve days earlier, Dmitry Volkov appreciated one of nature's obscure facts.

The Red Sea and the Mediterranean Sea had similar water levels, allowing for the Suez canal's construction without locks and for tankers to draw more than twenty meters of depth. Beyond that, he hated everything about his predicament between the two major bodies of water.

Ensconced within the innards of a Suezmax tanker, his *Scorpène*-class submarine, the *Wraith*, seemed imprisoned. Perched atop its conning tower, he dreaded his entrapment.

His boss, Pierre Renard, had paid for the customized cutting and re-welding of the tanker's holding compartments. With three meters of margin, a steel ceiling followed the submarine's contour, provided it constant illumination with recessed lights, and secured its mobile mooring with cleats. Nylon lines fanned out over the *Wraith* like a spider's web over its captive.

Cabling ran from a trapdoor above Volkov's head through a grating by his feet and into his surfaced submarine. Insulated wiring carried a high-speed Internet connection for telephone calls, news, and a secure connection to his boss.

He lifted a tablet fed by a wireless router in the control below. Checking the latest feed from Renard, he sighed and accepted the chaotic mess that was the Yemeni combat theater.

The Houthi and the secessionist Southern Separatists had together taken control of Aden, the nation's largest port in the Gulf of Aden. International pundits claimed that the United Arab Emirates, backed by Iran, supported the separatists. And although the Persians withheld visible military intervention, Volkov agreed with Renard that they'd sent submarines to Aden to serve joint Iranian-Emirati interests.

A tinny voice rang from below. "Dmitry!"

Lowering his tablet, the *Wraith's* commander scanned the waters on his ship's left side.

Seated cross-legged on the black metal, the dolphin trainer

held a tablet with a wire to a vertical stanchion, from which a thick cable tethered a submerged audio transducer.

"I hear you! Yes, Vasily?"

"It's break time! My babies need sleep!"

"Hold on!" Swiping his tablet to his nautical chart, Volkov calculated less than an hour to Port Tewfik, the canal's terminus. Knowing he could have the trainer push the dolphins harder, he instead opted to rest them.

The upcoming Red Sea held many adversaries, ranging from the apathetic Israelis with one of their three naval squadrons, the antagonistic Egyptians with five of their bases lining Volkov's southerly trek, and the American-backed wildcard Saudis with their four aging but dangerous *Al Madinah*-class frigates. He decided that his mammalian security force had patrolled for unwanted divers long enough and needed rest for future threats.

Aiming his voice downward, he shouted. "Very well, Vasily. Order them back to the torpedo tube!"

The trainer swiped his tablet, and then Volkov heard recorded cetacean sounds reverberate through the water, into the *Wraith's* hull, and through his hands and feet.

Quieter than the order, the dolphins' response seemed silent, but their trainer's reaction confirmed it.

Vasily stood, disconnected his computer from the stanchion and headed towards the submarine's entrance hatch.

When the trainer disappeared, Volkov returned his attention to Renard's feed.

Houthi rebels controlled the Red Sea port of Al Hudaydah, through which normally flowed seventy percent of the supplies for the famished nation's populace. From that stronghold, they'd commandeered more ships than the proper government had retained under President Hadi, and they used their small navy to resist Saudi maritime interference.

Little better than the Houthi rebels, the Saudis effected their own stranglehold in Yemen's eastern al-Mahra directorate in their claimed attempt to prevent Houthi weapons smuggling.

Reality differed from the anti-smuggling claims, as Riyadh controlled the strategic region from a financial hunger to build an oil pipeline to the port of Nishtun.

Nishtun.

A tiny village of twelve hundred people. A final refuge for the inflow of supplies for people suffering from poverty, austerity, and failing commerce.

Somehow, the mercenary fleet's patriarch had negotiated and arranged affairs to allow the *Wraith's* commander to right grievous wrongs by providing escort services to the coastal hamlet of Nishtun, Yemen.

But the hamlet was distant, and Volkov thought of his immediate concerns–getting through the Suez, transiting the Red Sea's fourteen hundred miles, slipping through the tight Bab el Mandeb strait, detaching his submarine from its host tanker, and then patrolling hostile waters.

Never had he felt so dependent upon the simple ruse of concealment against so many dangers. With six days separating him from his detachment point, he feared he'd go mad with the helpless waiting.

He also feared the Houthis' recent capture of Aden would break the Yemenis' will to fight. Pockets of underground resistance slowed the clenching of their rebellious fist around the city, but time worked against the surrounded proper army, which battled on multiple fronts against the Houthis, Al-Qaeda, and the Southern Separatists.

A selfish thought harassed him.

For a moment, he wondered why he risked himself for strangers when civilized nations failed to help.

He then wondered why he hesitated to commit himself to a humanitarian mission. After dedicating his adulthood to naval submarine warfare, he'd expected to heed a continued calling to service. And with his rise within the mercenary fleet, he'd seen himself as a champion of justice.

Seeing himself as a strong helper of the meek, he'd enjoyed his short but impactful tenure with the fleet.

But then, something had happened.

A force from Great Britain had arrived.

Danielle Sutton.

For lack of a better term, she was his girlfriend.

For lack of a better diagnosis, he was smitten.

They'd agreed to move slowly and had gone on five dates during a month in Southern France's romantic Provence region. A religious man, he'd forced himself to keep his passions in check and to court her like a gentleman. But there had been one long passionate kiss, and its memory clung to him like dewfall.

The thrill of their nascent relationship consumed his attention and entangled his thoughts about anything else–including his duties.

He caught himself daydreaming, tucked his tablet under his arm, and began a slow descent down ladder rungs into the control room where he anticipated new reports, idleness, and a test of his patience.

Four days later, at the southern end of the Red Sea, Volkov staffed the *Wraith's* watch stations as if he were independent of the behemoth tanker above him.

But he wasn't free, and he was glad for it.

An unexpected sonar system blared from the direction of Perim Island, the landmass marking the northeast end of the Bab el Mandeb strait. Closer to the Djibouti side of the fourteen-nautical-mile-wide passage, Volkov marked the acoustic demon's distance at eight nautical miles.

He aimed his voice at his sonar expert. "What system's that?"

Anatoly shrugged. "No idea yet. It's coming from Perim Island, though. It's probably land-based."

"Like Houthi rebels made some Yemeni engineers patch something together and dangle it off the end of a pier?"

"Yeah. Probably. It's the right frequency to reach all the way to Djibouti, but not much farther. So, it's not superhigh accuracy–not enough to detect us as anything different than the tanker, like a scanning sonar could, but it could detect a passing submarine."

Volkov frowned. "Whose?"

"Us? In case Egypt actually let us through Suez. Just guessing."

Volkov could only wonder if his boss had bribed the Egyptians into letting him pass undetected under the tanker. "Maybe. That or Egyptian or Israeli. We and they are the only ones who'd be coming from the Red Sea. Coming the other way could be anyone. I admit it makes sense for the Houthis to listen. Fortunately, that's why we're still underneath this tanker. And lucky that Mikhail and Andrei are still in the torpedo room."

"Vasily would've died if they'd been cooked."

"Right." The *Wraith's* commander reached for his console and enjoyed through the host ship above him the luxury of a high-speed communication to his boss. "Pierre?"

In his screen, the aging but handsome Frenchman stood and turned, whipping his blazer's tail across his desk.

"Damn. He's walking away." Volkov tapped an icon hailing Renard.

The Frenchman spun back and leaned into the monitor. "Yes, Dmitry?"

Leaving his translator unperturbed, he attempted simple English. "Found a sonar system. I send data."

Renard's features revealed his surprise. "Yes! Send the data. Is it a threat?"

"Threat. Threat. What does 'threat' mean?"

"Danger."

"Oh, no. Safe under tanker."

"Good, my friend. You worried me. Keep your wits about you and listen."

"Listen. Yes. It comes from the island. Look." Volkov sent the upload from the Subtics system.

Renard frowned at the screen. "I'll check the archives here. The history, I mean. It looks like an older sonar system. It's probably Russian. I'm surprised you don't know it."

Volkov batted his fingers towards the Frenchman's image.

"Bah. Not a student of old hardware history."

"Regardless. It's nothing. Keep going."

Two days later, Volkov anticipated his departure from the loud and busy transit lane heading into the Arabian Sea. Although he'd miss the luxury of high-bandwidth connectivity, he wanted to shrug the giant tanker off his back.

To avoid suspicion by slowing the behemoth underneath prying aerial or satellite eyes, Volkov needed to match its speed of seventeen knots before breaking free. But with his exhaust duct relieving to the confined atmosphere underneath his host, he left his diesel power untapped and had to drain the *Wraith's* battery to keep pace.

Atop the conning tower, he looked down at his team of four sailors who wore harnesses strapped to the submarine's back. He spoke into a short-range radio. "How's your progress?"

Serguei, his executive officer, looked up from below. "That's all the lines except for the final four."

Volkov's panoramic check showed unraveled lines dangling from the tanker into the water flowing by the submarine's sides while one line each retained the submarine's four diametrically opposed cleats. The strain on the taut ropes seemed to place them within mere kilograms of snapping and made their wraps too tight to unravel, and the *Wraith's* commander ordered his deck team to finish the job creatively. "Very well, Serguei. Douse all remaining lines for removal."

Two men poured a bucket of diesel fuel over the wrappings around one cleat, and then they aimed another sloshing load on its twin. Carrying the half-full container, they waddled forward, around the conning tower, underneath Volkov, and to the two remaining exposed forward cleats. Again, they dumped oil over the raveled nylon, and their executive officer shared the progress. "All four ropes are doused for removal."

"Very well. Set them ablaze and head below."

After marching rearward, one man each held a lighter to a rear cleat, waiting for the fuel to burn while another pair of men, including the executive officer, did the same up front. As the fires caught, the men escaped into the submarine.

Locking the hatch on his way down, Volkov descended the ladder into his submarine. "The bridge is rigged for dive."

A grey-bearded man standing at the station controlling the *Wraith's* ballast and buoyancy digested his commander's statement and then reported. "The ship is rigged for dive, Dmirty. I recommend submerging below the tanker."

"Not yet." Volkov grabbed a microphone and sent his voice throughout his submarine. "The mooring lines are on fire, and we're getting ready to drop from the tanker. If your station isn't stowed for sea yet, I suggest you do it now. And hold on and strap in. We will take some very odd angles."

He stowed the microphone, walked to the foldout chair on his elevated conning platform, and sat. After strapping his seatbelt, he looked to the grey-bearded veteran at the ship's control station. "You may want to strap in, too, when you can."

"I will, sir. May I submerge us?"

Volkov realized the request was impossible. "Submerge us, per se, no. We're still tethered to a tanker. But open the vents and flood the main ballast tanks as much as you can."

Moments later, the man replied. "The vents are open. The main ballast tanks are filling."

"Very well." Volkov looked to his sonar guru. "Anatoly, let me know when they're flooded."

Keeping a muff pressed against one ear, the sonar ace answered. "Aye, sir. Soon. And... the after group is flooded, up to the sea's level, at least. Okay, now the forward group. I hear both groups flooded. We'll submerge once the lines release us."

"Very well." Volkov addressed the grey-bearded veteran. "Let's make ourselves heavy. Tell me how much water you're flooding, and I'll command by negation if I disagree."

"I'll start with five hundred kilograms into our central trim tank."

"Very well."

The grey-bearded man lifted a finger to a control, waited, and then reported. "I flooded five hundred kilograms. I hold us five hundred kilograms heavier than neutral computed trim."

"Very well."

Nothing happened.

"I think I'll flood five hundred more, Dmitry."

"Very well."

After a repeated effort, the grey-bearded veteran spoke. "I hold us one thousand kilograms heavier than neutral computed trim."

"Very well."

After a few seconds, a snapping sound filled the room, and the deck rolled left and back. Volkov slapped his rubber sole against the conning platform for balance. "I believe that's one line broken, three to go."

Seated, Anatoly confirmed it. "We heard that on sonar, but at least it's airborne noise. It won't travel far in the water if anyone's listening."

"Very well, Anatoly. Keep listening. We've got–"

The second snap interrupted Volkov and burdened his thoughts with the worst-case detachment scenario. "*Blyad!*"

With the port mooring lines yielding first, the tanker above him dragged his ship by two starboard cleats and placed a forty-degree list on the semi-submerged submarine.

Having grabbed a console for balance, the grey-bearded veteran reached his seat. "Time on the battery is ninety-four minutes. I recommend slowing to preserve battery charge and to use drag to snap the final lines."

"Very well." Volkov aimed his voice towards another sailor who manned the helm, rudder, and planes. "All ahead two-thirds, make turns for ten knots."

The helmsman obeyed but complained. "We've slowed, but this angle worries me."

Envisioning the hydrodynamics, the *Wraith's* commander used his angled rudder as a stern plane. "Well, turn us to the right, then. Use fifteen-degrees rudder and hold it there."

"Aye, sir. The rudder is right, fifteen degrees."

As the list eased, the deck dropped backwards with the canted rudder pulling the stern under.

Then a third snap, and the world tipped forward.

Like a rollercoaster ride, hands flailed about and sought holds while men screamed in a combination of fear and delight. Above them, the tanker pushed forward, dragging them by a single cleat on its starboard stern, making the *Wraith's* deck list hard left and forcing its bow to swing right and downward fifty-degrees towards the abyss below.

Bent forward over his lap, Volkov stuffed away a submariner's mortal terror of an inescapable dive and ordered his ship's safety. "All stop! Pump water from fore to aft! Shift your rudder to left fifteen!"

"Left rudder? Don't you mean right?"

"No! We're moving backwards!"

"Understood, sir! My rudder is left fifteen degrees."

Moments later, the last line snapped, and the deck dipped.

But first, the top of the rudder smacked the tanker with grating anger, and then it grinded its huge host before sinking below it.

With momentum dragging the *Wraith* backwards, the down angle corrected itself to an annoying but safe fifteen degrees.

Volkov sighed. "Everyone, hands off your stations and analyze."

After several minutes, he had control of his level ship and headed north towards Nishtun at five knots.

Anatoly, his sonar ace, shared the obvious. "The entire world heard our detachment, Dmitry. And now we have four loud and exposed cleats, probably with ropes still wrapped around them. I recommend a limit of five knots."

"Agreed. We'll surface and turn them over at night."

"Are you ready for us to begin our search, then?"

Volkov replayed the plan in his mind. "Yes. Launch drones one and two. Have both drones swim at an offset of forty-five degrees relative to our heading, lead and lag respectively."

Minutes later, two wire-controlled drones pushed ahead of

their host submarine at eight knots. Once they reached five nautical miles ahead of the *Wraith*, Volkov had them match his ship's speed and course, and he had them broadcast short bursts of acoustic energy into the water to assist their passive listening.

Moments later, the dolphin trainer appeared at the front of the control room. His face twisted in indignation, he strolled towards his commander, dripping water from his wetsuit. Behind him, a torpedo technician followed with a smirk.

Volkov protested. "You're getting water everywhere."

Reaching his boss, Vasily folded his arms. "I forgive you—barely. But you'll have to apologize to Mikhail and Andrei personally!" He turned and retraced his wet, barefooted steps.

Unsure of his crime, the *Wraith's* commander respected the trainer's anger enough to agree. "I'll apologize to them after dinner. I promise."

His smile waning as he spoke with reverence, the torpedo technician showed his commander a picture from his phone. "Say what you want about him, but the man's an athlete."

In the picture, Vasily wore his dive gear and was submerged in the tank with his dolphins. One arm hugged Andrei while he locked Mikhail in a figure-four leg hold. A palm against one corner of the tank and the balls of his foot against an edge, the trainer gave his babies the leverage to keep themselves in their container against the ship's harsh angles.

After admiring the image, Volkov dismissed the sailor and then set about to searching the waters for danger.

An hour passed.

Then another.

Then the long hours of submarine boredom that tested every undersea sailor began to stack up.

But within the fifth hour, while Volkov considered checking out the ship's dinner menu, a sonar technician shared his excitement.

"Active return, submerged target, drone one."

As Volkov stood, his sore muscles protested having sat. "Stop the active transmissions from both drones. Send drone one to-wards the active return."

Anatoly stepped behind the younger sailor who controlled the first drone, uttered commands, and confirmed his com-mander's desires. "The drone is six miles from the target."

"Very well. Helm, slow to turns for three knots. Anatoly, slow both drones to three knots."

As men followed his conservative orders, Volkov walked to the central chart and studied the new contact's location.

If it matched his expectations, the submerged contact was guarding the entrance to the port of Nishtun, the best access to delivering aid to the Saudi-strangled al-Mahra region. He ele-vated his voice over his shoulder. "Anything passive yet?"

"Not yet."

Volkov allowed for the patience required of a submarine commander. After thirty minutes, he returned to his seat and sensed his mind wandering.

Danielle Sutton was smiling and devouring him with passion-ate eyes. *Blyad. I'm smitten*, he thought.

After another fifteen minutes which passed as moments in his lovelorn trance, he earned his reward for a slow hunt.

The young sailor controlling the first drone was elated. "I hear reduction gears from the submerged contact! Now, I hear a five-bladed screw. It correlates to six knots on a *Ghadir*-class sub-marine."

"Very well."

The young sailor continued. "If I can get another active ping from the drone, I can confirm the speed against the contact's track."

"No!" Volkov glared at Anatoly. "Passive, unless we can't fig-ure it out passively."

Understanding his boss, the sonar guru nodded and corrected the junior man. Then, after another ten minutes of the adversar-ial submarine making propulsion sounds, Anatoly confirmed the finding. "It's a *Ghadir*, Dmitry."

Volkov smirked. "We found an Iranian submarine. Get a communications buoy ready for Pierre with a Subtics upload on the *Ghadir* and launch it with a thirty-minute delay. Terry needs to know about this before he deploys the Yemeni commandoes to Socotra tonight."

## CHAPTER 5

Like most aviators, Captain Ali Sharifi considered himself an elite pilot–except during his quietest moments of contemplation. It was then when he accepted himself as mediocre–even substandard.

Born into the ruling tribe of the Emirate of Abu Dhabi as a second cousin of President Khalifa bin Zayed Al Nahyan, he'd been gifted a coveted spot in the UAE's air college.

At least 'gifted' was the term his father had used. Sharifi preferred the term 'coerced', with the loss of his birthright's inheritance at risk if he'd refused.

Luxury and privilege had been his since birth, and he'd expected a life of ease and power. Then, as the UAE grew stronger and more expectant of military strength, his father had burdened him with the unexpected obligation of service.

Complaining had been pointless, and Sharifi had accepted his fate. Resigning himself to the minimum commitment time, he'd decided to enjoy the act of flying, which he admitted provided unparalleled excitement, and to expect the praise of others for his efforts in having earned his wings.

Reclining on a bunk in the UAE's Socotran air field's ready room, he thumbed through a tabloid on his phone. "Did you hear something?"

His squadron leader, a major, lowered his tablet. "No. Did you?"

"On this accursed island, I'm sure it was just the wind."

With winter gusts from the east and summer winds from the south, the runway faced north by northwest. Military priority gave his squadron of four F-16 Vipers the best storage location off the tarmac's southern tip, where a chain link fence with concertina wire encircled the tiny installation. Though an imperfect barrier, the fencing protected Quonset huts, revetments, fuel tanks, and a storage shed of spare parts and munitions.

Under whipping gusts, noise was a frequent problem.

Returning his face in his computer, the seated major frowned.

"You wouldn't complain about the wind. Anything else, yes, but not the wind. Unless you were on the runway, of course. Then I'd expect you to complain about it, your remaining military service time, or your dislike of whatever mission we're about to undertake. Am I accurate in noting that you complain incessantly during every takeoff?"

Sharifi groaned and convinced himself he'd heard nothing. But he thought something more nefarious than wind had caught his ear, and doubt nagged him. "You didn't authorize a drill, did you?"

"If I did, I wouldn't tell you." The major placed his tablet on his desk and looked at his wingman. "Now you're worrying me. Seriously, what did you hear?"

Upwind and to the south, a blast confirmed Sharifi's fears. He leapt from his bunk and stooped by a window. In the barracks housing the two dozen soldiers who guarded the small installation, he saw successive flashbang grenades and teargas smoldering. "We're under attack!"

The major raced to his side, glanced through the window, and barked his order. "To our aircraft!"

Though the attack on the barracks seemed less-than-lethal, bullet splatter from the two sentries outside the building proved the assailants' deadly resolve. In an instant, Sharifi agreed with his boss' order to reach their cockpits.

Their two aircraft were poised to fly within fifteen minutes of rousting their pilots, and while fleeing for his life, Sharifi was certain he'd compress that timeline. He zipped his g-suit, grabbed his helmet, and ran out the door behind his major.

Adjusted to the ready room's low lighting, his eyes adapted to the tarmac's shadows. Fear compelled his feet, and he gained ground on the older, slower major. Emotional dichotomies pounded him as the hoped safety of his jet contrasted his panic and as the anger of victimhood conflicted with the strange new feeling of pride.

Having felt useless and isolated on an island that his nation had placed on a military backburner, he interpreted the surprise assault as an unintended boosting of his self-importance. From the monotony of drills, training, and uneventful air patrols, his life had taken on instant and profound meaning.

Thinking he'd reach his aircraft, he gasped as blood splattered from his boss.

Keeping his pace, he glanced at his fallen comrade's face. The corpse's lifeless eyes stared into oblivion, and Sharifi's instinct for self-preservation precluded his remorse. Focused on the ladder to his cockpit, he accelerated to an all-out sprint.

Trying to recall his rudimentary understanding of his ground crew's final pre-flight preparations, he was relieved to see an airman crouched behind a start cart. He called out between his heaving breaths. "Remove the wheel chocks and standby to remove the starter air hose!"

Terrified, the man stared back with wide eyes.

Sharifi repeated himself. "Wheel chocks and starter air hose!"

The airman remained a statue.

The captain ran to his side, crouched, and tried to slow his breathing.

Finally, the young ground crew member squeaked his question. "What's going on, sir?"

"It's some sort of ambush. I need to get in the air before they steal this jet."

"What about me, sir?"

The captain looked into the distant shadows of the compound's perimeter. "You can make a run for the fence. Once I get this plane moving, they won't be looking behind it for a man on foot."

"Agreed, sir. I'll get you airborne. Get in."

Sharifi darted towards his jet. Bullets whizzed by him as he grabbed a rung and scampered upward. Leaping, he landed in his seat, tossed away the ladder, and closed the canopy. Unable to think in detail, he let muscle memory guide his ignition of the jet's propulsion.

As the engine came to life, the linesman removed the starting air hose and took cover.

Releasing the brakes, Sharifi taxied the jet forward as he strapped himself in. Unsure of his assailants' intent, he feared a grenade or rocket landing in his lap. But as he gained speed and angled the fighter towards its runway, he noticed a lack of weapons coming his way.

He let himself hope he'd already earned his escape.

When his front wheel reached the runway, he glanced to both sides. Every warrior showed him his back, suggesting that they'd given up on stopping him. The unobstructed canopy also gave him a view of the carnage, and he saw five motionless soldiers on the asphalt. Four were his countrymen, but one was evidence of his security team's competence in fighting back.

Pride.

As he gained speed and knew he'd achieve flight, he noticed that a bullet had grazed his thigh. Keeping his hands on his aircraft's controls, he checked the injury with mental awareness. His skin burned, but his leg seemed functional.

At the pre-dawn hour, he saw no civilian aircraft blocking his run. Facing a ten-knot crosswind, he achieved lift at one hundred and twenty-five knots with his air-to-air loadout. In case his enemy prepared a missile against him, he stayed low and kissed the wave tops until his overrun base was five miles behind him.

Then he selected the afterburner and climbed.

He breathed and tensed his body against the acceleration, and the familiar stresses brought his panic under control. As he regained his calm awareness, he reflected upon the appropriate responses to his military installation's defeat.

Communication rose to the top of his list.

He flicked on his radio and yelled into his helmet's microphone. "Al Dhafra, this is Viper Thirty-six. Over."

A concerned voice from his fighter wing at Al Dhafra Air Base, Abu Dhabi replied. "Viper Thirty-six, this is Al Dhafra. We read you. Go ahead. Over."

"They attacked the base. Over."

"Say again, Viper Thirty-six. Over."

"We're under attack in Socotra, Al Dhafra! I barely escaped. The major's dead. At least four of our security team are dead. The base was overrun. Over."

"Understood, Viper Thirty-six. We had a distress call from the security team, but they didn't have any status on the assault force. We've lost contact. Over."

Anger and pride. "I'm heading back to Socotra, Al Dhafra. Over."

"State your intention, Viper Thirty-six. Over."

"To gather intelligence. I'll see what I can see. Over." Heeding his own advice, he checked his combat radar systems for proper function. Then he banked hard and turned back towards the military airfield he now considered hostile.

"Very well, Viper Thirty-six. Gather intelligence and then return to Al Dhafra. Over."

"Understood, Al Dhafra. Viper Thirty-six, out."

Although he aimed his anger towards his newfound enemy on the ground, he scanned the dark skies for danger.

Nothing.

Then he checked the water and ground ahead, and he saw three dark, rakish forms bobbing in the littoral waves.

Warships.

He checked his radar and committed the three vessels' numbers to his short-term memory. "Al Dhafra, Viper Thirty-six. I have three warships off the coast of Socotra Port. On my datalink, contacts seventeen, eighteen, and nineteen. Do you see them? Over."

"I see contacts seventeen, eighteen, and nineteen on the datalink and understand them to be warships. Can you identify the class of warships? Over."

Paying for his past laziness as a student, Sharifi was hampered. He described what he could. "They have large missiles. Huge compared to the ships' sizes. All three warships. Over."

"Styx missiles? Over."

"Yes. I think so. Over."

"Be advised, Viper Thirty-six, those are probably *Osa* missile boats. There's also a *Tarantul* with the Yemeni loyalists. None of those ships are equipped with anti-air systems, but beware of shoulder-launched weapons on those ships and from the forces that overran our base. Over."

Sharifi dove and readied his gun as he approached his former base. Unsure what to expect, he ingested everything he could see. His magnified forward-looking infrared sensor showed most of his security and support team in a forced march with their hands zip-tied behind them. Based upon the assailants' preparedness to usher prisoners in formation, he trusted his countrymen would survive.

As he saw his major's F-16 turning onto the runway, he hoped one of his squadron's aviators had reached their fallen boss' cockpit. But a sinking feeling compounded the g-forces as he leveled over the installation's covered revetments. The shadowy curves he'd seen in the pilot's silhouette were unfamiliar.

Even in the cockpit, the seated man was taller than Sharifi's fellow UAE aviators.

From lessons he'd considered boring about who was retraining pilots of the Yemeni Air Force, he remembered his nation handling much of the now self-defeating work. He also recalled a note about Egyptians teaching them how to handle F-16s.

He concluded the assailants were Yemeni and that they were stealing UAE aircraft. "Al Dhafra, Viper Thirty-six. I see a foreign pilot trying to take off in Viper Thirty-three. I also see our ground team being shepherded towards our aircraft in the revetments. Over."

"Understood, Viper Thirty-six. Do you see any signs of other hostile activities?"

"That's a negative, Al Dhafra. Just the three warships and the ground force on our base. Over.

"Very well, Viper Thirty-six. Come to Al Dhafra base immediately. Over."

"Coming to base..." Unwilling to leave in unqualified defeat, Sharifi let his anger blossom as he flew over a mountain and then banked back towards the tiny airfield. "No. I'm taking out Viper

Thirty-three. Engaging with a heat-seeking Sidewinder. Over."

"Negative, Viper Thirty-six. You could hit civilian targets at the airport. Do not engage! Do not engage! Acknowledge. Over."

Sharifi silenced his radio and flipped switches to assign the weapon under his right wing to his major's former jet. His fire control system discerned the roaring heat of the targeted airframe, and he let the Sidewinder fly.

Like a bottle rocket, the missile shot ahead.

Bright exhaust traced a line towards his quarry's engines, waned as the missile gained speed, and then left a contrail pointing towards the exploding Viper Thirty-three. An ejection seat shot upwards into the darkness.

Uncaring to look for his enemy's parachute, Sharifi accelerated over the water and turned around for a pass at the revetments to destroy the last two captured F-16s. As he prepared missiles for the task, he reconsidered.

By marching the ground crew into the aircrafts' berthing areas, the assailants had protected their last two captured fighters.

As the captain sought ideas to help his countrymen, he saw two intruders lifting a cylinder onto one of their shoulders.

The assailants had brought shoulder-launched surface-to-air missiles.

Recognizing the mortal danger, Sharifi decided to escape. Turning his Viper away from the SAM threat, he opened the distance and evaded. A parting glance showed smoldering wreckage on the asphalt.

Excited about his courage and initiative, he energized his radio. "Al Dhafra, Viper Thirty-six. Viper Thirty-three is destroyed. I couldn't touch Viper Thirty-four or Viper Thirty-five due to our ground crew being used as human shields, but I sent one Sidewinder into Viper Thirty-three and left it as wreckage on the runway. Over."

A new, stern voice replied. "You idiot! You just disabled that runway and stranded five thousand of our expatriates."

"Sir, I–"

"Shut up, rendezvous with a refueling tanker I'm having sent out, and get your aircraft back here."

Furious, Sharifi shut off his radio and aimed his aircraft towards Al Dhafra. He considered the senior officer's complaint the result of a frightened, political careerist but knew his fellow pilots would applaud his bravery.

To spite the senior coward in Al Dhafra, he wanted to push his position. With two Harpoons and four anti-air missiles remaining on his hard points, he could sink at least one of the warships and damage radar and weapon systems of the others.

But then he recalled the rules of engagement which he'd ignored when attacking Viper Thirty-three. He couldn't confirm the identity of the assailants as Yemeni any more than he could know who operated the darkened warships below him. And if he could penetrate the close-in defenses of three ships to land his Harpoons, he doubted the value of eliminating one small warship against the political fallout of killing an unknown crew.

Then he checked his conscience and admitted his hesitation to turn a ship into a tomb. As his anger fell, he considered his retaliation against the assault team's pilot justified, and when his military intelligence could verify his enemy's identify, he would strike back harder against those who'd wronged him.

And he needed the challenge.

For the first time in his life, he felt like he'd earned something–respect. And for the first time in his life, he had a purpose–revenge.

He'd fight the administrative battles on land, calling in his father's favors if needed, to assign himself to the retaliation force that would retake the base on Socotra–if his leaders had the courage he expected.

And if they didn't, he promised himself to rally a strike force of his own.

No matter what, he vowed to come back.

Tickling his aircraft's skin, unwelcomed electromagnetic radiation tripped an alarm. He gasped but then became curious about the flying newcomer that broadcast unfamiliar frequency patterns. His Viper's radar painted the object, which moved at thirty knots above the island behind him.

A helicopter. Or a rotary wing drone.

He made note to call attention to the aircraft during a debrief he dreaded, depending who attended it.

As he received permission to fly a corridor through Omani airspace, he heard a new voice hail him. "Viper Thirty-six, this is Al Dhafra. Over."

Recognizing his squadron commander speaking in an early-morning-rousted gritty but non-accusative tone, he took the bait. "Al Dhafra, this is Viper Thirty-six. Go ahead. Over."

"Viper Thirty-six, this is the Third Squadron Commander. Report immediately to the debrief room after landing in Al Dhafra. Over."

"Understood, sir. Over."

The colonel lowered his volume. "I assume you already heard the general's opinion. I'll reiterate the salient points of his message in private upon your return. Out."

Sharifi sighed and smiled. His squadron commander supported his aviators taking initiative, and reading the message between the message, he knew that an ally backed up his actions.

# CHAPTER 6

His heart pounding, Commander Andi Amir heaved a heavy sigh. "The fighter jet is gone, sir."

"Very well. Break defensive formation and return to our off-boarding operation."

Surprised how cool Captain Damari remained against an aircraft with the firepower to sink their flagship, Amir wondered if his new commodore was human or molded from steel. "I'll recommence the offboarding immediately, sir."

"I'm sure the pilot saw us. Make haste."

The *Tarantul's* commander lifted his voice to an open microphone. "Tactical center, verify that we're still in communication with the infiltration team."

His executive officer sounded shaken from the surprise F-16 that had escaped the commando raid. "They just called us to make sure we're coming ashore. They still control the shore facilities, and the second team still holds the airfield."

Rerunning the evening through his mind, Amir recalled an uncontested taking of the harbor that a mix of Emirati sailors and Socotran employees had yielded without a fight. Combined with a victorious procurement of the air base that had left six Emiratis and one Yemeni commando dead, the infiltration had succeeded.

The only flaw had been the escaped pilot and his F-16 Viper, which had exposed an occupying navy that might have otherwise remained concealed until daybreak.

Amir needed to unload his human cargo before the Emiratis regrouped and came back. But with the uncontested harbor he expected to accomplish the landing's goals.

He accelerated his ship to the pier and sent a boat crew ahead to climb ladders and handle ropes. With a backing bell, he brought the *Tarantul* to a stop, had it mated with mooring lines, and connected it to dry land with a walkway.

Letting the captain leave first to confer with the commando leader, Amir stayed behind to assure the families debarked into ordered groups.

When his feet reached solid concrete, he shouted. "Everyone, please listen to your assigned officer. Your assigned officer will share details as we learn them." He grabbed his lean second-in-command. "Keep them in tight formations and tell them what you can when you can. Hopefully Captain Damari will return with good news and some soldiers to lead them."

"Where will you be, sir?"

"I'm checking on the *Osas* and the surface-to-air missiles. After that F-16 escaped, I fear the Emiratis may retaliate sooner rather than later. We need to get these ships back to sea."

"Right, sir. I'll tend to the families."

Amir trotted to the first missile boat, whose sailors were lowering its brow between their ship and the pier. Saluting as he placed his foot on the steel girder, he kept his stride while pretending to expect an answer. "I request permission to come aboard."

A sailor returned his salute.

"Radio Commander Gulla that I'm coming up to see him."

"Aye, sir."

On the small ship, Amir reached its bridge within several breaths and found his friend standing by a window.

Gulla grunted. "You seem in a hurry."

"We need to talk, Najib."

Raising his voice, the *Osa's* commander brought privacy to the space. "Everyone, clear the bridge. Executive officer, get the families off first."

Amir protested. "Hold on. That's what I want to talk about. We need to get the air defenses assembled first."

"But we've always put the families first."

"And we still are. That F-16 pilot may change his mind and come back. Let's protect the skies."

"Good thinking." Gulla turned to his second-in-command. "You heard him. Anti-air missiles first. Then the families."

Alone with the *Osa's* commander, Amir shared his concerns. "Has Captain Damari told you anything about our Socotran contact?"

Gulla frowned. "Yeah. During the same briefing he gave you. It's Nuha Shaman, the loyalist resistance leader."

Amir reflected upon the female icon whom President Hadi had let rise to power as a thorn pinching the patriarchal emirates' sides. While the UAE had lavished Socotra with infrastructure and commerce to win its people's hearts and minds, she'd formed the resistance in response to the tightening of controls and dependence on foreign investment. She was an image of courage and principles. "But what do we really know about her?"

"We know she's taking in our families. We're in her debt."

"As long as she doesn't turn against us."

"You know as well as I that she's on our side."

"Today she is. Tomorrow may be a different story."

"Damn it, Andi! Don't be an ass."

Amir corrected himself. "Sorry. I'm letting my family's safety bother me. I can hardly remember why we dragged them with us when we're going to be constantly deployed."

"Because it's easier to hide three hundred people on an island of sixty-thousand people as opposed to any town on the mainland." Gulla stepped towards the exit. "Come on, Andi. We're going to have to trust those who are helping us if we want to protect a home worth retuning to."

Standing on the pier, Amir saw progress.

The second *Osa* had moored, and its strongest sailors held tarps carrying the final six-hundred-pound Russian R-27T Alamo air-to-air missile towards its makeshift launcher.

Soldiers had arrived with trucks holding single-rail launchers in their beds and had assisted the sailors in hoisting the weapons to their racks. With the weapons from Commander Gulla's *Osa*, there were sixteen Alamos moved onto eight trucks with each vehicle holding one reload.

Though disadvantaged with ground launches and with their forward-looking-infrared guidance systems mounted on truck roofs, the surface-based attack using R-27T missiles had proven effective when Houthis had shot down Saudi jets.

The UAE Air Force could outsmart sixteen Alamos, but losses were probable, and they'd have to consider losses before striking from the sky.

A junior officer from this *Tarantul* called to his boss. "Commander Amir, sir? The families are leaving now. The executive officer sent me to tell you. Your family's last in line, per your orders."

Amir turned and stepped towards the lines of people moving beyond the waterfront port authority building and towards civilian vehicles creating a traffic jam at the gate.

Losing count of the times he'd bid farewell to his family under the weight of mortal danger, he found his children and his wife and gave them goodbye kisses.

Wanting to get to the open sea's safety, he sought his commodore where he expected to find him. He saw discussions underway among groups in disparate clothing in the port authority structure, darted to the building, and pushed his way into its lobby. A circle had formed around a woman who appeared shorter and wider than her pictures suggested.

A voice halted him. "Commander Amir!"

The *Tarantul's* commander turned and saw his commodore entering the building behind him. "Sir?"

For the first time, the navy's new commodore seemed flustered. "A word, before we meet the resistance."

"Of course."

"I spoke to one of President Hadi's aides. He knows of our success in taking the island and will use the Emirati detainees as a bargaining chip. I've arranged for the few Emiratis here to be transferred to the barracks at the airfield. That will be our holding pen until we have access to a proper brig."

Unsure why his boss seemed uneasy, Amir listened. "Understandable, sir."

"For us, that changes nothing. We still need the air defenses posted here and at the air base. I'm negotiating with the army's

Special Security Forces teams to have a third of the trucks moved to the air base, and a third sent up the mountain with four shoulder-launched teams joining them."

"Negotiating? I thought you were in charge."

Damari snorted through his hawkish nose. "It's an endless struggle for power between ground and naval forces. Since we're on an island, I have the upper hand, but the army sent a colonel with them. I need to overpower him to keep ground soldiers from taking control of things they don't understand."

The *Tarantul's* commander gulped. "Like the sea and air battle."

"The problem is, they understand the air battle, but only from the perspective of defending or attacking ground positions. They'll lose sight of the maritime elements unless I assert myself."

Growing louder, the din behind Amir beckoned. "They already have the relationship with the resistance. The army arranged for all our families to hide with them." He glanced through a window and saw one of his officers ushering two families into the waiting automobile of a resistance member.

Damari lowered his voice. "But the colonel has the personality of a train wreck. I'm sure he's making no friends."

"I'm sure you can do better, sir."

"No, commander. You can."

Amir's heart raced. "Me? I need to get my ship to sea."

"Soon. Spend fifteen minutes with her and win her over. I'll introduce you as my chief of staff, answer a few questions, and then leave you with her."

Wondering if his boss sought to shirk his duties, Amir frowned.

"I know what you're thinking, and you're right. I should be doing this, but I can't be two places at once. I need to get in front of the colonel and his people and get them used to obeying my orders. That leaves you with her."

"Well, yes. But, sir–"

"Look at me, commander. Do I seem charismatic to you?"

"Um… Not really." Amir grasped the commodore's intent. "I see your point, sir."

"You have a quality about you that wins people over. Just don't mention the mercenaries yet. I don't trust her completely."

"I–"

"Let's go." Damari stepped towards the audience and pushed through it. Taking a space by a desk which served as the port authority's center of power, he stopped, spun, and faced the small crowd. "Good morning, everyone. For those of you who don't know me, I'm Captain Rami Damari, fleet commodore. And this is Commander Andi Amir, my chief of staff and commanding officer of the *Tarantul.* which is the largest of our three warships."

Uncertain how to behave in front of his boss, a handful of camouflaged commandos, and an icon of the pro-Hadi resistance surrounded by her six closest followers, the *Tarantul's* commander nodded and remained silent.

Wearing a hijab dyed a regal purple, Nuha Shaman folded her arms and offered a slight bow. "I'm glad to meet you in person. Has everything been going to plan?" She eyed the special forces colonel who made sure he and his supporting officers stayed in her vision.

Damari was respectful. "Not perfect but successful, ma'am. The team seized the port and the air base with minimal casualties. One fighter jet escaped to the UAE and one was destroyed along with a large patch of runway, but I'm sure our engineers can patch the runway by the end of the day."

Shaman scowled. "By the end of the day, there'll be a thousand Emirati citizens lined up for flights home, and my people will have nothing to tell them. Shall I say that your attack stranded them in a terminal next to a military installation that changed ownership to their state's enemy overnight?"

"I agree that it's an unwanted outcome, but I assure you that Colonel Mohamed's soldiers performed admirably in their task."

Amir noticed the colonel's tightening body and reddening face, suggesting that he'd interpreted Damari's veiled compliment as a jab for letting the runway get bombed.

Shaman seemed to agree. "The escaped fighter jet has placed a strain on my people. We've accelerated the evacuation of your families to our ranks, but as you can see, it's hectic."

Glancing at the exodus, Amir saw cars losing their order and camouflaged men serving beside sailors as overwhelmed traffic cops.

In a condescending tone, Colonel Mohamed replied. "Moving forward, we'll establish anti-air defenses so that no aircraft can threaten us."

Shaman eyed him and then faced Damari. "Do you agree? Will no aircraft be a threat to the island?"

The commodore was diplomatic. "I believe what the colonel means is that we'll optimize our air defenses before sunrise and that we'll have the strength to dissuade any opposing air forces from escalating hostilities."

Either predicting his political defeat or demonstrating his disdain for the competition, the colonel excused himself under the pretense of directing the air defenses and left one underling to represent the army.

Shaman addressed Damari. "I'm helping you now because your families are desperate and because I wanted the Emiratis off the island. What guarantee can you give that you won't make our lives worse than the Emiratis did?"

"No guarantee. Just my word to protect the seaport and the airport and to otherwise stay out of your affairs."

"But by taking the ports, you're already in our affairs. I want to better understand your intent."

"Of course. Commander Amir has my full confidence and can explain in detail, but I need to help the colonel establish our air defenses. If you'll excuse me." Damari left the *Tarantul's* commander with the resistance.

Shaman unbalanced him with an unexpected question. "Tell me about yourself, Commander Amir."

"Uh… I'm a career naval officer, but I have no political connections. I'm going to command my ship until it's no longer mine to command."

"And then?"

"And then I expect my career will end. Then I'll probably work as a fisherman until I hopefully become an old man watching my children grow."

"And why are you here?"

"To protect my family."

"Not just your family. Many families. With a well-stocked warship under your command, you could have sought refuge in easier places. Why Socotra?"

"It's strategic."

She rolled her eyes. "So said the Russians, the Americans, the Saudis, and the Emiratis. I'm more interested in how you see this latest iteration of violence affecting my people."

He realized that only candor would appease her. "If I had a magic wand, you'd have any peaceful future you choose. But as you implied, larger nations will never leave you alone. My hopes are that you can join a united Yemen."

An underling leaned and whispered into her regal fabric. Dismissing her aide with a nod, she challenged the officer. "You're from a southern tribe. Why do you want a united nation?"

"President Hadi is from Aden, like me. I know nothing of him personally, but I support his policy of remaining unified. We need strength to stand against so many oppressors. Divided, we're weak."

She continued digging. "You had an admiral in charge of your fleet, and I know personally that President Hadi trusted him until he was supplanted. How do you explain Captain Damari's rise?"

Unable to lie to her, Amir shared everything. "The admiral was incompetent and would've put our entire fleet and families at risk. I supported the transition."

"The mutiny, you mean."

"Yes. If we must name it."

Her gaze paralyzed him. "I'll tell you what I see when I look at you, Commander Amir. I see an honest man who believes in a cause greater than himself. I don't know yet with Captain Damari because he's too reserved, and I know a tyrant when I see one in Colonel Mohamed. But as long as you are standing against the Emirates, you and the navy have my support. My people will also pressure the soldiers to fall in line."

"Thank you, ma'am."

Another underling lowered a cell phone and then whispered in Shaman's ear.

She nodded. "Join me, commander. There's an argument happening outside. Let's see if I can settle this divide among your forces." Her people repositioning to her flanks, she spun around and marched towards the door.

Amir trotted to catch up to her, and he was surprised to see Colonel Mohamed screaming at his naval counterpart. "Any idiot knows that you consolidate defenses."

Damari's voice was forceful. "Not when you're protecting multiple locations."

"We don't need to protect the damned port! It's just a bunch of water and walkways."

Shaman raised her voice. "Ninety-three percent of our food and medical supplies arrive through this port. And, if I understand your plan, your occupying ground troops will be arriving here, as well."

Colonel Mohamed scowled. "You may know politics, woman, but you don't know armed combat!"

"But this woman, as you call me, knows common sense. The port is valuable. Something valuable must be defended."

In a silent huff, the colonel marched away.

The captain faced his rescuer. "Thank you, ma'am. There's no time to waste arguing. Daylight's coming, and we need to be in our optimized posture by then."

"How do you define your optimized posture?"

"Our families hidden among your people. Our navy hidden at sea. Half our air defenses at the air base, half here, spread around each location to prevent destruction by any single bomb. One F-16 in the sky, another F-16 ready to launch within five minutes."

"Even with a broken runway?"

"It's only broken for passenger aircraft. An F-16 can manage with a small fraction of that runway."

"Very good. My people will be watching. If Colonel Mohamed gives you trouble, call me directly." She turned and walked away with her entourage.

Damari watched her depart. "Impressive. She has more power than I'd thought. What did you say to her?"

"I just told her the truth, sir."

"Best to never lie to her, then."

"Absolutely not..."

"Come, Amir. Gather the crews. We've won enough land-based battles tonight. Let's get underway and prepare to fight at sea."

## CHAPTER 7

In the Al Dhafra airbase commander's office, Sharifi stood at attention with his jaw clenched shut.

The general's breath stank of coffee. "Don't pretend you were out of radio contact for one instant. You thought you'd play the hero, and all you did was create political pressure! How do I explain one of my pilots disobeying a direct order from my staff and putting Socotran civilians at risk?"

Sharifi risked answering. "I didn't put them at risk, sir. It was a safe shot. I never put civilians in danger."

The general yelled. "It was a rhetorical question, you idiot! Politicians don't care how safe it was! You launched a weapon at a civilian Socotran runway that we borrow based upon very delicate agreements. In case you're too stupid to figure it out, delicate agreements and missiles don't mix!"

Since the runway was no longer in UAE possession at the time, the young captain had to bite back his desire to correct his general again about 'borrowing' being in the past tense.

The senior officer lowered his volume. "If I didn't need every pilot I've got, I'd take your damned wings right now. Do you understand me?"

"Yes, sir!"

Turning to the Sharifi's squadron commander. "Do you have anything to add, colonel?"

"I'll use him in our counterstrike, but after that, Captain Sharifi will wish he hadn't been born by the time I'm done disciplining him, sir."

"Good. Dismissed!"

Sharifi spun and marched out the office behind the colonel. In the hallway, he risked talking to his squadron commander. "You don't really believe–"

"Shut up, captain."

"Yes, sir." In the uncomfortable silence, the walk to the briefing room seemed twice its normal distance.

Outside the secure door, the colonel stopped, glanced in all directions, and then leaned towards the young pilot. "I'm not going to rip into you like the general wants, but there will be repercussions. Putting a Sidewinder on target like you did was clever, but it may have been too clever. Disobeying orders is a quick way to lose your wings. You should've known that."

"Sir, I–"

"You need to shut up and listen."

Sharifi took the hint. "Sorry."

"In the heat of battle, I don't expect you to do everything perfectly every time. But all your missile did was shut down the civilian flights and add havoc to an island we've spent years trying to win with kindness. And you just infuriated thousands of the natives."

Wanting to protest, Sharifi pursed his lips.

His tone softer, the colonel continued. "But your decision to take out Viper Thirty-three on the runway was excellent, and your fellow pilots will revere you for it. Don't let the admiration cloud your judgment."

"No, sir. I won't."

"Get in there and accept your accolades because I know the guys are impressed–and even jealous, which is good. You're helping to keep them hungry. But you need to understand that restraint and following the rules of engagement are paramount to success."

Sharifi had to say something. "May I speak, sir?"

"Go ahead."

"There were no rules of engagement. I was surprised, I barely escaped with my life, and I had to watch people die. I think I responded admirably, sir."

The colonel straightened his back. "I'm not going to coddle your ego, son. But you did see some nasty stuff, and it's okay to be rattled."

"I'm not rattled, sir. I'm furious–at the Yemenis and the general for treating me like a dog for it."

"The general won't get in your face about it again, and the other pilots will worship you for all of about two minutes. After that, you'll be alone with your thoughts, and all your cocksure swagger won't matter an iota. You'll realize that you're rattled, or else you aren't human."

Absorbing the wisdom, Sharifi remained silent.

The colonel finished his lesson. "When that happens, make sure you can look in the mirror and accept everything you did out there and make sure you're ready to fly again. Until then, keep replaying what you saw in your mind and make sure you don't forget. You'll want to remember every detail, for your own sanity. Come on."

Sharifi followed the colonel into the room.

As the squadron commander moved to a display screen, a dozen admiring pairs of eyes looked up. The other pilots revered the young captain, and pride displaced his anger.

"Captain Sharifi?"

The hero turned. "Sir?"

After the squadron commander invoked a satellite view of Socotra, he extended a remote control. "Plan the counterstrike."

Warm butterflies flitted in Sharifi's stomach as he accepted the controller. "Me, sir?"

"I want to see what you propose with the battle fresh on your mind."

"Of course, sir."

"Note the following changes since you left the island. We've got a reconnaissance drone monitoring the scene, and the Yemenis brought two MiG-29 Fulcrums to join the two F-16s they took from us. They've also deployed ten to twenty Alamo missiles on the backs of trucks. The MiGs and F-16s are working round the clock on combat air patrols, probably using extra pilots to allow the high operations tempo."

The UAE's latest hero considered the defenses surmountable. "We can handle all that. Do we have a goal for a counterstrike?"

"The goal of the joint naval and army strike group is to win back the airbase and the seaport with zero civilian casualties. Our job from the air support perspective is to soften the defenses to allow paratrooper and maritime force landings."

"Soften. Meaning, we hit first?"

The colonel shrugged. "That's what we do. The Navy may be able to sustain battles farther from home, but we strike the fastest. We need to open the way to allow boots on the ground, and the only way to get them there is to drop them or to disembark them. Since we lost control of the airfield, we can't land heavy equipment on the island like we may have preferred."

The comment inspired the young captain's defense. "Neither can the Yemenis until they clean the runway, thanks to me."

The colonel grunted. "Good point, but don't mention it again outside this room. Nobody above my rank wants to hear it. In fact, I don't want to hear it again."

Sharifi frowned but nodded his agreement. "Yes, sir."

"Regardless, the general has informed me that we need to land troops from the air into each base. The landings must be within the perimeter of each installation, as shown in the red borders on the map. Sea landings are a second priority."

"Can we have the airport terminal abandoned?"

"Probably, at least while they repair the runway."

Sharifi swallowed and recalled his ground support team being marched to the aircraft parked on the ground in Socotra. "What about the prisoners on the air base?"

"The ground troops will work an extraction plan–provided we open up access for them. Please proceed, captain."

The young pilot walked to the screen and pointed to its top left corner. "We send in two fighters from the northwest, just like anyone defending the island from us would expect, but we'll do it as a diversion."

"Good so far. Keep talking."

"The main force will pass low and fast from north to south and then double back from the southwest."

Animated, the colonel stepped beside the captain and elevated his arms towards the screen. "Let's split that force in half. Five aircraft will come from the west to attack launchers at the seaport and five from the southwest to attack those at the airfield."

As he absorbed the tactics, Sharifi understood why his squadron commander wanted him involved in the planning. It helped wipe away the chaos of reactive combat and forced him to think intentionally. He'd needed that. "Right, sir. We'll want cluster munitions for the Alamo launchers and for any grounded aircraft, which should be our secondary targets. Concise timing where we strike in unison will be key to overwhelm the defenses."

"Good job, Sharifi. Take a seat."

Calmed, the young captain obeyed.

The colonel looked at him. "I assume you intended for the diversion fighters to pull the Yemeni combat air patrol to them?"

He had. "Yes, sir."

"The diversion fighters will have an air-to-air load." The colonel looked at a pair of young captains. "You two will handle it. You haven't trained in bombing runs as much as the others, but I trust your dogfighting skills as well as anyone's."

With bravado masking their fear, the pilots nodded.

The squadron commander looked to his executive officer, a short lieutenant colonel with a wide nose. "You'll lead Strike Team Two against the seaport. I'll lead Strike Team One against the airfield. I expect more resistance from the air base, given the importance they've placed on keeping their air patrols. I'll assign two anti-air missiles and a full gun magazine to each of the main strike force jets, in case the Yemeni jets pose a problem. But the rest of the loads will be cluster bombs."

Emboldened by his string of success in action and thought, Sharifi challenged. "Is there any chance we can go after the Yemeni Navy?"

"We don't know where they are, and we're not going to look. If they want to create trouble, we have enough support from Iranian submarines to stop them."

Until this morning, Sharifi had ignored naval developments, much less events happening under the waves. "There's nothing of ours available to dissuade the Yemenis?"

The colonel shook his head. "No. However, there's a task force being mobilized against Socotra now, but our softening run will be done long before it arrives. If there's anything remaining of the Yemeni Navy when the task force arrives, they'll call on us again, I'm sure."

Sharifi felt small in a growing cauldron of combat.

The squadron commander continued. "And you can avoid the Yemeni Navy by keeping your distance. They have nothing to reach you except shoulder-launched weapons. Your threat is on land, and your targets will attempt to blend in with the countryside, which is why we'll attack before sunset. You'll need visual confirmation of targets."

A pilot seated across the room made the snide remark that had been circling in the back of Sharifi's mind. "If we'd kept the damned garrison on Socotra, they would've already retaken the ports, and we could all stay home for dinner."

As his comrades issued nervous chuckles, Sharifi wondered if the abandoned garrison would've prevented the Yemenis from conducting the raids that had reshaped his career and his perspective. But he remembered the native islanders protesting an overage of Emirati power on the island, leading to the disbanding of the five-hundred-man barracks.

Feeling his overused adrenaline subsiding, he sank into his chair and digested the lecture.

Hours passed in planning, and when a good approach took shape, the colonel departed to share his intent with the general. An hour later, the squadron commander returned with irrelevant changes the general had inserted to assert his power. But the basic plan stood.

Attack with the sun behind them and soften the ports' anti-air defenses.

An hour before sunset, Sharifi guided his F-16 Viper in the trail position of a five-aircraft formation. Since he'd joined the squadron as an outsider from its overrun Socotran detachment, he flew behind his unfamiliar partners.

Over his radio, he heard the ruse working. "Viper One, this is Viper Eleven. Viper Twelve and I have two bogeys coming for us at five hundred knots. Over."

Leading Sharifi's group of five, the colonel replied. "Viper Eleven, this is Viper One. Draw them away. You may engage if threatened, but keep them away from the strike teams. Over."

"Understood, Viper One. Viper Eleven, out."

The colonel's tone intensified. "Viper Six, Viper One. Is Strike Team Two ready to attack? Over."

Leading the second team, the short lieutenant colonel replied in a gritty baritone. "Viper One, Viper Six. Strike Team Two is in position and ready. Over."

Raising his voice to imply an audience of ten aircraft, the squadron commander ordered the assault. "Strike Teams One and Two, this is Viper One. Follow me down to two hundred feet, airspeed four hundred eighty knots."

After the jets ahead of him dived, Sharifi tightened his muscles against the g-forces and angled his accelerating fighter behind them. With the low horizon, a minute passed before the Hajhir mountains became visible. His heart raced as the airfield, and then the first targeted launcher truck, came into view.

"Strike Team One, Viper One. Energize your fire control systems and arm your cluster munitions."

As Sharifi flipped switches to prepare his aircraft to drop bombs, he saw the closest truck kick dust.

"Viper Five, Viper One. The truck located at ten o'clock is target one in the system. Target one is yours. Confirm. Over."

Sharifi acknowledged his new call sign with his new formation and glanced at the icon on his fire control display. "Viper One, Viper Five. I confirm target one is mine. Over."

"Viper Five, Viper One. Detach and engage target one. Over."

"I'm peeling off." A gentle turn aimed Sharifi and his cluster bombs towards the victim of his vengeance.

A thirst for revenge fueled him, but as the number of anti-air warheads poised against him danced in his mind, something made him hold his breath.

Fear.

His squadron leader had been correct. He was rattled, and he welcomed the colonel's voice in his helmet as he assigned the next visible trucks to the other pilots. "Viper Four, Viper One. You have target two at one o'clock. Over."

"Viper One, Viper Four. I have target two. Over."

"Viper Four, Viper One. Peel off and engage target two." The colonel then narrated his concerns. "Strike Team One, Viper One. The targets are moving. They're not going to sit still to be bombed. Adjust your targeting. But why aren't they firing yet?"

Sharifi found the question perplexing until pandemonium answered it.

Within seconds, half a dozen panicked men were shouting.

"Something's locked onto me. Inbound missiles. At least six! I can't see anything!"

"I'm spiked! I've got inbounds, too. But I don't see anything!"

"They're not coming from the island. They're coming from the water. French Thales guidance radar."

"I see it. Dark and low in the water. Three o'clock!"

Attentive, the colonel drew a wise conclusion. "Ambush! Strike Teams One and Two, break off. Abort! Abort! Abort!"

Having broken first from the formation, Sharifi had the greatest distance between himself and the hostile weapons. He pulled his Viper hard away from danger, rolled out, and accelerated it to its best speed.

Amid the turmoil, he heard each teammate fighting for his life, and Sharifi felt alone. Nobody would encourage him, nobody would help him watch the inbound death seeking him at twice his speed, and nobody would advise him how to escape.

With a wide panorama, his cockpit allowed him a line of sight to the chaos behind him. Crossing contrails laced the sky, and the missile coming for him eluded his eyes. But as the high-speed weapon illuminated its seeker, it revealed itself as a French MICA.

Sharifi feared he'd become the most interesting international death statistic. Recalling his day, he anticipated being the first

Arab pilot to die from a French missile after shooting an American-made jet operated by the UAE on a Yemeni runway. His aircraft's g-forces prevented his laughing at himself.

Then his fighter reached its top speed, eased its pressure on his ribs, and sent wave tops by him in hypnotic rhythm. Increasing distance from his hidden assailant weakened the lock of the mystery ship's French radar system on his fuselage.

As seconds ticked away and the deadly MICA attempted its own lock, distance and geometry allowed Sharifi to angle his F-16 from the reaches of the missile's seeker.

Having grasped the weapon's general direction, the young captain scanned behind himself for it. Seeing it over his right shoulder, he broke hard towards it, fought for consciousness while enduring the acceleration of eight gravities, and hoped.

The weapon dropped its lock and overshot.

Safe, he turned farther west and saw the missile falling off miles behind him. As his awareness expanded beyond his mortal terror, he considered his comrades. He climbed to see the battle and, to his dismay, to count parachutes.

Seeing two billowing canopies, he marked his position and the distance and direction to both floating pilots. After annotating his comrades' positions in his combat system, he switched channels and radioed his base. "Al Dhafra, Viper Five. We're under attack by MICA missiles. Over."

"Viper Five, Al Dhafra. We're aware of the attack. Your strike team has identified the shooter visually. You're facing a mercenary combat transport ship, *Goliath*-class. Over."

Wishing he'd paid better attention during his briefings, Sharifi was stymied. "Al Dhafra, Viper Five. Advise me on *Goliath*-class capabilities. Over."

"Negative, Viper Five. You're not to engage the *Goliath*-class, and this channel is open for damage assessment. Five Vipers have been hit. Can you see any parachutes? Over."

He was unable to see anything other than smoke trails from his squadron mates' doomed aircraft. "Negative, Al Dhafra. Over."

"Keep looking, Viper Five. Over."

"I want to engage the *Goliath*-class ship. Tell me what I'm up against. Over."

"Negative, Viper Five. The *Goliath*-class ship has already submerged. Regroup on your squadron commander to the west. Al Dhafra, out."

Sharifi switched channels and sought his leader. "Viper One, Viper Five. Radio check. Over."

Nothing.

"Viper One, Viper Five. Radio check. Over."

The colonel's voice revealed his unease. "Viper Five, Viper One. You heard Al Dhafra. Rejoin on me to the west. Over."

Sharifi wanted to destroy the *Goliath*-class ship that had surprised his squadron. The mercenary ship's presence with the misfit Yemenis seemed like cheating, but he knew better than attacking a semi-submerged ship with anti-air guns.

He obeyed his boss and escaped.

## CHAPTER 8

Cahill noticed his shaking leg, saw Walker noticing it, and allowed it to continue draining nervousness through his rubber sole and into the *Xerses'* deck plates. "That was almost unfair."

"It's war, Terry."

"We hit at least four of them. That's four widows."

"You don't know that."

With the dome under dark water, Cahill watched low-bandwidth data trickle in from Toulon, France, relayed through the guyed submarine-communication masts of Rosnay, a continent away, as his Yemeni clients fed their information over higher-speed channels to Renard. Lacking the long antennas needed to penetrate the water, the Yemenis relied upon the Frenchman's rented assets.

An update revealed Cahill's success in knocking five Emirati aircraft from the sky. And since he cared, he let his eyes burn on the number of parachutes seen.

Only two.

He'd killed three men.

Walker tried to make light of it. "Only three widows. It could've been worse. You unloaded all eight missiles."

Cahill found himself measuring life against life, his faceless victims against the faceless survivors his mission's humanitarian aid sought to feed and medicate.

His executive officer prodded him. "You've killed entire crews before. What gives?"

The *Xerses'* commander revealed the weight on his heart. "Ariella's pregnant. Uh... don't share that with anyone. It's too early to announce."

"Damn! You made quick work of it. Congratulations." Walker extended his arm.

Cahill shook his comrade's hand. "Thanks, mate."

"I guess that changes your perspective."

"I had no idea until I started killing again." The *Xerses'* commander stopped himself from sharing his deepest concerns.

With his wife bearing new life, he'd changed his criteria for bravery and the taking of human souls. He felt three-times as courageous, representing a growing family of three people, but he felt time-times as protective.

"It's about time. I wouldn't trade kids for anything."

Cahill considered his second-in-command a rock of serenity. "How do you do it? How do you face the danger with a family depending on you?"

"I just do it, mate. Killing. Fear of being killed. You've got to compartmentalize it."

"If you say so. It doesn't feel right."

"Well, feeling right or not, we're at war, and the data feed says you've still got F-16s circling above you. We're out of MICAs, but you can surface and take shots with the cannons and knock out a few more of them."

"And help the hidden Iranian submarines get a better targeting solution on us?"

"The drone hasn't heard anything about Iranian subs, and neither have we on our organic sensors."

"Doesn't mean they're not out there. You want to risk this ship, this crew, and this mission on a few buckshot opportunities?"

"Your call, mate. That's why you're in charge."

Telling himself any Iranian submarine coming for him with appreciable urgency would make noise, and verifying that nothing hostile appeared from the Israeli submerged drone's arcing patrol pattern, Cahill erred on the side of courage. "Bloody hell. Let's do it. Let me warn the crew."

"Like I said. You're in charge."

Cahill touched his nearest screen and flipped his circuit to the entire ship. "We're coming shallow to shoot down the remaining Emirati aircraft with the cannons. Set each of your next twenty rounds for splintering. I'll light them up on radar for you. Gunners report readiness."

Familiar voices replied over the speakers. "Port weapons bay ready. Starboard weapons bay ready."

"Drive us up, Liam, and keep us heavy with an up-angle. We won't stay up there long."

Walker tapped his screen, and the deck took a gentle incline. Cascading water became prisms shooting the setting rays through the dome. "Energizing the phased-array radar."

"Very well." Squinting against the light, Cahill saw a small swarm of aircraft dotting the sky above the setting sun, and his chest tightened. "Raise the railguns. Target the F-16s to the west."

"They're painting us with their targeting radar."

Cahill was surprised. "That was fast."

"They must've been watching. Raising cannons."

"No! Wait! Belay that!"

Walker lifted his fingers from his screen. "I'm waiting. Shit! Missile launch!"

"Damn. Get us back under."

Walker tapped keys, the deck angled downward, and water crept up the dome's sides.

But the small supersonic missile outpaced the *Xerses'* descent, and the warhead cracked above the submerging ship's stern.

Cahill barked. "Damage report!"

Nothing.

Walker shared his opinion. "I think that hit the starboard side."

The *Xerses'* commander called the starboard gunner by name. "Evans! Report!"

"I'm okay. Shit! That was loud."

"But you're okay?"

"Yeah. The railgun's fine, too. It was still stowed."

Tapping an icon to shift communication circuits, Cahill lifted his voice to the entire ship. "An anti-air weapon detonated above the starboard weapons bay. That's a small warhead. Evans is okay, and so is the railgun. We'll be staying under for some time."

Walker announced his instinctive damage assessment. "Anti-air warheads shoot strands of metal designed to cut aircraft skin. Our hull is thick enough to absorb that, and we were probably under enough water to have escaped damage."

"We'll check for damage later. My concern now is that the explosion just gave away our position to any Iranian submarine that's out there listening."

"Okay. I see your point. But there's nowhere to run. We're safest behind our drone's screen."

Although disliking the statement, Cahill agreed. "I got greedy. Trying to tag another jet or two with the cannons was too much." He raised his voice. "Sonar team, I'm going to hold five knots. Tell me how bad our flow noise is with the damage from the missile."

From the control room below, the supervisor replied. "We're already listening. There's nothing noticeable yet."

"Very well. Listen for another minute and then get back to your search plan for *Kilo* and *Ghadir* submarines."

Walker frowned. "You don't think the Iranians would risk getting this close to shore, do you?"

"Why not?"

"We've got the seaport and the airfield. We have helicopters ready to launch whenever those F-16s bugger out of here."

"But we don't have anti-submarine helicopters... not in the Yemeni order of battle."

"They may not know that."

"I've got a feeling the Iranians know as much about the Yemeni military as we do. Don't kid yourself. They'll have the guts to come close to shore, and I bet they've got at least one boat coming this way, if not more, now that they know we're here."

"Well, take a look at the data feed. Looks like the Emiratis are keeping their F-16s on station. Encouraging their downed pilots, standing up against the Yemenis. And they've probably figured out that we've shot our complete load of MICAs."

Cahill glanced at the deck and gathered his thoughts. "It's a quiet time, the calm between storms. But we'll need to stay on the bridge in case something develops. I'll have some dinner sent up."

Three hours later, Cahill considered splitting the midnight watch between himself and his executive officer.

A report over the slow data feed shifted his thoughts. "Bridge, control room. There's an unscheduled report from the drone coming in... it's found a submerged contact!"

Cahill snapped. "Enter the data into the system."

Finishing a yawn, Walker rubbed his eyes. "If this is a real detection, we may owe the Israelis our lives."

"Don't jump to conclusions yet." Cahill trusted the small nation's military hardware as the fruits of its hydrophones became the icon of an Iranian submarine on his display. "Bloody hell. *Ghadir*-class propulsion noise."

"Not good enough to shoot, though."

Cahill ran an aggressive geometry through his mind. "Not yet, but I'm shooting soon anyway. Assign tube three to the *Ghadir*."

Wide-eyed, Walker balked. "Tube three? A heavyweight?"

Having expected to face the decision, Cahill had wrestled with it for days. "Someone in our fleet needs to remind our enemy that we have teeth. They'll never be our clients, but they'll always be our adversaries. Assign tube three."

"I'm assigning tube three. Tube three is assigned. The system holds the *Ghadir* at eleven miles on bearing three-four-five, but bearing and range are both poor estimates."

"They'll get better, mate. Trust me." Cahill yelled into the open microphone. "Control room, set tube three with its slowest runout speed, passive search, submerged target mode."

As the team obeyed, the weapon's details appeared in a screen before the *Xerses'* commander.

"You're not going to shoot yet, are you?"

Cahill was itching to remove the submerged danger. "Soon. I may use the torpedo as a search tool during its run."

"Aggressive, especially given how few torpedoes we have."

"We can reload. And yes, it's aggressive. Let's move to a lag line of sight. Come left, steer course two-seven-zero."

Walker tapped keys. "Coming left to course two-seven-zero."

During the slow turn, Cahill read the final message from the Israeli robot stating it was heading deep to continue tracking the Iranian submarine. He expected an update from the drone in thirty minutes, unless the *Ghadir*'s behavior invoked an alert report.

Thirty minutes later, Cahill frowned at a display void of submerged contacts. "Control room, bridge. You've still got nothing?"

"That's correct, sir."

"What's the detection range to a *Ghadir* moving at five knots?"

"In these waters, less than three miles."

Cahill hoped the Iranian submarine moved faster than five knots. Otherwise, the *Xerses* would suffer an acoustic disadvantage–being detectable farther away than his adversary.

Walker voiced his growing knowledge of their new Israeli undersea warfare asset. "The Caesaron is the only reason we know about the *Ghadir*. It's due to report any minute now."

"Right. God willing, it's got something useful."

"It knows to maneuver towards a submerged contact automatically, doesn't it?"

Affirming what he'd read in the technical manual, the *Xerses'* commander nodded his agreement. Then, two minutes later, the Israeli drone's feed reached the Subtics tactical computer, placing a smile on Cahill's face. "That's a good bearing rate and a good bearing separation over time."

Walker scrunched his face. "In English."

"See how the lines of bearing from the drone to the *Ghadir* fan out like the spreading of fingers?"

"Yeah."

"That means it's really close to the drone, or it's going fast. But if it were going fast, we'd probably hear it. So, I believe it's a lot closer to the drone than to us. That's a guess–intuition, mind you, but I'm going to test it."

Seeming to warm up to submerged tactics, Walker sounded eager. "By turning towards the drone to reduce the distance?"

"Good guess, but no. If we weren't at war, I would. But this is combat, and I'm going to test my assumption with a weapon."

"Right."

Cahill raised his voice. "Attention on the *Xerses*, I'm shooting tube three at a *Ghadir*-class submarine detected by our Caesaron drone. I'm using a heavyweight to send a message about our seriousness as a warship and a fleet. We're on a lag line of sight, appropriate to evade counterfire. That's all. Carry on."

Walker's face was unreadable as he met his commander's stare.

"I'll do it meself, of course." Cahill looked to his screen, tapped icons, and then pressed the final graphic sending death towards unsuspecting Persians. "Shooting tube three."

The control room supervisor announced the weapon's initiation. "Bridge, control room. Tube three is away. Normal impulse launch. We have wire control."

"Very well, control room." Cahill sighed. "And now we wait." After waiting six minutes, he forced the outcome. "Damn it. Control room, set the torpedo to an active search, full power."

"The weapon is searching at full power, sir."

"Very well." Cahill flipped the view on a screen to show the torpedo seeker's raw transmissions and incoming sonic reflections. For a long minute that stressed his nerves, there was no return. "Bloody hell. Those small *Ghadir* hulls are problematic."

"Patience, Terry. You've taught me that."

Leaving the comment unanswered, the *Xerses'* commander glared at the screen.

A faint, fuzzy arc appeared. "Bridge, control room. Active return, bearing three-five-two. Range, three-point-four miles."

Cahill voiced a correction. "Steer the weapon left ten degrees."

"The weapon has accepted a left ten-degree steer. Active return, bearing three-five-three. Range, three-point-three miles. We've got a rough course and speed. Entering the solution into the system."

Cahill watched his victim's icon rise on a tactical display. The weapon had an advantageous geometry and adequate fuel. "Accelerate the weapon to pursuit speed."

"We're accelerating the weapon to pursuit speed... high-speed screws from the *Ghadir*. Gaseous countermeasures. It's trying to evade, but our weapon's on a good course."

Intense minutes passed as the torpedo closed in on the slow submarine.

The supervisor announced the enemy's fate. "Our torpedo's range-gating. We've got them."

As the explosion resounded throughout the bridge, Cahill lowered his head and accepted his decision to kill eighteen more men. "What can you hear, control room?"

"Nothing of the target. It's too small to break into compartments. I'm sure we vaporized most, if not all of it, sir."

Walker's tone was soft. "What's done is done. You made a decision, and nobody can fault you."

Thinking of his own fledgling family, the *Xerses'* commander pontificated. "There are women and children waiting for food and medical supplies in Yemen, and anyone who'd stop us from helping them now knows we're serious about it. The Iranians, the Houthis, the Separatists, the Emirates, and the Saudis." Speaking to convince himself, he continued. "Someone had to send the message. We're dead serious."

## CHAPTER 9

After two days of tracking an Iranian *Ghadir* off the coast of Yemen's eastern region around Nishtun, Volkov appreciated the resiliency of his crew and of the air-independent-propulsion variant of *Scorpène*-class submarine. Although the MESMA system ranked lowest on his list of AIP solutions in terms of efficiency, it let his *Wraith* outclass any *Ghadir*-class ship in a sustained battle.

Keeping his submarine slow, the *Wraith's* commander had avoided snorkeling while his adversary was shallow and charging its battery with diesel power.

He stooped over his sonar guru's shoulder. "How loud is it?"

Anatoly slid a muff behind his ear. "Snorkeling, loud enough. But you know it's touchy once it goes deep again."

Having lost and regained the Iranian submarine three times, Volkov wanted to shoot it. But he needed to wait, keep the mercenary fleet's presence hidden, and preserve Cahill's element of surprise in defending Socotra.

Seated at a far console, his radio operator announced the desired permission from the low-bandwidth feed. "Dmitry! Pierre says the *Xerses* has attacked Emirati aircraft and an Iranian submarine, with a heavyweight. You're free to engage any and all Iranian submarines."

Volkov darted to the man and glared over his shoulder at the incoming trickle of characters. "What else?"

The operator read the words aloud as they formed on his screen. "And you're ordered to clear a path in and out of Nishtun. Destroy all hostile naval assets. Submarines are the priority."

"Finally!" The *Wraith's* commander wasted no time. "Assign tube four to the *Ghadir* in passive mode. I want it in a combined submerged and surfaced mode, since the *Ghadir* is shallow. I also want it to swim out and run in its slowest mode to minimize noise. It's an unmoving target, and it's time to strike! Warm up tube five."

Twisting in his seat, the sonar ace shot his commander a

harsh glance. "That's a heavyweight."

"I know. That burden's on me. Assign it."

Standing, Anatoly hovered over the junior operator seated next to his console and watched him enter the data. "Tube four is ready."

"Shoot tube four."

His sonar ace announced the Persians' pending demise. "Tube four is away in swim-out mode. We have wire control."

"Very well."

The weapon covered the short distance and jogged towards its prey. When the *Ghadir's* crew realized its fate, the acceleration, countermeasures, and probable prayers proved pointless. The *Wraith's* detonating torpedo pounded the Iranian hull.

During the resonating boom, Anatoly was somber as he announced the success. "Our torpedo has sunk the *Ghadir*. We're listening for damage assessment."

"You won't hear anything, will you?"

The sonar ace shook his head. "No. There won't be much left of a submarine that small, if anything."

As Volkov accepted the weight of liberating eighteen souls from their bodies, he called to his radio operator. "Prepare a summary for Pierre with our attack. Launch it in a communications buoy with a fifteen-minute delay."

Later that night, the waters off Nishtun's coast were quiet with the undersea explosion seeming to have slipped out of remembrance for anyone outside of Volkov's chain of command.

Atop the *Wraith's* back, he stood over his crouched executive officer's shoulders. "You can hardly notice it."

A flashlight in his hand, Serguei disagreed. "If you were a teenager and you put such scratches and dents into your father's automobile, you'd see his backhand across your cheek before you'd see the light of day again."

"Fortunately, I'm not a teenager, and Papa Pierre is in a control center far away." The *Wraith's* commander glared at the rudder, which had survived having sliced its way through the escort tanker's hull. "Hold the light steady."

Steadying the lantern, Serguei sighed. "We already know it's insignificant for our sound signature. We got lucky. Rather, we didn't get unlucky."

Blunted at its forward edge, the rudder looked otherwise undamaged from its scraping against the escort ship. "Yes, but I wanted to be certain it wasn't any worse. There aren't any dangling parts. So, let's call it structurally sufficient and get on with our lives." Volkov turned and stepped away but heard only the lapping waves. He glanced over his shoulder. "Aren't you coming?"

His second-in-command had extinguished the light but remained crouched in the moonlight.

"Serguei!"

The executive officer stood, turned, and ambled to his commander. "Sorry. I was caught in a daydream."

"About what, if I may ask?"

"The dualism of our lives. It's so peaceful up here, and it's so quiet under water. But then I consider the violence we inflict. Terry just used a heavyweight. You just used a heavyweight. We're in an all-out war now."

After living with the outcome, Volkov judged the deadly decisions wise. "We both did the right thing. Pierre told us to be willing to use the heavyweights to prove that we're capable. In a way, I'm glad Terry did it first. It means I can share the burden with him."

"It also means our enemies will be desperate during situations where they wouldn't otherwise be mortally terrified. I'm not sure if we should have used humane weapons instead, but complaining now is pointless."

"Pierre considered it before instructing us, and so did I before shooting. And I assume Terry did, too. What's done is done. We have a convoy to escort to Socotra." Aiming his eyes in the distant darkness behind his submarine, the *Wraith's* commander spied the dark form of the ancient *Polnocny*-class troop transport ship and the two *Barbe*-class landing ships flanking it. "Say goodbye to the fresh air and head below."

Thirty minutes later, Volkov stood over his central tactical chart in the *Wraith's* submerged control room. "I don't like it. The waters are too quiet."

Across the table, his executive officer looked up. "I would've said they're too loud."

Understanding his second-in-command's point, the *Wraith's* commander clarified his statement. "I mean it's loud with fish and trawlers and tankers. I agree about that. It's the lack of sounds from hidden Iranian submarines that bothers me."

"We destroyed two of their small submarines when they didn't even know they were fighting us. They may not have any other assets in the area, or they may be unable or unwilling to challenge our convoy."

"We could never be so lucky."

"Do you want to deploy the dolphins?"

Volkov wanted to use the cetaceans constantly, but the risk of losing them–especially to the Persians who understood dolphin communications and how to counter them–forced his conservatism. "I intend to hold them aboard the *Wraith* until we reach Socotra."

Serguei lowered his gaze back to the chart. "I assume you conferred with Vasily?"

"Of course. I'm no fool. I want to keep him happy."

"Good choice. Happy trainer, happy dolphins. Happy dolphins, the better the chance they keep us alive when we need them."

Volkov thought he sniffed a challenge. "We don't need them now. Two drones and our organic hydrophones will suffice."

"Then what are we waiting for?"

"The convoy's go-ahead. Come to think of it, what are they waiting for?" The *Wraith's* commander called to his Arabic translator. "Ask them what we're waiting for?"

With the periscope raised above the water and its low-power, high-frequency voice antenna energized atop it, the translator exchanged phrases with the Yemeni convoy's commander. "He says they're getting a tally of equipment and personnel aboard all ships."

Volkov straightened his back. "Remind him we're racing an enemy. The Emiratis and Iranians will return to Socotra in force. Best that we get there first."

"I'll remind him." The translator relayed the message and heard its reply. "He doesn't seem to care."

Volkov's ire rose. "What did he say?"

"He said, before you give orders on his troops' movements, you should learn to carry a rifle first."

"Wonderful! Tell him when he learns to win battles in undersea combat, he can tell me how to operate my submarine, which is leaving now. I suggest he follows me if he wants an escort."

"Dmitry? I..."

"Tell him."

The interpreter conducted his two-way translation. "He says you have a commitment to protect the convoy."

"I know. Tell him I'll honor that commitment by scouting ahead. The sooner he follows, the safer he'll be."

After a long sigh, the translator relayed the message. "He says you need to stay where you are and obey his commands."

"Tell him, goodbye. And hurry."

The interpreter obeyed, listened to a loud tirade, and then summarized the verbalized angst. "He swore in ways that are hard to translate."

"Don't bother." Volkov stepped to the elevated conning platform, leaned into a console, and brushed aside the translator. "Lowering the periscope. Helm, all-ahead two-thirds, make turns for eight knots. Make your depth thirty meters. Sonar team, accelerate both drones to eight knots, matching our course and speed until I say otherwise."

As arms and fingers flitted about screens, Anatoly smirked and yelled above the rising din. "Dmitry?"

"Yes?"

"The convoy's starting up behind us. It looks like they decided to follow close behind us after all."

Four hours later, weariness clawed at Volkov's body. Given the full day required to transit to Socotra, he let his executive officer manage the escort during the remainder of the darkness. so that he could be fresh during the riskier daylight hours. "Serguei?"

His face sagging from sleep deprivation, the second-in-command looked up from the chart. "Sir?"

"You're ready to handle the ship for a few hours?"

"Of course."

"Maintain our course and speed. Wake me if you detect any war machine, submerged, surfaced, or flying. Wake me if any of the transport ships fail to turn on a scheduled anti-submarine leg. Barring those events, wake me an hour before sunrise." Volkov started to turn away.

"Dmitry!"

"Yes?"

"Do you think there's another Iranian submarine out there? I mean, we've already... handled... two of them between us and Terry. They didn't know we were here until twelve hours ago. Even if they are sending more submarines from Bandar Abbas, they can't reach here yet."

The *Wraith's* commander had considered the question all evening. "I run the numbers in my head incessantly, and all I can do is guess at probabilities. But with the sheer number of *Ghadirs* patrolling these seas, I can only assume we'll run into trouble before we reach Socotra. Stay alert." He turned and walked to his quarters.

Five hours later, Volkov awoke with his mind and body hovering between fatigue and vigor. After swigging mouthwash and sponging himself with moist wipes, he walked to the control room.

A bleary-eyed Serguei joked. "Is it morning already?"

"Tell me what's going on, and then you can get some food and sleep."

The executive officer walked to the central chart and pointed at the history of the convoy's trek. Flanked by the pair of *Barbe*-class landing ships and a half dozen fishing ships that supported the soldiers' exodus, reminiscent of the World War II Dunkirk rescue, the *Polnocny*-class troop transport had been cutting sharp angles into the water behind the *Wraith* all day.

Volkov liked what he saw. "Good. Perhaps we can hope for continued quiet all the way to Socotra. Get your food and rest."

Two hours later, the *Wraith's* worried sonar ace cried out. "Super-cavitating torpedo, bearing two-seven-seven."

Volkov's heart landed in his throat. There was nothing he could say or ask to avert the instant and unfolding disaster. Instead, he lifted a headset and pressed one muff against his ear.

The shrill hiss was ominous.

Anatoly narrated the tragedy. "Now it's bearing two-eight-two. Assuming it's at least three miles from us, it's moving faster than one hundred and six knots."

Recognizing the VA-111 Shkval rocket torpedo, Volkov lamented Russia's supplying of technology to the Iranians. Though he doubted the gesture's efficacy, he opted to warn the surface ships. "Bring us to snorkel depth." As the deck took a gentle angle, he stepped to his console. "Raising the periscope."

After a quick automated sweep, he viewed the panorama on his screen while the translator raised a handset to his mouth. "Tell the convoy's commander that we've discovered a torpedo and to begin torpedo evasion maneuvers."

The interpreter rattled off the message, begetting a hasty reply. "He wants to know which ship is targeted."

"Tell him—"

Anatoly interrupted his commander. "We hear a second super-cavitating torpedo. Coming from the north. Bearing rate is less than the first, but it's drifting towards the convoy."

"Very well." Volkov faced his translator. "Tell him that multiple ships are targeted. All of the ships in the convoy must begin torpedo evasion maneuvers."

His throat dry with tension, the interpreter obeyed.

Volkov analyzed the geometry. "Now tell him I'm going deep to fight off these submarines."

As the Arabic exchange finished, the first weapon exploded underneath a fishing trawler. The blast echoed throughout the control room.

Cringing, Volkov lowered the periscope, ordered his ship deep, and turned the *Wraith* back towards the convoy. As the deck leveled, he called out more orders. "Show me your best solutions to the shooters."

Anatoly protested. "I've got little to go on. Just guesses of the bearings to the weapons launched."

"Give me your best. In the system, now!"

Two icons appeared on the central chart. "Assign tube five to the first shooter. Assign tube six to the second. Set both weapons to active search modes."

Anatoly managed two junior personnel in addressing his commander's order. "Tubes five and six are assigned in active search modes."

The second Iranian super-cavitating weapon detonated underneath a landing ship. With soldiers aboard each destroyed vessel, Volkov counted nearly one hundred drowning, vaporized, and burning men.

Hoping to save the remnants of the convoy, the *Wraith's* commander took shots in the dark. "Shoot tubes five and six."

As the *Wraith's* weapons sought to harass invisible enemies, the sonar ace announced a worsening of the tragedy. "High-speed screws. Bearing two-seven-eight."

Volkov began to understand the challenge. "Just one set of screws?"

"Yes."

A junior technician called out. "Another set of high-speed screws, bearing three-four-four."

The *Wraith's* commander announced his conclusion. "I believe we're facing two *Ghadirs*, the first shooter from the west, and the second shooter from the north. If they were larger ships, we'd see more torpedoes, but I believe each *Ghadir* had one Shkval and one heavyweight in its tubes. They have no reloads. The priority now is surface ship evasion. Anatoly, have our technicians steer our weapons without waiting for my inputs."

"The technicians will steer our weapons, sir."

Volkov moved to his sonar guru's side and crouched. "It looks like the heavyweights are going for the trailing fishing ship and the remaining landing ship."

"Agreed. The troop transport was adequately flanked by the other vessels. At least the biggest ship is safe."

Seeing no way to save both targeted ships, Volkov made the hard decision to play God. "Bring us back to snorkel depth smartly." As the deck nudged upward, he stepped to the elevated conning platform and raised his periscope."

The translator appeared spooked.

"Can you talk?"

"Yes!"

"Tell the convoy's commander we've discovered two more torpedoes, targeted at the trailing fishing ship and the second landing ship. There's no escape. Cease torpedo evasion maneuvers and have the targeted fishing ship and the landing ship drive towards each other. If he listens to me, he can time it right so that the fishing ship absorbs both weapons."

The interpreter balked. "Dmitry! You can't–"

"I can't what?"

"Okay. I'll try it." The translator relayed the message in Arabic, and the reply was somber. "I don't believe it. He agreed."

Having feared a wasteful quarrel, Volkov was relieved the convoy's leader had heeded him. He wondered if the mercenary fleet's reputation for last-ditch defenses had reached the man's ears prior to the *Wraith's* commander proposing one. "Good. Anatoly, what's your confidence in the solutions to the hostile torpedoes?"

"Good for the western one. Not as good for the northern."

"Can the targeted ships converge at their maximum speeds

before either weapon hits them?"

"Yes. I think so."

"Give me those solutions in the system." Volkov faced the translator. "Bring the two targeted ships towards the western torpedo. Course two-four-four for the landing ship, course two-six-two for the fisher. Send every other ship to Socotra."

The interpreter obeyed.

Five minutes later, one torpedo exploded underneath the fishing ship, and then thirty seconds later, the second hostile weapon vaporized the wreckage.

The landing ship escaped.

Finding no targets, the *Wraith's* counterfire torpedoes exhausted their fuel.

Volkov sighed. "Have the convoy continue towards shore now with anti-submarine legs."

The interpreter frowned. "You think there are more submarines out there?"

"I have no idea, but it seems the Iranians have sent every *Ghadir* in their fleet to thwart us, and they just hit three out of four targets. They know what they're doing, and we must remain alert."

# CHAPTER 10

During his final time-consuming, anti-submarine zigzag leg, Andi Amir reminded himself of an important fact.

Speed hinders submarine attacks.

The one hundred and twelve soldiers and mariners who perished during the transit from Nishtun to Socotra suffered for their ships' limits. Slow movement had made them easy targets. As he led the *Tarantul* at forty-five knots, he doubted even a Shkval super-cavitating torpedo, with its wide turning radius, could threaten him.

Then he reminded himself of another fact.

His outdated and oversized Cold War vintage anti-ship missiles flew faster than those of his Emirati adversaries. In sheer attack power, his ship rivaled any single ship within the UAE fleet.

But he lacked defenses.

Designed for packing a huge punch from a small hull, his *Tarantul* and its tiny *Osa* escorts carried oversized Styx missiles, struck with ferocity, but were restricted in their defenses to sprinting from harm. Knocking down incoming threats to protect themselves was an afterthought.

Backfitting modern point-defense systems left the Yemeni fleet with last-ditch hopes against an incoming missile or two. But its air protection was pathetic compared to the Emirati adversary, which carried an integrated system of anti-air missiles that could knock down incoming weapons, especially old Styx missiles with huge radar cross sections and negligible anti-jamming.

Against the incoming UAE naval task force, his only advantage was speed, and although swiftness could save him from a submarine's torpedo, it was useless for outrunning anti-ship missiles. Attempting to face his enemy head-on would have been foolish.

Instead, he intended to use environmental factors, such as the mountains which extended the range of the anti-air missiles parked atop them and the island's shallow southern littorals for the laying of anchored mines off the coast.

He sighed in relief as he pulled within sight of the Socotran shoreline. The dangers–the enemy aircraft flying on the edge of strike range, the Emirati naval task force coming for him, and the hidden Iranian submarines–receded from his mind as he neared the seaport.

A *Polnocny*-class troop transport ship provided the first sign of positive developments since he'd hidden his tiny fleet at sea two days ago, and it lifted his spirits. Then, as it came into view, the single *Barbe*-class landing ship reminded him of its lost twin from the Iranian submarine attack on the convoy.

Slowing, he brought the *Tarantul* beside the transport ship and ordered the two *Osas* with him to nestle against moorings as well.

When he crossed the brow from his ship to the concrete, he stood within controlled pandemonium.

His first task was verifying that his crew ran lines from a fuel truck to his tanks. After seeing his lean executive officer watching over the refueling, he sought the officer in charge of the transport ship. Meandering between platoons of camouflaged soldiers, he found three petty officers standing by a folded mooring line. "Sailors, are you from the transport ship?"

The senior one answered as the group saluted. "Yes, sir."

Amir returned the gesture and then lowered his arm. "Where's your commanding officer?"

The sailors shrugged as one answered. "I think he's with the captain. Probably in the headquarters building."

The *Tarantul's* commander stepped away, dialed his commodore, and placed his phone to his ear.

"Damari."

"Sir, it's Commander Amir. I'm trying to find the transport's commander to begin loading the mines."

"He's with me. Headquarters desk. Join us." The captain hung up.

As the *Tarantul's* commander walked towards the waterfront building, he wished he could see his wife and children. But the

102

soldiers in charge of shore security had judged the risk too grave of moving family members between the bases and their safe-houses. The reunion would have to wait.

Entering the waterfront building, Amir felt an unpleasant power-struggle déjà vu. Two colonels were arguing with the captain while the lower-ranking officers hovered behind their leaders. Worse, the promised commanding officer of the transport ship was absent, probably scared away by the bickering leaders.

Keeping quiet, Amir crept around the fringe and listened.

Colonel Mohamed, the boisterous officer who'd challenged Damari about placement of the anti-air defenses, was loud about the same subject. "The Alamos stay where they are! There's barely enough coverage for our assets now, and we just landed one hundred and seventy more troops. Do you want to leave them exposed to an air attack?"

Damari glared at the senior soldier. "They'll have adequate coverage. I only want three trucks sent to the south side of the island to protect the mine-laying ships. That is, unless you want enemy troops landing on unprotected shores."

When the second, shorter colonel spoke, his tone suggested deference to the taller braggart, and he stuck to verifiable information instead of declaring his opinions as facts. "We have no intelligence about the Emiratis attempting any landings on the island, much less on the shallow side with the hard surf."

Amir felt the precious hours of darkness ticking away.

The loud Colonel Mohamed compounded the argument. "The threat is from the air–not from the sea. If we weaken our Alamo footprint at the bases, we'd be inviting an air attack. I can't believe you used cargo space on the transport ship for mines that could have been used for more ground weaponry. Do you think four tanks are enough? This mining mission of yours is foolhardy."

Damari barked. "The mines are here because I ordered them and because we need them! You'll thank me when brigades of Emiratis don't make landfall and start marching across the island."

"You're making wild speculations, captain!"

Undaunted, the commodore continued. "Without the mines, that's exactly what will happen, and you'd have enemy assault teams hiding among the local populace until they're ready to kill you in the dark. Or you'd have fire squads running door to door uprooting our families. It takes only one small ship to sneak through. Is that what you want?"

"I'm not answering your hypotheticals!"

"It's not hypothetical. It's trivial for the Emiratis if we don't mine the littorals. What's to keep a fishing boat full of commandos from landing just like we did?" Damari answered his own question. "I'll tell you. For the deep approaches to the bases, it's our ships, our aircraft, and our troops. For the rest of the island, it's mines and nothing else."

The argument's logic bore into the tall colonel. "Since you already brought the mines, you may as well lay them. But you can't have three trucks."

"I'll make do with two."

Puffing his chest like he'd won the negotiation, Colonel Mohamed bragged. "Fine. I'll give you two." He lifted his phone to his ear and barked. "Yes. Get two trucks refueled and ready to provide air cover to the navy throughout the night." He hung up. "You've got your trucks, captain. Can I get on with organizing my men?"

"Yes, colonel. Excuse me." Damari marched to the *Tarantul's* commander and grabbed his arm. "Get out there and start laying mines as soon as you can. Your air cover's only going to last until he gets scared about another air strike. You need to hurry."

Unsure if the army would abandon him, Amir balked. "Loading all three ships for mine-laying operations will take hours."

"So, don't load all three ships. Start with one *Osa*, then the other, then your ship. Start laying when you've got the first ship loaded."

An alarm rang in Amir's head. "I planned on having us lay them in formation, staggered, three abreast."

"You no longer have that luxury. We may end up with only a half or a third of a minefield by the end of the night, but it's better than no minefield at all."

"The precision navigation required for doing this one ship at a time without blowing ourselves up, sir. It's..."

"I know."

"With the speed at which we'll be moving, sir? We have to do this at flank bells in choppy seas so that we don't become submarine fodder. There's no room for error."

Damari folded his arms. "Are you challenging my order?"

Respecting the dangers of laying mines and then navigating around them, Amir held his ground. "I guess I just did, sir. I didn't say I was intent on disobeying–"

"But... I'll finish your thought for you. It's dangerous work, and you could do it. But you shouldn't have to. I have a better idea."

Relieved, the *Tarantul's* commander nodded. "Yes, sir."

"You'll keep your cannons aimed at our Alamo trucks."

Targeting his army's assets caught Amir off guard. "Sir?"

"You're not going to shoot them. In fact, you're not even going to really target them. You'll take target practice in the wildlife reserves, and the explosions will remind our army friends what you can do to them if they abandon their posts." Damari smirked. "Think of it as a subconscious bluff to keep them honest and awake. I'll make sure the colonel knows about it before you head out there."

At the docks, the *Tarantul's* commander saw a pile of mines forming next to a crane beside the transport ship. He found the nearest naval officer. "Lieutenant, are you in charge of this unloading of mines?"

The stocky young man looked at Amir and saluted. "Yes, sir."

"How do you plan to get them onto the surface combatants?"

"Sorry, sir. That's not my responsibility tonight, but I can tell you how we normally–."

"Do you have your commanding officer's phone number?"

The lieutenant lifted a satellite phone from his pocket. "Yes, sir."

Remembering that he outranked the transport ship's commanding officer, Amir relayed an order. "Call him and tell him to call me. I'll dictate my number once you have him on the line."

"Yes, sir." The officer lifted his phone, spoke to his commander, and then looked at Amir. "He's ready for your number, sir."

The *Tarantul's* commander recited his phone number and awaited the call that arrived moments later. "Commander Amir."

"Lieutenant Commander Qureshi, calling as ordered, sir."

"What's your plan to get the mines onto the surface combatants?"

The transport ship's commanding officer hesitated as if Amir had asked him humanity's dumbest question. "Uh... it's rather standard, sir. We make an offloading pile. Then we sort them and move them into smaller loading piles next to each ship."

"Does that mean you'll move every mine three times? From your ship to shore, from an offloading pile to a loading pile, and then from a loading pile to its deployment ship?"

Again, a pause. "Of course, sir. That's how it's generally done."

"Wouldn't it be faster to move the ships around the piles instead of the other way around?"

Another hesitation. "You mean, move my ship?"

"Yes. Leave the big pile where you've already started it, but since my ship's taking half the mines, you can stop halfway through unloading, move to a different berthing, and then I'll take your berthing spot to load. That lets you move half the mines twice instead of three times." During another short wait, Amir feared he'd confused the man.

But the transport ship's officer proved his initiative. "If you're really in a hurry, sir, I've got an even faster option."

"Go ahead."

"You may have noticed that the offload pile is really two piles being created by two cranes."

Amir stepped from an overhead lantern's artificial orb and then scanned the pier along the transport ship's side. As promised, another crane lowered a mine from the vessel's far end. "I just noticed."

"I can have the offload pile kept in halves so that the same two cranes can load them onto the *Osas*, if they take my spot in the berthing. You should be able to get those smaller ships close enough to allow that. Then you and I will dock our ships back to front and move mines directly from my cargo hold to your rails."

Amir appreciated someone thinking creatively. "I like it."

"If the cranes would reach, I'd suggest having you moor inside me, and we could use two cranes. But they don't have the reach."

"That's fine. We've just cut this logistical nightmare's duration in half with one conversation. Get me an estimate of when you'll have the first half of your mines unloaded, and I'll inform the *Osas*."

After moving the *Tarantul* to the pier's other side beside the newly berthed transport ship, Amir clutched his crew's latest welding work and yanked with all his weight. The mine-laying rails held firm to the fantail. He scrunched his hardhat against his head and then urged his team into motion. "Load them up! Get going!"

After he retreated to the superstructure, he watched a crane lift the first Russian-made weapon from the transport ship's hidden cargo hold and into the artificial lights. The load block canted as it swung the mass over the water, and then it steadied as it lowered it to the corvette.

Like threading steel needles, the work crew aboard the *Tarantul* pushed the railings through the mine's top eyehook. Once the top rail bore the cargo's weight, the sailors ordered the crane's line slacked and detached. They then slid two locating holes over lower guiderails and then latched a winch's chain to a final hook.

With the mine connected, a sailor whipped his arm in a circle, ordering a winch motor into motion and pulling the mine deeper into its storage rail.

Seeing the first keel-cracking warhead aboard its dual-purpose storage and launch rail, Amir wanted it off his ship. As the winch pulled the next mine beside the first, he wished to get rid of both ship killers. The night offered tedium and danger, and he wanted it in his past.

He lifted his phone and called his executive officer.

"Sir?"

"Where are you?"

"I checked on the diesel fuel loading status. They're topping off the last tank. I'm going to check on the food stores now."

"Hold off on that. Come watch over the mine loading."

A minute later, the lean second-in-command stepped through a watertight door and onto the fantail where he watched the fourth mine steady in its railings. "Reporting, as ordered, sir."

"Call me if they run into a problem or slow down."

"Where will you be, sir?"

Expecting an exhausting effort, Amir sought rest. "First, I'm going to make sure the *Osas* are loading mines, too. Then I'm getting three hours of sleep. After that, it'll be your turn to get some rest."

Seven hours later, Amir stood on the *Tarantul's* bridge as the corvette sliced the dark waves and raced to lay mines before sunrise would expose his fleet to shallow submarines. The *Osas* were in a line abreast off his starboard flank as he rounded the island's western tip. Lifting his voice to an open microphone lined up to a radio channel, he called out. "Commence mine-laying. Release mines every three minutes."

Through a closed-circuit, he watched a black and white rendition of his crew dropping the *Tarantul's* first mine off the fantail. After the first weapon splashed, a team hurried to attach a motorized winch to pull the next one down the rails while another team stood ready to drop the next mine from the rails on the other side.

The *Osas* reported having deployed their first mines.

Fearing the unseen threats below the waves, Amir welcomed the update from the Israeli robot.

His second-in-command updated him over the loudspeaker. "Bridge, tactical center, the submerged drone is shallow and communicating a status."

"Very well, tactical center." As the weird data trickled over a staged laptop, he glanced at the foreign translator. "Does that make sense to him?"

The interpreter exchanged words in English with the commanding officer of the *Xerses*, who'd boarded the *Tarantul* to understand the incoming undersea data and to provide a gesture of shared risk between the Yemeni and mercenary fleets. "Yes. He says the drone has no submerged contacts."

With anti-submarine zigzag legs impractical, Amir could only trust the Australian and his Israeli hardware. Although he would have preferred the mercenary submarine's protection, the *Wraith* was occupied preventing enemy attacks on the moored ships at the seaport.

The translator added Commander Terrance Cahill's commentary. "But he says the drone doesn't have the speed to search our entire operational area. He's programmed it to search to the east, but we will become increasingly at risk to an attack from the west during the morning. He chose the east to put the sun in the eyes of any submarine that would use a periscope after sunrise."

As he watched the next mine slide off its rails, Amir shifted his fears to the air. "Excuse me." He slipped by Cahill and the translator to a console showing him the icons that his combat system generated. Amid the activity, he saw relative safety.

A pair of Yemeni jets paralleled two Emirati fighters to the north, and a half dozen drones from multiple countries overflew waters off the island, watching local military developments.

The executive officer announced the three-inch, AK-176 cannon's readiness. "Bridge, tactical center, the cannon is ready for gunnery exercises."

Having selected with the concurrence of local park authorities a patch of grass to pummel, Amir started the live-ordnance evolution. "Very well. Twenty rounds. Check targeting between fires. Commence gunnery exercises."

The muzzle popped, and the bridge windows shook.

Two hours later, dawn's rays crested the horizon and Amir anticipated releasing his final mines.

His executive officer sounded concerned. "Bridge, tactical center, the mercenary UAV sees a vessel deploying from Socotra and heading towards the minefield."

Amir had verified the notice to mariners before beginning the mining run. Someone was foolish enough to ignore it. "Raise it on the radio! Warn it away!"

Minutes passed without an answer, and then an explosion sent a plume of water into the violet light behind him.

Amir grabbed his phone and called his boss.

"Damari."

"Sir, we're finishing mine-laying operations. I need another fifteen minutes to complete the field."

"Good work, Amir."

"Bad news... I assume it was a local fisherman who just blew himself up in the field."

The captain remained hard to read, especially over the phone. "Continue laying the mines. I'll call you back."

Twenty minutes later, the last mine was anchored to the seafloor, and Amir aimed the three combatants around the island's eastern side, completing the circle around the landmass and heading towards the relative safety of the seaport.

The commodore called.

Amir answered. "Yes, sir."

"Don't worry about the fishing ship. I called Nuha Shaman, and she verified that its captain is a known drunk. He probably ignored all the warnings. The crew's death is on his hands."

Though tragic, the news comforted the *Tarantul's* commander by verifying he'd done all he could to prevent the disaster. "Understood, sir. Thank you for finding out."

"In a bizarre way, this works in our favor."

"How so?"

"The Emiratis know we were laying real mines. Your mission this morning wasn't about blowing up Emirati ships–it was about deterring their arrival. I believe you've accomplished that, and you avoided Iranian submarines. I call that a success–one we needed."

## CHAPTER 11

Captain Sharifi stared at the wall-mounted display showing a chart of Socotra. To prevent civilian casualties, black lines marked most of the island as a no-fly zone, leaving him to wonder if the rules of engagement left him any chance of winning his revenge.

Then he wondered how many indigenous islanders wanted him dead and would oblige the Yemenis with another prisoner if he were shot down over their homes.

Although the best path to attack would have sent him over Socotra's densest population center, he accepted the need to avoid the populace and instead overfly the Yemeni Alamo mobile SAM launchers.

With reliable surveillance from aerial drones, reconnaissance aircraft, and UAE sympathizers among the Socotrans, Sharifi was confident that he and his squadron mates faced sixteen missiles spread across eight trucks. If his strike team moved fast enough, they'd wipe out the mobile launchers with their spare weapons unused.

Ignoring reloads, at most eight of the thirty-six aircraft of the strike group would need to dodge the inferior Alamo missiles. Sharifi was hesitant to risk an eight-in-thirty-six chance of facing mortal danger again, but regaining the small airfield on the annoying island consumed his focus.

His memories of wasted hours and long boredom during his assignment on Socotra had become distant and murky. Now contested, the island had value, and he would embrace the Yemeni threat, especially the greedy mercenaries who'd downed his colleagues.

Anger swelled within his chest as he envisioned carrying out his part of the coordinated air strike–suppressing the deadly *Goliath*-class warship, *Xerses*.

His squadron commander's voice sliced his daydream. "Is that clear, Sharifi?"

The young pilot replayed the colonel's words through his

mind before repeating back what he'd heard. "Yes, sir. I'll be the wingman for a two-plane team on the island's east side as an overwatch for the *Xerses*. I see the boundary for the western overwatch team, and I acknowledge the altitude separation."

"And what else?"

After the destruction the mercenary vessel had caused, Sharifi would attack it with a pistol if he thought it could damage the bastard ship. But he played along with his commanding officer's order. "And I won't waste an anti-air missile on the *Xerses* unless I'm out of anti-ship missiles. We assess zero damage based upon the last anti-air missile slammed against it."

"Good." The colonel lifted his chin to address the full audience of thirty-six pilots, which included six members of the allied Yemeni Southern Separatists whom the UAE had trained. "The *Xerses* surprised us once, but it won't have any MICA missiles this time. It's empty, and it hasn't reloaded. We've been watching. If it surfaces, we'll have the overwatches engage it. Everything else we're doing is a simple and direct challenge designed to overwhelm the Yemeni defenses with sheer numbers and firepower."

Sharifi sent sideways glances to the pilots around him. He could smell the fear and anticipation.

The squadron commander finished the briefing. "Any questions? No? Good. First wheels are up in sixty minutes."

As the pilots walked out of the briefing room with the innate confidence of military aviators, Sharifi noticed fear lurking behind the thin masks of bravado.

Three junior pilots, roughly his age, were grouped in a side conversation. He recognized them as virgins to combat, like most of the assembled cohort.

As he walked by, they looked up, and the one with the cockiest visage addressed him. "Sharifi?"

"Yeah?"

"Everyone's talking about you."

Unsure where the conversation was heading, Sharifi stood his ground to hear more. "Okay."

"What's it like to get shot at?"

The young captain remembered running from bullets and running from a MICA missile. "I guess that depends. Do you mean when I was on my feet or in my jet?"

The inquisitor sneered. "In your jet, of course. None of us here is planning to be shot at on our feet."

The other two pilots gave nervous chuckles.

Sharifi lost interest in coddling his comrades. They'd have to figure out their reaction in combat for themselves, as he had. "And I wasn't planning on getting shot at on my feet or in my jet, either. Just do what you've been trained to do, and the rest will take care of itself. Good luck up there, guys."

Their fears unaddressed, the trio of pilots watched in silence as the combat veteran walked away.

Watching them over his shoulder, Sharifi pitied them for their fear. His was spent days ago, and he smirked as he realized it wasn't coming back.

Combat had hardened him, and anger now fueled him.

He reached into his pocket to turn on his phone, which he'd silenced during the briefing, and he noticed that his father had called. Unsure why the family patriarch had reached out, he returned the phone call and awaited the answer.

"Ali!"

"Yes, Father. It's me."

"I was worried when you didn't answer."

"You know I have obligations. I can't answer the phone at all hours, or did you forget that I'm in the military?"

"Of course, I know you're in the military. I put you there. And from what my colleagues are telling me, you're making a name for our family. But why must I hear it from others and not from you?"

Sharifi knew his father cared more about rank, image, and reputation than his own family's well-being. But out of habit, he played the obedient son. "Operational security, Father. I can't confirm nor deny anything I've done."

"You can at least call me to let me know you're okay."

"Aren't the rumors among your colleagues sufficient?"

"Why, yes! They're wonderful. I hear that you've flown in combat on multiple missions and were the only surviving pilot from the outpost on Socotra."

Sharifi hoped the two pilots who weren't shot dead on the tarmac like his former commander were still alive. "I'm glad you heard good news about me. I can't comment about survivors, of course."

"It's just good that you're alive."

Doubting his father cared as much as he claimed, Sharifi sought the conversation's end. "Thank you, Father. But I need to go. You'll have to excuse me. Work calls." He hung up.

Two hours later, Sharifi cruised at a high altitude among an airborne armada. To assist the flying warriors in placing eyeballs on their moving targets, they approached during daylight.

With Oman disallowing attack flights through its airspace, the strike team came from the northeast of Socotra and headed south to place the risen sun at their backs.

Two hundred miles from the island's eastern edge, the colonel ordered the first break in formation. "Overwatch teams, prepare to detach from the formation. Western Overwatch first."

A pair of aviators on the far side of the formation answered in order. "Western One, ready."

"Western Two, ready."

The colonel gave the team bound for the island's far end parting advice. "If you see that accursed *Xerses* ship, don't hesitate. Send it to oblivion. Western Overwatch, detach!"

Two F-16s dived, turned, and accelerated.

"Eastern Overwatch, you're next. Report readiness."

The major leading the eastern-bound two-aircraft team responded. "Eastern One, ready."

Sharifi followed, using his mission's call sign. "Eastern Two, ready."

The colonel offered an abbreviated version of his advice. "Send that ship to oblivion. Eastern Overwatch, detach!"

Ahead of Sharifi, the major banked his F-16, accelerated ahead of the formation, and descended. "Follow me, Eastern Two."

Breaking from the larger formation, the young captain kept his leader in front of him.

On his leader's diving left wing, Sharifi nosed his jet on a gentle decline, and the landless panorama became more isolating as the blue horizon receded around him. The lower altitude left him enough vantage for finding the *Xerses* within any credible range it had of engaging him or his colleagues with its farthest-reaching weapons—its railguns.

When the island's mountain peaks pushed above the western edge of his view, his leader called to him. "Eastern Two, we'll stay on this course until we're twenty nautical miles from the island."

Understanding that none of the missiles could reach him at that distance, Sharifi obeyed. When disadvantaged by overcoming a ground-based, motionless launching, the jury-rigged anti-air Alamo missiles suffered a halved range limit.

The squadron commander announced an update. "We've got company. Bogeys bearing two-one-four, twenty-five thousand feet."

The voice of the lead officer assigned to fend off enemy aircraft carried exhilaration. "This is Dogfighter One. I request to detach and engage the bogeys."

"Negative, Dogfighter One. The bogeys aren't challenging us."

The dogfighter sounded hungry for action. "That doesn't make sense, sir. Why aren't they challenging us?"

"I don't know. Cowardice? Poor training? They're lucky to even get those F-16s airborne. It doesn't matter. Stay in formation and be ready to drop ordnance." A minute later he added an order. "Eastern Overwatch, I just got a message from Al Dhafra. They say there's new activity at the airfield and the seaport. Get eyeballs on it."

Although the mountains blocked his view of the Yemeni

strongholds, Sharifi tapped a display to invoke a view through a drone's camera. With intense interest in Socotra, his nation had several unmanned vehicles watching.

The first drone showed two jets taking off from the airfield, and he announced his findings. "This is Eastern Two. I'm looking through UAV-two's camera. The second two Yemeni fighters just took off from the airfield."

The major flying in front of the young captain agreed. "I concur. That's good intelligence for the airfield, but I still want our naked eyeballs on the seaport. Follow me."

The squadron commander acknowledged the report. "Concur, Eastern Overwatch. I see the new bogeys on radar. They're heading away from us, as well. Dogfighters keep a watch on them in case they find their courage and challenge us."

His head on a swivel, Sharifi checked the waters for the *Xerses* and saw nothing but three fishing ships and two tankers passing in a shipping lane. He then switched to another drone's view of the seaport. What he saw shocked him. "This is Eastern Two. I'm looking through UAV-three's camera. Does anyone have eyeballs on the seaport?"

The squadron commander answered. "Negative. We're too low in altitude. I'm calling up UAV-three now myself."

While awaiting his commander's digestion of the image, Sharifi followed his leading major around the mountain and into a line of sight to the port. Four shipping containers rested at equal intervals spaced along the pier, and a half dozen merchant container ships were scattered at anchorages around the abandoned wharf. Only the troop transport and landing ships remained docked.

After being infuriated by two ambushes, Sharifi had run multiple possible scenarios through his mind during his few free hours. One of them included all the Yemeni ships abandoning the pier to avoid being attacked.

But keeping two ships by the pier was an anomaly. "Eastern One, Eastern Two. Do you see two noncombatant ships still tied to the pier and those four rectangular containers?"

"I see them. I don't know what to make of them."

"Me neither." Sharifi studied the concrete wharf.

"Watch yourself, Eastern Two. You're too close to my wing."

The young captain snapped his head forward and then backed off the throttle. "Sorry." He glared at the pier again, and this time something caught his attention.

An antenna.

He returned his concentration to flying in formation. "Eastern One, Eastern Two. I see an antenna sticking up from the closest container." He looked back at the pier. "And I see them from the others. Damn it. There might be missiles inside them."

The major's voice rose half an octave. "Squadron commander, Eastern One. Did you hear Eastern Two's assessment?"

"Yes. What's your assessment? Do you agree? UAV-three isn't focused well enough yet."

"I agree with Eastern Two, sir. They could be MICAs. They could be anything."

Motion caught Sharifi's eye. He craned his neck, and his heart skipped a beat as he saw white water forming and then cascading off his target, a stone's throw from the pier. "The *Xerses* just surfaced, at least partially. I see the rear sections!"

"Follow me in, Eastern Two. Let's hit that ship hard!"

Sharifi turned behind his leader and brought the enemy in front of him. His heart pounded as he raced to shoot his anti-ship missiles before the *Xerses* and the mysterious containers could spring whatever trap the Yemenis and their mercenary pets had planned.

He tried to lock his weapons on the enemy combatant, but his radar system hopped between the docked ships, the *Xerses*, and the nearest container. "We need to get closer."

The major's afterburner created a circular mirage. "Hurry!"

Accelerating, Sharifi looked ahead, and new motion caught his eye. On the forecastles of both moored ships, men in bright, reflective clothing appeared. Their hands bound, they seemed imprisoned. Another glance showed two of the captives being marched in front of the crates. "Eastern One, we can't shoot!

They have our countrymen on those ships and next to the crates."

"Damn them! Agreed. Break off."

Straining and breathing for consciousness during a high-acceleration turn, Sharifi followed his leader to the north.

The squadron commander added his final order. "Get out of there, overwatch teams. All aircraft, abort mission! Abort! Abort! Abort!"

Sharifi's anger compelled his complaint. "Squadron commander, Eastern two. We can still attack the missile trucks, sir."

"No! I won't risk hitting our own people. They may have scattered some prisoners with the trucks, too. Damn them for using human shields! Strike team follow me to course zero-three-five."

Above the young captain, his colleagues angled their jets away from the island and descended in hopes of escaping below the *Xerses'* limited radar horizon.

Sharifi wondered how close he'd been to tipping over a hornet's nest of anti-air missiles, and he wondered how close he'd come to shooting his own people.

As he rejoined the retreating armada, he wondered if his growing anger against an enemy he'd considered an inconvenience a week ago would ever find satiation.

# CHAPTER 12

Cahill sighed. "They're gone."

Walker smirked. "Remind me never to play poker with you."

"You think that was a bluff?"

"Of sorts."

Although three of the containers on the concrete wharf were empty false targets, the *Xerses'* commander had considered the fourth crate of eight MICA missiles his assets for defeating the incoming raid.

After a freighter carrying other goods to the island had brought the weapons, work crews had lacked sufficient time to load them aboard his ship, but the wireless electronic connection with their vertical carrying cells was solid. "Eight MICAs plus the eight Alamos would've ruined their day, I think."

The executive officer grunted. "I'm not sure you're doing the math correctly. There were more than thirty incoming aircraft. That attack would've been doomsday if they'd followed through."

Cahill doubted the foregone battle's hypothetical outcome, but to boost his confidence and that of his executive officer, he argued in his allies' favor. "You're forgetting the six shoulder-launched missile teams in the mountains. The railguns would've made them think twice, too. They can hurt aircraft in splintering mode."

Walker folded his arms across his chest. "Well, I'm glad we didn't have to test our defenses, especially the MICAs. I'm not sure this remote firing scheme would work."

Cahill had faith in the engineering team from France that had mated the French missiles to the Subtics fire control system aboard the combat transport ship. With the technician Renard had sent alongside the first eight weapons, the *Xerses'* commander had verified the full electrical connection himself. "We'll have control of pier-launched MICAs when we need it."

"I sure hope so, because the UAE may come back in force again, and we're running out of surprises and tricks. We'll need the ability to shoot our backup MICAs from the pier."

"Right." With the fear of combat draining from his body, Cahill checked the fleet's logistical situation. On the nearest screen, a freighter destined for Socotra with an inventory of thirty-two backup MICAs was coming towards him. The ship also carried a quarter billion euros worth of goods, all of which replaced the broken supply chain from UAE merchants to consumers on Socotra. "We'll test one live if a UAE drone gets too close to the island."

Walker placed his hands against the nearest railing. "Maybe I'm worrying about nothing."

"We've got plenty to worry about. It's just that worrying doesn't help." Cahill mentally replayed his recent tactics. "But I am a bit disgusted, truth be told. The human shield thing's leaving a nasty taste in me mouth."

"Yeah, me, too. But in our defense, those ships are appropriate places to keep prisoners."

"Don't rationalize it, mate. Using the prisoners as human shields is a valid tactic, but it sickens me. I'm pretty sure it's illegal, too, depending which conventions are agreed to."

"Well, in our defense, we didn't think of it. That idea was the brainchild our Yemeni colleagues."

Cahill became cynical. "Right, mate. We just eagerly went along with it all."

"Okay. You're right. I'll stop denying it. Just give me time."

The *Xerses'* commander made himself forget the use of UAE prisoners as pawns to free his mind for the next steps in the campaign. "Surface us completely and drive us to the pier for MICA loading. I'll call Pierre and let him know what's going on."

"Aye, sir. I'll surface us and drive us to the pier for MICA loading."

As daylight broke through the rising dome, Cahill tapped a screen to bring up his boss.

Smiling, the Frenchman's face appeared. "I see that you've fended off the attack. Well done!"

Cahill couldn't match Renard's enthusiasm. "We're far from

feeding the hungry masses, though, aren't we?"

"All in good time, my friend. Patience. Keep holding Socotra, and it will be a perfect staging ground for humanitarian operations."

Wary of his boss' latest machinations, Cahill fed Renard an open comment. "I noticed your freighter of additional MICAs... and valuable commercial products... coming our way."

The Frenchman's smile waned. "Very well. I won't evade the question I believe you really wish to ask. I admit to profit motive with the consumer goods I'm shipping to Socotra along with your spare weapons, but I was candid that I'd be seeking subsidies for this mission. The Socotrans need the substituted goods which I broker from my network to replace those from the UAE and other sources which are no longer reaching the island."

Having been consumed with warfare, Cahill wondered how many freighters had turned back to their ports of origin after he'd helped secure the seaport for the Yemenis. As expected, the UAE was boycotting trade with the island, but a host of other nations had paused their trading. "Thanks for sharing, Pierre. I have to admit I was curious about that."

"It's not all about money coming into our fleet. I also have to keep the Socotrans supplied if we're going to keep using their island."

"I don't suppose I can blame you for making money when the chances arise."

Renard smirked. "I assure you I undertook this mission from a desire to feed the hungry. That I keep stumbling upon opportunities for profit is beyond my control, and I'd be a fool to forego them. The income helps support the mission."

Cahill wondered how much money the Frenchman stood to lose–or gain–in the campaign. "Understandable."

Next, Renard seemed to brag, and his tone made the Australian wonder if his boss offered a veiled confession. "The irony is that my command post in Toulon is inside the headquarters of the company that's building the Emirati Navy its next four warships. I was at first concerned about the conflict of interest, but a trusted executive assured me everything was fine. In fact, it is desired."

"You're joking?"

"Not at all. What better way to make boost your customer's urgency to buy your warships than to have someone destroy his inventory?"

The *Xerses'* commander found the economics almost as shameful as human shields. "You mean, if we sink UAE ships, the Naval Group company is going to write you a big fat bonus check?"

Again, the Frenchman sneered. "You know I spare my staff the burden of my financial goings on. I've said too much already about it. I just want to assure you that everything is aligned between your mission parameters and our fleet's future. Again, I reiterate that this is a humanitarian mission first and foremost."

Although the plan remained solid in Cahill's mind, he began to doubt his boss' charity as his sole motivator. "But the humanitarian phase is next, right? There's nothing else delaying it now."

"Correct. You're now only awaiting the subsequent freighters which will be carrying humanitarian aid for Nishtun."

The *Xerses'* commander accepted Renard's explanation. "Right. It's consistent with our plan."

"Indeed."

"Well, thanks for sending the extra MICAs. They're gems we bloody well needed given that half the UAE air force is working against us."

"Yes, of course. My pleasure. You'll be a veritable mini-Aegis destroyer, at least while operating under the coverage umbrella of the missiles from your pier."

"This is quite a departure from being a submarine commander."

The Frenchman issued a smug smile. "You and Liam are teaching each other well."

Cahill recalled the automation he'd needed in shooting MICAs during his surprise attack against the first wave of UAE aircraft. "The technology handles it without a hiccup, thankfully. It happens so bloody fast, though. It's the opposite of submarine warfare... I'm not used to so many things moving, such rapid speeds, and all the information overload."

Smirking, Walker entered the conversation. "Maybe it's the universe rebalancing itself after making me play submarine advisor to Danielle."

Grasping the segue, Renard shifted the discussion to the team's other tandem of warships. "Speaking of our newest commander, she and Jake are on the southern side of Ascension Island and are on schedule to arrive in theater with you in eleven days."

Thoughts of his comrades' laborious grind across two oceans distracted Cahill from the bitterness of having killed UAE pilots with a button press on the *Xerses'* MICA system, of having used human shields, and of Renard's profit motive undermining a humanitarian mission. "How are our esteemed globetrotters? I imagine morale is a challenge with the tedium."

"Jake seems to be struggling with it more than Danielle. I think it's because she's eager to learn the *Goliath* and transfer her knowledge to the *Xerses*. So is her new crew. Would you believe she even recruited a new member to her team while in Ascension?"

The news startled Cahill. "Seriously?"

"A jet turbine technician was set for discharge from the Royal Navy in less than two months. After a few drinks with Danielle, he decided to forego the job he'd lined up back home and join her."

"I imagine he'll make more money during this campaign than in one year of civilian work?"

"More like two years. I had to make a small donation to the Officer's Club on Ascension to get the man's commanding officer to accelerate his departure from the Royal Navy, but the new recruit is aboard the *Goliath* and contributing."

"Danielle sounds like she's growing an appreciative team."

Renard nodded. "Indeed."

"But you're still going to make me give up the *Xerses* and take back the *Goliath*, right?"

"Of course. It's your ship, and the *Xerses* is hers. You've switched for this mission only while she ramps up her knowledge."

"Sure. I want the *Goliath* back. But no deal, unless you give me MICAs! They're addicting."

Renard's smile was genuine. "I promise. As soon as I can get it into dry dock."

"Thanks, mate."

"Jake's crew is doing fine too, but the honeymoon ended years ago. They've been together so long that they're probably having nightmares about finishing each other's sentences."

Cahill snorted. "Yeah. If I ever get fatigued, I think about how long they've all been at it."

Spurred by a memory, Renard perked up. "Oh, before I forget. Ariella has requested bandwidth for a private conversation. I can give you twenty minutes."

The announcement made the *Xerses'* commander uneasy. "Did she say why?"

"Not really, and I didn't pressure her. It's the first time she's asked for it, and I granted her request without question. I assume she's missing her new husband. That's all from me. If you have nothing else…"

"No, we're good here, right Liam?"

The executive officer shrugged. "Yeah."

"Very well, gentlemen. I'll leave you to it. Ariella's standing by." The Frenchman's face disappeared, and a blank screen replaced it.

Cahill's heart fluttered. "She'll be calling any second, I imagine."

Walker took the hint. "So, I'll just run off to the loo, then."

The *Xerses'* commander stopped him. "No. I'll take this in me quarters."

"You're sure? I can give you privacy up here."

His emotions churning in unfamiliar directions, Cahill wanted seclusion. "No. You can dock the ship without me. Port side to the pier, obviously, to allow missile loading."

"I'll take care of it."

Cahill turned, walked down the stairs, and shut the door behind him. After quick greetings with staff members in the control room, he found his way to his stateroom.

He logged into his laptop and saw a request for a video call. Tapping an acceptance icon, he invoked his wife's face on the screen.

Ariella beamed at the sight of her husband, but something in her voice was somber. "Hi, Terry."

Happy to see his wife, Cahill forgot his gnawing unease about the mission. "Ariella! It's great to see you."

"You, too." The smile and color fell from her face.

"What's wrong, honey?"

Tears welled in her eyes. "I... I lost the baby."

He was in disbelief. "What?"

"It was a miscarriage."

"Oh. I... uh."

"I'm sorry, Terry. I'm sorry." She sobbed.

Inwardly, Cahill wept with his wife. But he stuffed down the whirlwind of emotions. His voice was weak. "We'll be okay. I promise. Everything will be fine."

She'd never appeared so vulnerable. "I'm sorry."

He recalled a statistic that at least twenty percent of pregnancies end in miscarriage. "Don't be sorry. It's not your fault. Don't even think of it as a fault. It's just a horrible fact of life."

"I wanted to give you a child!"

"You will. I promise. We'll try again. We'll succeed."

"How can you be sure? What if I can never give you a baby?"

"I'll love you no matter what."

The comment seemed to ease her pain. "I know you will. You're a wonderful man. I don't deserve you."

He snorted. "Bloody hell, woman. I don't deserve you."

She wiped her tears. "Thanks."

"I wish I was there to help you feel better."

She shook her head. "No. I shouldn't have bothered you while you're on duty. I knew better. I was being weak."

"So says the strongest woman on the planet."

She leaned off the screen and blew her nose. She reappeared with her nostrils reddened. "I don't feel strong."

Unsure of the trauma his wife suffered, Cahill encouraged her. "You are."

"Enough about me. How are you doing?"

He scoffed. "Don't ask. There's something about this campaign that give me the willies."

"Don't say that! Now you're scaring me."

Waving his palm, he countered. "No, it's not so much about being safe. The danger I'm facing is becoming frightfully normal, if that makes sense."

Talking about her husband's danger seemed to distract her from her sadness. "It does."

"It's about what I'm doing. I'm killing people, and it seems a lot easier than it should. And I'm not even sure I'm doing the right thing."

"What do you mean?"

"Who's to say we shouldn't just let the Emiratis take control of Socotra and as much of the Yemeni mainland as they can? Who's to say that's a bad thing?"

"Consider what happens if you don't."

He tried to make sense of the political mess. "It would be a battle between the Houthis, that Southern Separatist group, and the Saudis."

Her military intelligence mind kicked into gear. "If you were leaving a power vacuum, I might agree. But Pierre has a plan to prevent that."

He recalled the twist the mercenary fleet had never used to its advantage in a campaign–the media. "I'll have to trust him, and apparently that's not as easy as I'd hoped. We're expecting the media to serve our purpose of helping the humanitarian cause. I mean, it makes sense to me, but I don't know if anything we'll do can merit enough attention to matter."

"Trust Pierre. I do, with your life every time you leave home."

"I know."

She lowered her gaze and then looked up again. "I'm working today. I should get back to it."

"Right. And don't worry about anything. We'll get through it. Together."

"I love you, Terry."

"I love you, too."

The screen went blank.

Alone with his thoughts, Cahill felt a surge of angst and frustration.

Surprising himself with his loss of self-control, he stood, screamed in anger, and punched a cabinet. When he withdrew his stinging hand, he saw blood dripping from abraded knuckles.

He flopped into his chair and considered the death of the entity within his wife's womb.

Though unsure about what fate had stolen from him, he found himself in deep sadness with the loss. His wife's senseless suffering bothered him, and it made him question the sanctity of life and the sanity of creating it anew.

Perhaps, he wondered, the world was unworthy of his offspring. Perhaps a childless marriage would spare his unborn children from the needless suffering of existence.

His mind fracturing under unfamiliar stimuli, he leaned forward, placed his head in his hands, and cried.

## CHAPTER 13

Dmitry Volkov finished his plea. "And please bless your children, Terry and Ariella, in their time of strife. Let this tragedy strengthen them and help guide them to the truth. Amen."

He pressed his fingers together, tapped his forehead, and then completed the sign of the Christian cross in front of his body. His prayers complete, he rose from his knees and then returned his Russian Byzantine crucifix to a cubby.

His Orthodox Christian faith anchored him when faced with his own helpless suffering or that of his friends.

When a personal message from Cahill had arrived ten minutes earlier, he'd been shocked by the bad news. After reading about the miscarriage, he'd typed a rapid response of support to the Australian, sent it, and then set about to calling upon his god for help.

As with any inexplicable shock of suffering, Volkov felt the miscarriage testing his faith.

As he'd wrestled in his young adulthood about accepting or rejecting his faith, he used to argue that if God is omnipotent, he can't be perfect since he permits evil and suffering, and there was no point in worshipping him. Therefore, the Russian feared during his religious formation that his clergy was asking him to pursue a weak god, one incapable of eliminating evil.

Replaying the anti-god argument in his head as he sat, he recalled the strength of its emotional appeal.

But to the *Wraith's* commander, only a benevolent creator God could explain needless suffering. It was the trickiest of theological arguments, but it was the only logical explanation of evil.

Per his belief, evil began when people declared themselves the ultimate judges of right and wrong.

Therein lies the rub.

Shutting his eyes and pinching the bridge of his nose, he forced himself to remember that every human being is an imperfect judge of right and wrong. Nobody can see the entirety of the universe, and nobody could declare pain, sadness, or loss as evil.

Miserable, yes. Horrible, yes. Suffering feels terrible, but feelings are not truth. To declare it unfair or wrong is to appeal to a perfect judge of fair and right.

It's an appeal to God.

And having finished his appeal to God on Cahill's behalf, Volkov accepted that human understanding of right and wrong, of justice and mercy, was flawed.

To a perfect God, the miscarriage was justice. Somehow. And only divine revelation could reveal why.

He lowered his head into his hands and sighed.

He couldn't understand how bad things could happen to good people, but he knew that answering the question was hopeless without insertion of his creator into the argument.

Hoping to make something good from the lost child, Volkov probed his thoughts and emotions.

Forcing optimism to his mind's surface, he felt closer to his friend. Yes, Cahill was a friend, one who'd sought Volkov's solace during strife and who'd requested secrecy about the issue.

The Australian's note stated that he hadn't told anyone else about his loss, not aboard the transport ship or beyond.

Not even Jake.

Having struggled in his earlier missions with acceptance, Volkov now felt elite.

The numbers–the unofficial scorecard of submarines defeated–favored the Russian as the mercenary fleet's best commander. But now, the commander of second seniority, when faced with a personal crisis, considered him, the commander of third seniority, more approachable than Jake, the primary and assumed next-in-line behind Renard to lead the fleet.

And both men shared a bond of having destroyed two *Ghadir* submarines, ramping up the death tolls of the fleet's enemies and shouldering a shared burden of guilt.

As the lingering, nagging doubts about his belonging on the team faded, Volkov turned his thoughts towards those he'd killed and those whom he might soon send to watery graves.

He leaned back in his chair, shut his eyes again, and considered his role as judge, jury, and executioner.

Even trickier than digging through soundbite-level arguments against God was trying to discern the creator's will.

Were he and Cahill justified in sinking *Ghadir*-class hulls? Was he correct to hunt more Iranian submarines? Was doling out death a warranted cost for getting humanitarian aid into Yemen?

He could only wonder, hope, and pray.

But he knew these were passive tasks, and his ship was approaching waters that required action.

With the Israeli Caesaron submersible drone protecting the Socotra port from meddling *Ghadirs*, Volkov was leading his *Wraith* submarine on a hunt.

Although the human shields and MICA missiles had turned back the air strike, the Emirati naval task force continued towards Socotra. The remnants of the legitimate Yemeni Navy, hiding in the open ocean, were steaming to intercept the inbound enemy.

But the old Yemeni combatants lacked the defenses to battle the superior UAE ships.

Enter Volkov and the *Wraith* to give the Yemenis an advantage in the upcoming battle. But first, he had to find and eliminate the Iranian submarines hiding in support of their UAE allies.

Unsure if killing Emirati or Iranian sailors was proper, Volkov lamented his humanity's limited intellect. He knew he could rarely be certain of the absolute righteousness of his cause, but a warrior in battle lacked the luxury of philosophy. So, the *Wraith's* commander considered it merciful that combat under orders let him sidestep the questions of right and wrong.

He valued loyalty, and he was loyal to his fleet—his family. And his family's present goal was turning back the Iranian submarines suspected of protecting the encroaching Emirati task force.

A harsh knock on his door startled him. "Dmitry!"

"Enter."

The dolphin trainer clicked open the latch and then stepped into the room. "There's someone broadcasting false dolphin signals!"

The *Wraith's* commander sprung from his seat. "We found another *Ghadir*?"

Vasily extended his palms. "No, no. Not like that. At least, Anatoly and Serguei think it's not a submarine."

"What do they think it is?"

"They're guessing it's a sonobuoy."

"A lone buoy or a buoy field?"

"I'm not sure, but they weren't panicked."

Volkov's pounding heart slowed. "Okay. It's probably a lone buoy, which can be avoided. You excited me for a second."

"Sorry, Dmitry. I didn't mean to. You know how anxious I get about my babies."

Volkov recalled the dolphins' status as being deployed and scouting two miles ahead of the *Wraith*. "I know. Are they okay?"

"They're fine, but I did pull them back to a mile ahead of our track."

"Good move. But not any closer. I can't guarantee that I won't need to go active on the sonar."

"I know. I won't let you deafen my babies, much less cook them."

"I'd never cook your babies, but I intend to cook this sonobuoy–or do something worse to it. Come with me to the control room." The *Wraith's* commander led the trainer to the ship's nerve center, which buzzed with human energy.

His executive officer greeted him. "Dmitry! We've got what looks like a sonobuoy, bearing zero-five-three, sending out dolphin calls. Well, it's a repeated dolphin call, just one. Someone managed to record our range-report request and is now sending it out in an infinite loop."

"Like the Israelis did in the Med."

"Right. Except the Israelis stole our return-to-home message.

I guess one of the Iranians captured our range-report request instead."

"Of course. What makes you think it's a sonobuoy?"

"Anatoly's got the team listening to it, and there's nothing coming from it other than the calls. Assuming it's dead in the water, I've got a loose range estimate of four nautical miles."

The news alarmed the *Wraith's* commander. "If it shifts from dolphin-fooling mode to submarine-finding mode, it could get a return off our hull. And who's to say the Iranians aren't using dolphin calls as sonar?"

"They might be, but at those high frequencies, we're too far away for the sonobuoy to be a threat."

"Let's first verify what we're up against." Volkov slowed the *Wraith* from its zigzag hunt for Iranian submarines and then faced the trainer. "Send the dolphins for a photograph."

During an hour of carving a slow hole in the sea, the *Wraith* absorbed the suspected sonobuoy's false cetacean signals.

The noise became a frustrating, repetitive torment. Wanting to silence the annoyance, Volkov instead allowed it to continue to assure that multiple ears listened for his dolphins' proper communications.

When he thought he'd lose his mind if he heard another false mammalian call from the sonobuoy, a new pattern of cetacean chirps and whistles rang from the overhead speakers.

Vasily announced the meaning. "That's my babies. They've identified a submerged contact. I'm ordering them to approach it for a flash photograph."

"Very well. Order the photograph."

Five minutes later, more chirps and whistles arrived, and the dolphin trainer announced the message. "They've taken the picture. I want to order them back to the ship."

"Very well. Order them back."

Vasily tapped keys and reported his progress. "I just ordered them back to ship."

"Very well. Where's my picture?"

Seated at a Subtics console, the trainer turned his head. "It's coming. We need about three minutes before there's anything useful, even at low resolution."

The *Wraith's* commander stepped to his foldout chair on the elevated conning platform. "Show me what's already come in."

"Okay. Here it comes."

A grainy image appeared showing a murky abyss of black surrounding a fuzzy blob of reflected brightness. Volkov glared at it, willing it to materialize.

An artificial sound–a perfect sinusoidal note–whistled through the speakers, and the sonar guru revealed his sullen face to his commander. "The sonobuoy just went active at a valid search frequency."

A pit of despair formed in Volkov's stomach. "Chance of detection?"

"Greater than fifty percent."

"Damn it! All-ahead two thirds, make turns for ten knots." After accelerating, he ordered an opening course to drive away from the sonobuoy. "Left ten-degrees rudder, steady on course three-three-zero. Vasily, use range checks and return-to-home signals liberally with the dolphins to get them back here."

"I already am! They'll catch up to us if you don't increase speed."

"I won't unless I have to." Noting an eerie silence over the loudspeaker, Volkov raised his voice. "What's the sonobuoy doing?"

The sonar guru shook his head. "Nothing. No more dolphin calls. No active transmissions." Another sinusoidal signal–a loud, concentrated musical death note, like a final confirmation of the *Wraith's* position–rang throughout the room. "And there's your next active transmission. It's got us, Dmitry."

"Understood. We'll stay at ten knots and slip away before anyone can react."

Anatoly yelled. "Torpedo in the water!"

Another sonar technician echoed the call. "I've got a torpedo in the water, too! No. Wait. Two more torpedoes in the water!"

Volkov's chest tightened. "Anatoly! Figure out how many torpedoes are out there, with bearings and bearing rates, and enter them in the system!"

During a long minute that tested his commander's patience, the sonar ace stood and walked behind his two seated technicians. When done gathering the data, he looked at Volkov and shook his head. "We're in trouble, Dmitry."

The *Wraith's* commander stepped to the central plotting table and studied the incoming danger. Four torpedoes arrived from opposite directions. He whispered to himself. "A trap."

Anatoly waved for his commander's attention. "Counterfire?"

"Yes. Tubes one and two. Give me your best solutions in thirty seconds and inform me when the weapons are ready."

"They'll be guesses. Bad shots."

Volkov yelled. "Get them ready anyway!"

"Aye, sir. We're preparing tubes one and two. I've got the full sonar team coming to the control room."

The *Wraith's* commander studied the bearings to the incoming weapons. Instead of converging on him, they fanned out. "These torpedoes aren't threats to us."

Supervising the counterfire assignments, the sonar ace replied over his shoulder. "Agreed, but they could be steered towards us at any second. They're boxing us in from four sides."

Volkov concurred and made a counterintuitive decision. "Helm, all-stop!" As the ship slowed, he glanced at his sonar guru. "My weapons, Anatoly?"

"Tubes one and two are... yes. Both are ready."

"Shoot tubes one and two!"

Back-to-back impulse launches whined into the control room and popped Volkov's ears.

"Tubes one and two are away, normal launches. We have wire control." Anatoly straightened his back. "But we have a bigger problem. There's another torpedo in the water, bearing zero-one-nine. Bearing rate is nearly zero."

Any doubts remaining in Volkov's mind of a trap dissolved.

Anatoly repeated himself. "Dmitry. Another torpedo."

"I heard you. Put it in the system. Assume a range of four

miles." As the icon appeared as a fifth hostile weapon, the *Wraith's* commander barked orders. "Prepare tube five against the launcher of the fifth weapon. Assume the launching submarine is five miles away on the torpedo's bearing."

While the speed gauge showed the ship slowing below four knots, the team bristled with nervous energy.

Volkov wrestled with a decision and then announced it. "Use our remaining speed to bring us shallow. Come to periscope depth, and prepare to abandon ship."

The control room's din subsided, revealing the quiet background drone of electronics.

"You all heard me. We're boxed in and defeated. This was a brilliant trap. Anyone who wants to live, get ready to abandon ship. Get a communication buoy ready for Pierre with our situation and launch it with zero time delay."

Surprising the *Wraith's* commander, the dolphin trainer stepped by his side. "I have an idea."

Volkov grunted. "You're a miracle worker?"

"Not me. My babies. A torpedo is just another underwater contact to them. Fast, yes. But they can maneuver between us and the fifth weapon."

Volkov grasped Vasily's meaning. "And they can sprint up to twenty knots, right?"

"Twenty-one! I've clocked them."

"The torpedo is coming at more than forty knots and will accelerate to over sixty if it reaches terminal mode."

"But my babies aren't chasing it. They're approaching from the front, and then the side. They'll figure out how to intercept it. Nature designed them to defend their families from mako sharks, and those go faster than thirty-five knots."

"You'd have them plant detonators on it?"

Vasily seemed assured of his cetaceans. "Yes! They can do it!"

"You'd bet your life on it?"

Doubt erased the trainer's veneer of false confidence. "Well, no. But I see no other choice."

Volkov appreciated the honesty and agreed. "Make it happen.

Give them the order to arm themselves and attack the torpedo."

"Thank you, Dmitry!"

"But I'm still preparing to abandon ship."

Vasily hollered over his shoulder while striding to his console. "Give my babies a chance to impress you!"

Anatoly shifted his commander's focus to his counterfire. "Tube five is ready!"

"Shoot tube five."

The impulse launch was normal, invoking a third outgoing weapon in the central chart.

As the *Wraith* steadied at a shallow depth, the deck rolled from side to side, and Vasily updated the cetaceans' status. "Mikhail and Andrei have confirmed an intercept course for the torpedo. I have them converging on it in four minutes."

Volkov saw little margin for error. "The torpedo will hit us in five minutes."

Anatoly challenged the timing. "Not if you turn and run."

Though terrified, Volkov admired the intricate trap. Three Iranian submarines had formed a triangle around the baiting buoy, and their response was executed to preplanned perfection. Two submarines had sent their combined four weapons to prevent running while the third enemy sent the kill shot. "If I run, I'll attract one of the other weapons."

"Just five knots, Dmitry. It'll keep us away from the outer torpedoes but could buy us half a minute."

"Very well, all-ahead one-third, make turns for five knots!"

The sonar ace examined his screen and then looked to his commander. "Five and a half minutes to impact, roughly. It's just an estimate."

Loud clanks rang from the crew's accommodation room.

"I know." Volkov turned to see the source of the noise. Sailors were dragging shotguns to a raft staged below the hatch. Instead of correcting them for making banging noises, the *Wraith's* commander appreciated their zeal to get off the submarine.

Vasily announced his babies' progress. "The dolphins report short-range detection of an underwater object on their clock's direction to the torpedo. They hear it, and they're in position ahead of it. I'm having them arm themselves."

"Very well."

A minute later, the trainer announced each cetacean's success in lifting a suction-and-magnetic mountable explosive off his partner's back to his nose for deployment. "The dolphins are armed. I've ordered them to plant their detonators."

Contemplating the timing of surfacing the *Wraith*, Volkov let the mammals finish their attempt. "Very well."

Half a minute later, the chirps and whistles came, but the trainer remained silent.

Volkov barked. "Vasily!"

"I don't know what happened! Andrei's saying 'yes'. Mikhail's saying 'no'. I don't understand them, Dmitry. They've never disagreed!"

"*Blyad*! Mikhail missed, but Andrei did it! Order the detonation!"

"Right! Right! Okay. I'm ordering it."

A muff pressed against his ear, the sonar guru half-leapt from his seat. "Single detonation on the fifth torpedo's bearing! It's flooding! It's sinking!"

Volkov sighed in relief. "Dear God. They did it. Or at least one of them did."

The sonar ace showed shrewd eyes to his commander. "We hear high-speed screws on the bearing of the last shooter. It's a *Ghadir* making its best speed. Your counterfire was accurate."

"Very well. Guide our weapon to it, and send that *Ghadir* to the abyss."

Anatoly seemed hungry for vengeance. "Do you want to go after the other two shooters? If they're *Ghadirs*, they're out of reloads."

"Do you still hear the *Ghadirs*?"

"One just faded as we opened distance, but we're faster. We could go after the other and then come back for the first."

Volkov weighed the risks–and the death toll. "I wouldn't be surprised if they kept a submarine or two hidden in reserve as a second trap. Surviving one trap is enough for one day. There's no need for any more mortalities today just yet. But to be sure, line me up to talk to Pierre. I need advice from above."

## CHAPTER 14

Commander Amir watched the icons representing the Emirati task force's ships slip closer to his *Tarantul* and its two *Osa* escorts. Needing speed for his attack, he'd abandoned the slower supply ship, leaving it to rely upon a large ocean for its continued concealment from the enemy.

And the enemy was changing.

In his favor.

Carrying a printout of the latest update from his squadron commander, he yelled across the bridge and addressed his executive officer, who navigated the *Tarantul*. "Exec?"

The thin second-in-command lowered his binoculars from his face and strode to his commander. "Sir?"

In disbelief, Amir unfolded the paper and aimed it at his thin colleague. "It's from Captain Damari. Tell me I'm reading it correctly."

The executive officer's eyes opened wide as they flitted across the page. "The mercenaries destroyed another Iranian *Ghadir*-class submarine."

"Keep reading."

"Can this be true? The Iranians have withdrawn completely from the battle, and the Emiratis have given up on retaking Socotra."

Amir folded the paper and tucked it in his breast pocket. "Correct, if you believe the intelligence report."

"I don't know if I believe it, but it makes sense. The Iranians have lost three submarines and gained nothing. And if they've really retreated, the Emiratis can't defeat the undersea assets of the mercenaries around Socotra. But to believe it all, since it's good news... that's another thing entirely."

"Captain Damari has ordered us to behave as if it were true. We'll be repositioning closer to Nishtun now, to defend the incoming humanitarian freighters."

"What intelligence revealed all this?"

"Supposedly, the commander of that transport ship is married to an Israeli Aman officer. Captain Damari suspects the Israelis have spies in the Iranian military that watch their naval movements, especially their submarines."

"And the Iranians are smart enough to suspect this, I imagine. This could just as easily be disinformation."

"I don't think so. Like you said, they've lost three submarines, and those loses have been for a war they don't need to fight. Iran can win by letting other people fight it for them."

"The Emiratis may come back to Socotra right after the mercenaries leave us."

Amir eyed the screen again. "Not if we defeat them soundly before then." As he watched, a warning popped up telling him the robotic helicopter was returning to Socotra for refueling. Instead of risking the drone as a tracer bullet going the wrong way and landing on the *Tarantul's* fantail, the mercenaries programmed it to complete the roundtrip to the harbor. "We're losing our aerial coverage for four hours."

"I sure hope it gets back on station before we encounter the UAE. It's nice being able to watch them."

"It will. We're still six hours from their extreme missile range. And I don't expect many missiles coming at us."

"You seem confident about that."

Amir shared the unwritten news. "Captain Damari told me over the phone that the French ambassador to the United Nations is aboard the first freighter."

The executive officer scowled. "Seriously?"

"Apparently, Mister Renard has the political clout and arranged it, most likely with a generous bribe."

"Okay. That sounds like a good thing, but what's the implication for us, sir?"

Feeling the battle shifting in his favor, Amir smirked. "It's a fantastic thing, especially since President Hadi's chief of staff informed the Emiratis about it."

The thin officer's face flushed with recognition of the value. "A one-man human shield?"

"Yes, and a visible one. His presence assures us that the

freighters won't be harmed any worse than being disabled."

"That's great. We only need to get to Nishtun first and keep the UAE task force out of cannon range of the freighters."

Amir recalled the second part of his conversation with his commodore. "Uh, not quite. Captain Damari suspects a spy working against us in Socotra. You didn't think we'd be the only ones benefiting from espionage, did you?"

The thin officer folded his arms. "Not at all, sir. Given the island's history, I'd expect that half the population wants to work against us."

"Right. A few locals have been asking dangerous questions, and we think they've figured out and shared with the UAE the arrival timing and destination of the humanitarian freighters."

"So, the Emiratis can find them on the high seas?"

Amir shrugged. "Probably. They can backtrack from Nishtun and make logical guesses. Regardless, we're going to snuggle up with the freighters and escort them in."

"So, now we're using human shields to protect ourselves, too, just like the shore defenses did with the prisoners?"

The *Tarantul's* commander tasted the same bitterness he suspected his shore-based colleagues felt while thwarting the UAE's air assault on Socotra. "I'd like to say you're wrong, but that's part of it. Still, I'd like to think the primary reason to take station on the freighters will be to conceal our radar return from the Emiratis. It'll give us the element of surprise when they challenge them."

"After learning about the UN ambassador, you think they'll still attempt to disable ships carrying humanitarian aid?"

"They'll claim we were smuggling in weapons to the Houthis. That's how the Saudis have shut down the eastern half of our nation's commerce."

"But we hate the Houthis! They're the damned enemy! Everyone knows that."

Amir wished everyone knew, but his nation's crisis seemed unwatched. "The world doesn't know or care, and if the ambassador's presence draws the attention Mister Renard hopes, it could just as easily backfire."

"Why would it backfire, sir?"

"France supplies weapons that we and our mercenaries have used against the UAE, such as MICAs against their pilots, and they can point to that. If we end up in a battle at sea, there'll be a subsequent political spin battle it in the press."

The thin officer cast his glance to the deck. "Politics."

"Politics matters, but Captain Damari has given us the freedom to do anything to protect the convoy, including sinking every UAE combatant we encounter. And we can strike first. From his perspective, we're at war."

"Bless him and his courage."

Amir felt justified about having supported his commodore's rise to power. "Absolutely." He shifted his focus to navigation. "Chart an intercept course to take station on the convoy as quickly as possible."

The second-in-command nodded. "I'll see to it, sir." He stepped towards a charting table.

Amir strode to the bridge's starboard side.

A lone lookout greeted him. "Hello, sir!"

"And hello to you. What do you see out there?"

The young sailor pointed through the windows towards the rising sun. "*Osa-1* is there, ten miles off our beam, right where it's been for the last hundred miles, sir."

Amir scoffed. "What else?"

"There's an oil tanker dropping off the horizon behind us. If you look hard, you can see it, sir. Other than that, I can't see any other contacts, although I know we've got *Osa-2* on the port side where I can't see it. But from what I hear over my headset, other than that, we're alone."

Hoping the Iranian submarines obeyed the retreat order a friendly spy network had intercepted, Amir agreed with the youngster. "That's how I like it."

The sailor lifted a sound-powered phone's mouthpiece to his lips. "Course two-zero-five, speed forty-two knots, aye." He looked across the bridge at the second-in-command and then to his commander. "The executive officer recommends course two-zero-five at forty-two knots to intercept the convoy. We're going after our own convoy, sir?"

"I'll explain it to you and the entire crew soon." Amir raised his voice. "Executive officer, I concur with course two-zero-five and forty-two knots. Order the turn when all ships are ready"

The lean officer faced his commander and nodded. "Understood, sir. Tactical center, bridge. Inform the *Osas* of the fleet's new course and speed, prepare to turn as we turn."

After a minute, the officer on duty in the tactical center informed the bridge of the *Osas'* agreements.

The executive officer barked. "Helm, left standard rudder, steady on course two-zero-five. All-ahead flank."

Moments later, the sun slid rightward across the sky, and the small *Osa* missile boat drifted from Amir's twisting vantage point. As the other missile boat, *Osa-2*, came into view through the port bridge windows, the *Tarantul* commander's ire rose. "Damn." He glared at dark smoke rising from *Osa-2's* superstructure and the ship's decaying wake. He stepped across the bridge to his executive officer. "Any word from *Osa-2*?"

His attentive second-in-command lowered the binoculars he'd aimed at the distressed ship. "Not yet, sir. I'm giving them a minute to contact me."

"Half a minute was plenty. Hail them."

The thin officer grabbed a radio handset and contacted their comrades. After a rapid exchange, he learned that one of *Osa-2's* three diesel engines had failed. "They're investigating the failure. They're taking the inoperative diesel offline and are limited to two engines, maximum speed of thirty-six knots, sir."

"I don't want them pushing their two remaining engines any harder than they have to. Recalculate an intercept course using thirty knots."

The executive officer marched to a charting table, uttered words to a quartermaster, and then watched the young sailor recalculate the Yemeni Navy's direction. Apparently confident in the new track, he looked up at his commander and nodded. "We can still get there well before the Emiratis."

"Show me." Amir strode to the chart and studied the geometry. Assuming the UAE task force could identify the humanitarian aid freighters and intercept them, the aging Yemeni ships would arrive first and meet their enemy on the high seas, free of clutter in the shipping lanes, out of sight of land, and far from fishing havens. "This looks good. Lucky for us that *Osa-2* can still hold more than thirty knots."

"The laws of power and speed are odd, sir. You need eight times the power to double your speed."

The *Tarantul's* commander reflected upon the proportionality. "That's a brutal engineering challenge when you're trying to build ships as fast as ours."

"But it's one of the few blessings we have, sir. These ships were designed for it, at the expense of just about everything else."

"And when you lose a third of your propulsion like our *Osa-2*, the loss in speed is acceptable. At least, I hope it is. I'll need to account for their speed limit while developing a battle plan, unless they can fix their diesel."

The executive officer scowled. "I haven't heard from them for a few minutes. Let me check their status."

Keeping his eyes on the chart while pondering his future tactics, Amir nodded. "Go ahead."

Minutes later, the thin officer returned, his head shaking. "They blew a piston, sir. Repairs are impossible until we're back in port. And even then, we don't have the spare parts."

The *Tarantul's* commander tried to stuff away the bad news as a minor speedbump on the route to victory. "Thirty-six knots as their maximum speed will have to do."

Attempting rare optimism, the second-in-command sounded encouraged. "I think the Emiratis will be surprised to find us next to the convoy's ships, if they can even figure out which ships those are. Heck, even if they do find us, they may want to avoid the danger. They know we can fight, and we could get the convoy to Nishtun without further combat."

Tempted to agree, Amir remained cautious. "Other than showing up with the freighters, we have no more surprises. They're aware of the *Wraith* and *Xerses*, they know about our anti-air missiles, and I'm sure they've figured out we're using a helicopter drone. They'll probably shoot it down as soon as it's in range."

"Agreed. But we'll probably be in organic-sensor range when that happens, sir. We'll have them on shipboard radar systems, short-range hovercraft, and possibly even visual."

Amir considered the tactics and dared to hope. "You may be right, and we can also negate their technical advantages using the freighters as shields. The Emiratis can't launch anti-ship missiles without risking unwanted international attention."

"But they could blame us if they damage the freighters. They could say they took legitimately targeted shots and claim that we hid like cowards next to the bigger ships."

"Perhaps, but they have more to lose. We're a failed nation. They're a rich nation trying to take us over, and they're easily connected to Iran and the Houthis. The less international attention for them, the better."

The second-in-command shrugged. "Perhaps, sir. But we'll be ready the best we can to deal with incoming missiles."

"Of course. But if we play this smartly, we can keep it contained to a gunfight. Cannon shot verses cannon shot. Speed, maneuvering, and gunnery skills can win the day."

"Agreed, sir."

"Alright, gather the tactical team and have them assemble in the wardroom. It's time to plan for battle."

Hours later, Amir stooped over the wardroom's dining table and stared at lines penciled onto a paper chart. He liked what he saw. "This might work. We might enjoy a tactical advantage for once."

Standing by his right, the executive officer concurred. "I'm looking for holes in the plan, but I don't see any." He raised his jaw towards the other officers and senior enlisted technicians who circled the table. "Anyone else see a flaw?"

Heads shook.

A knock came from the room's door, and Amir yelled. "Enter!"

A young petty officer standing in the passageway read from a sheet of paper. "Captain, the officer of the deck sends his regards and informs you that our aerial drone is back on station and sees the UAE task force."

"Did he send the task force's information?"

"He wrote it down, sir. I..." The befuddled youngster extended the paper to the nearest officer, who handed it to Amir.

Reading the update, the *Tarantul's* commander saw his future converging on a spot in the water.

Identifiable by their shared, rapid twenty-six-knot transit speed, five enemy ships veered from a trajectory towards Socotra and now aimed towards an intercept point ahead of the humanitarian freighters heading towards Nishtun.

Amir snorted. "Thank you. Tell the officer of the deck I'll be on the bridge shortly. Dismissed."

Relieved, the youngster darted away.

The *Tarantul's* commander extended the paper to his right. "You were hoping they might not figure out which freighters are ours?"

The executive officer read the update. "I did, but it was obviously a fool's hope. They've turned towards the convoy and accelerated to their slowest ship's maximum speed, sir. They're coming."

## CHAPTER 15

As the reloaded *Xerses* pushed away from the pier, Cahill let Walker handle the maneuvering while he absorbed news from the Frenchman. "You're not serious, are you, mate?"

In the display, Renard gave a broad smile. "Have you ever known me to lie?"

"Yes! God, I hope so. You're an international gangster."

The Frenchman blushed. "I don't know whether to be honored or offended."

"It's all the same to me."

"I'll choose to be honored, and no, I'm not lying. Dmitry encountered three *Ghadirs* and destroyed one of them."

"And the other two got away?"

"No, actually. He could've taken out the other two, but he contacted me for advice, and I stopped him."

Walker looked to the screen and raised his eyebrows. "Wow. Seriously?"

The *Xerses'* commander chided his companion. "Keep your eyes on the ship's movement. Let me talk to Pierre." He faced the computer display. "Yeah, Pierre. What Liam said. Seriously?"

"I stopped him because he scared away the Iranians."

Cahill doubted the good news. "It's too good to be true, but if he took out a third *Ghadir*, it makes sense for those mongrels to cut their losses."

"I understand your doubt, but a certain Lieutenant Colonel Ariella Dahan shared with me that a spy has confirmed the cease-and-desist order for all Iranian submarines that were tasked with helping the Emiratis against us."

Cahill folded his arms. "I think you owe me an extra bonus for me wife's contributions."

"Perhaps, but we'll celebrate after the aid reaches those in need."

The *Xerses'* commander looked through the windows at the receding Socotran wharf.

In addition to the eight MICA missiles loaded within his port hull, three containers of eight spares lined the pier. The freighter which had carried them from the Mediterranean Sea remained tied up while cranes lifted goods from its deck to the island's awaiting consumers. "Right. Liam's got us underway. Too bad we couldn't bring all the MICAs with us. Those things are gems."

"You've got some distance to cover. If there were another ship in Socotra that could transport your spares fast enough, I'd use it."

"We'll get there in time. Both gas turbines are online, roaring like lions."

"Good to hear it. Your future isn't with the missiles you left behind. It's with the next three freighters arriving through the Indian Ocean, bound for Nishtun."

"Is the French ambassador to the UN really aboard one of them?"

"You've seen the picture, haven't you?"

Cahill recalled a photograph of the ambassador shaking hands with a short Pakistani man dressed like a merchant marine captain while both men stood on a huge ship's bridge. "Yeah."

"It was taken in Singapore when the ambassador toured the ship on his vacation. The ambassador also verified the manifests of all three ships as carrying only humanitarian aid."

"Those could be faked."

Renard shrugged. "Sure, they can. But the ambassador's oversight creates real pressure on any nation that would thwart the ships' arrival to the world's most notable humanitarian crisis."

The truth crept up on the Australian's doubting mind. "Then, there's no need to actually have the ambassador aboard any of those freighters."

The Frenchman frowned. "Oh, don't make me reveal my secrets. You never know who might be listening."

Cahill muted the connection and looked away from the screen. "Bloody Pierre's invented a half-truth to confuse the Emiratis. That ambassador walked off the ship right after the photo op."

"It changes nothing we're doing, but remind me never to play poker with him."

"What's your obsession with poker?"

"I'm terrible at it."

"Says the man who would bait me into playing for paychecks."

Walker smirked. "That's for you to find out."

Cahill unmuted himself to his boss. "Liam and I will be happy to defend the convoy with all urgency, regardless of its staffing."

"That's my ace talking. Charmed, like all my commanders."

Feeling more unbalanced than charmed, the *Xerses'* commander quieted his mind with thoughts of tactics. He ran the pending battle through his head before answering. "This is a good plan, Pierre. I'll grant you that. I haven't been as optimistic about a battle before."

"I appreciate the vote of confidence. However, you sound hesitant. Is something wrong?"

Ashamed his boss sensed his doubts from across the world, Cahill deflected. "Not at all. I'm good, mate."

"Perhaps mentioning your wife's name was my mistake?"

As his lost child resurfaced in the Australian's mind, he lied. "I'm fine. It's just the withdrawal from newlywed paradise. It's a normal letdown, I'm sure."

"If you say so, I won't belabor it. Let's get down to the intelligence report then, shall we?"

"Right."

"You see where Dmitry encountered the *Ghadirs*?"

Cahill looked to a screen showing the tactical overview. "Yeah. That happened far to the northeast, didn't it?"

"Indeed. He won't be able to catch the convoy. His positioning was based upon the premise of the Emirati task force transiting to Socotra. Now that's old news, but I count it as a blessing that he's already pushed away the Iranians."

"Right, mate. I never thought I'd say this, but we don't need Dmitry to win this one."

Renard grunted. "Before counting your easy victory, I'll share some noteworthy information from prying eyes in the UAE. Apparently, their navy has been studying defenses against our tactics, and they may have improved upon them."

"I don't like the sound of that."

"Nor should you. They were seen loading sandbags and what looks like some sort of modular lattice armor. Words won't do it justice, I'm sure, and our man on the ground was unable to take photographs without compromising himself."

"Then you've got some explaining to do."

"The sandbags will obviously go around propulsion equipment at a minimum. I wouldn't be surprised if they surrounded their close-in-weapon systems and cannons, too."

"We've seen that before."

"Indeed. But the way the lattices were described, you can picture models of molecules bound together by electrons, except with steel balls as the nuclei and rebar holding them together. I think the Emiratis are expecting them to work like nuclear shielding against your railgun rounds."

Having trained on diesel boats, the Australian misunderstood. "I thought lead was used for nuclear shielding because it's heavy."

"Ah. Against gamma rays, yes. But when shielding against large particles, like errant neutrons, water serves as a shield. The like-sized hydrogen atom's nucleus absorbs the neutron's energy. If a neutron hits a smaller object, the smaller object takes a tiny fraction of the energy, and the neutron continues. If the neutron hits a larger object, it reflects with most of its energy. But like-sized particles share their momentum."

Cahill understood. "And if our cannon rounds hit balls of steel of similar size, the kinetic energy is immediately halved and shared with the balls."

"Correct. And both masses, your incoming round and the defensive steel, move in directions other than towards the target."

"With that and sandbags, even our accurate shots may have no effect."

151

"And it's no good switching to splintering rounds. They were bringing two sizes of lattice–one sized for your intact rounds, and one sized for splinters. And from the amount they loaded, it looks like they can replace them as you would destroy them. They come in one-meter-square units, which appeared modular in design."

The *Xerses'* commander felt his advantage slipping. "You're sending me into a slugfest armed with the weakest cannons."

"I know. You may have to target the enemy's radar systems to soften their defenses."

Disliking the reliance on ships older than himself, Cahill countered. "Or, I could just play submarine and torpedo them all."

"I would normally agree, but they've also brought three anti-submarine warfare helicopters. I'm sure one will be deployed at all times, possibly all three when you meet them in battle."

"Why hasn't the drone seen them flying yet?"

"I think they're holding them back until needed, since they know that you and Dmitry are still beyond range."

"Is there any more bad news you want to give me?"

"Just a final review of whom you're up against. Along with a landing ship, which is serving as a stores ship, a helicopter deck, and probable flagship, the Emiratis brought four combatants–two *Baynunah*-class corvettes and two *Lürssen* TNC-45 patrol craft."

Cahill did the math. "Each of those has a full-sized cannon. That's four punchers in this boxing match."

"Right. And our team has only one, the *Tarantul.* Our railguns are more like jabs than punches."

"The patrol craft have compact turrets that shoot slightly slower than those of the larger ships, but you'll be essentially outgunned four-to-one in cannon shot."

"Is this your pep talk?"

"No, and it gets worse." Renard's glare became stern. "I'm not giving you permission to launch torpedoes. I fear it would entice the Emiratis to desperation, and they'd launch their anti-ship missiles without regard for the freighters."

The *Xerses'* commander considered the risk in human lives. "Damned if I do, damned if I don't. If I hit a ship with a slow-kill, it would only piss them off. If I use a heavyweight, I kill a complete crew and piss off their friends."

"I know. But at least you'll have the freighters as shields. Use them." The Frenchman's features froze in a warning about his seriousness.

"I hear you, boss. I'm ready to do what I must."

"I know you will." Renard relaxed his stare. "But hopefully, you won't have to. If deterrence wins the day, so be it. I'd be happier if your presence helps turn away the Emiratis as opposed to baiting them into a bloodbath. Remember, the mission is the landing of humanitarian aid, not the sinking of combatants."

Cahill wanted to put the pending battle–or the nonviolent standoff, however it evolved–behind him. "Understood."

Walker interrupted the conversation. "We're clear of the channel. We can accelerate to any speed when ready."

"Bring us to flank speed, Liam."

The risen sun bobbed off the starboard quarter as the *Xerses'* rakish bows sliced the waves.

After allowing the completed acceleration, Walker announced the transport ship's motion. "We're making thirty-four-point-two knots on course zero-four-one."

Three hundred miles from the Arabian Sea's convergence point of future warring combatants, Cahill did the mental math. "What's that? Just under nine hours?"

"Eight and three quarters, if we don't stop for gas or the loo."

After verifying in the tactical display that the Yemeni warships were scheduled to arrive long before him, the *Xerses'* commander decided to relax before the encounter. "We've got some dead time ahead of us. If you gents will excuse me, I'll take some personal time. You've got the bridge, Liam."

Ten minutes later, Cahill was seated in his stateroom, facing his wife's visage in his laptop. "You look good."

"I hope you think I look good. I'm your wife."

"That's not what I meant."

She scowled. "So, I don't look good?"

"You're twisting me words around."

Releasing her frown, she teased him. "Can't you tell when I'm playing?"

"I wasn't sure that you understood the concept. I'm always in fear of a lethal Krav Maga blow."

She chuckled. "As you should be. Finally, you're relaxing a bit. It's good to see."

"Sorry. I'm taking this separation from you harder than I thought. The... uh... our loss isn't making it any easier."

"Stop being a pussy, Terrance Cahill. It happened in my body, and I'm over it. Now it's your turn to let it go."

He wondered if she ignored her pain to her detriment, but he conceded that he'd married a strong woman. "Done. Your husband's no pussy."

"Good. Now, do what you have to, and come home alive. We'll have fun trying to get pregnant when you're home again."

"You're damned right we will."

"Nice try. But I can tell that you're still worried. What's wrong?"

"You see right through me."

"I do, and I'm listening..."

He sighed and contemplated thoughts from which he'd been hiding. "I think I've hit the point where I'm questioning life's meaning."

She scowled. "You're in combat. You don't have that luxury."

"I'm ready for this battle, and I'll review it once again with the team before I get there. I've got time to ponder things."

"What are you pondering?"

"At the moment, Jake Slate."

She frowned. "Why?"

"Because he's the prototypical model of a commander in this fleet. If I ever wonder what might happen to me, I look at him."

"He's an angry man who turned himself into a machine of destruction to get back at the world. You're not like that."

He entertained the idea. "Maybe not to the same degree, but we were all run out of our fleets as someone else's scapegoat. We've all got chips on our shoulders. If I admit it, I'm bloody well furious about how the Royal Australian Navy sidelined me."

"That was a long time ago."

"Not really. Jake's been harboring fury for more than a decade."

"Then he's a child. I didn't marry a child."

"I didn't say I was. You didn't let me finish me thought."

"Go ahead."

"He's changed. Or at least, he's changing. For the better. He stopped drinking, he's found his religion, and he just seems a lot more grounded and stable recently."

"Compared to his baseline, that's not saying much."

"True. But I think this fleet has a calming influence. Or it used to. Now, I'm not so sure. I used to be sure we were the good guys. Well, sure enough."

"You're on a humanitarian mission. What's wrong with you? What could be better than that?"

"We've used heavyweights. And despite Pierre's hopes, I may have to again."

"I know. Pierre keeps me informed."

"I'm sure you're relentless about asking him for updates."

"I am. But like I said, I didn't marry a pussy. If he said to use heavyweights, use heavyweights."

A fire erupted inside him. "Quiet, woman! That's enough."

She blushed. "I'd rather see you angry than afraid."

He snorted. "Good point."

"Did I snap you out of your doldrums?"

"Enough."

"Good. Go win your battle and come home."

## CHAPTER 16

In the Al Dhafra airbase's briefing room, Captain Sharifi scanned the fourteen other seated pilots.

Two of his companions had ejected from their aircraft during the surprise MICA attack and were later rescued, and their credibility among the squadron challenged Sharifi's. But the young captain sensed from admiring eyes that he retained his stock as the group's most battle-tested aviator, and he embraced the chance to prove himself again.

As the squadron commander entered the room, he spoke above the din. "Give me your attention, gentlemen."

The background chatter died.

"That's better. In case you haven't figured it out by my presence here, the general approved our maritime interdiction mission. We're a 'go' against the convoy."

Having taken a surprise beating from the *Xerses* followed by an aborted assault on Socotra, the aviators showed respect for their resourceful enemy by absorbing the news in silence.

The colonel continued. "Our primary target is the *Tarantul* corvette. Our secondary targets are the two *Osa* missile boats. There is no other seaborne target. None of you–I repeat–none of you will attack a civilian vessel. Is that understood?"

A chorus of murmurs answered. "Yes, sir."

"Good." The team's leader shifted his demeanor from drill sergeant to mentor. "Now, we've all flown in combat at least once, and I commend your courage. Each one of you has met the challenge of facing danger."

Murmurs rose as heads nodded.

"And each of you has lost someone close. That's a burden we'll all bear forever. But believe me, nobody takes it worse than me when an airframe goes down without a parachute."

Although he hadn't known his deceased teammates, Sharifi respected their courage. As the only pilot to have escaped the isolated outpost on Socotra, he also appreciated the camaraderie of shared battles.

After a warranted moment of silence, the colonel continued. "Maktoum, Galadri, Nayhan, and Salmeen."

The addressed pilots responded chorus. "Yes, sir."

"You four are flying combat air patrol. Keep Yemeni air power out of the way. And if any of you want to be heroes, you have the general's permission to engage and shoot down enemy aircraft. But don't get duped into chasing anyone. You're protecting airspace. You're not hunting. Understood?"

"Yes, sir!"

"Dawood, Bilal, Kashif, and Noor."

"Yes, sir!"

You're east and west overwatch respectively. You'll get sensor support and eyeballs from the task force's helicopters, but you'll do the shooting when the *Xerses* shows up. We know it's coming. Destroy the damned thing with your bombs. If you find yourself in a strafing run, aim for the port side forward, parallel to the bridge, and take out the MICAs from their vertical launcher. If all eight MICAs are launched, aim for the cannons. Understood?"

"Yes, sir!"

"Sharifi and Hamad."

The young captain's heart fluttered. "Yes, sir."

"You two are taking out the enemy's helicopter drone. Blind them from situational awareness."

"Yes, sir!"

"Captain Sharifi, since you outrank Lieutenant Hamad, you're flying lead. Congratulations, now you have a wingman."

Mixed emotions rose within Sharifi. "Will we be able to join the battle after we take out the drone?"

"You may target the combatants as secondary targets of opportunity, but the strike team won't wait for you."

"Understood, sir."

"I'm sure you studied your briefing packet, but in case you skimmed the boring parts, we use Schiebel Camcopter helicopter drones in our own military, and they have no defenses. It's an easy shot. Use your guns. Don't waste a missile on it."

"Understood, sir." Sharifi glanced at his new wingman and saw fear giving way to relief. Then he realized why he'd been sidelined to attacking a drone. He and the lieutenant had experienced mortal terror in combat, and the colonel was giving them a break from near death experiences.

"Helicopters from the transport ship will share overwatch responsibility for the *Xerses* within five nautical miles of the task force's center. Our east and west overwatch teams will patrol outside that, which leaves the remaining six of us to attack the Yemeni combatants. Counting me, that's two aircraft on each surface combatant, a strike leader and a wingman. I'll lead the strike on the *Tarantul*, which is the most dangerous target."

A brash captain called out. "So, what's the navy doing while we do their work for them?"

After nervous chuckles subsided, the colonel answered. "If we succeed, they'll stop the freighters and board them. They have infiltration teams ready to storm the vessels and search for contraband."

The brash pilot pressed for clarity. "Contraband?"

"Weapons." The colonel raised his voice. "But if for some reason we fall short, the task force will handle whatever's left of the Yemeni Navy. Then they'll storm the ships. Got it?"

The brash captain sat straighter. "Yes, sir."

"Your attacks will be laser-guided bomb runs targeting the anti-ship missiles followed by strafing if you find yourself close enough. You won't carry anti-ship missiles of your own."

A major challenged his boss. "Why not, sir? They'd work, since the Yemenis have weak anti-air defenses."

"They do, but... well, let me show you." The squadron commander stepped to a podium, grabbed a controller, and invoked a video on the huge screen.

Sharifi found the image's clarity of the transiting ships below the camera admirable, given the perspective from ten thousand feet above the open water.

The colonel narrated. "Our naval task force sent a drone over the enemy convoy, and here's what we've got. The three freighters have moved within half a nautical mile of each other, and the Yemeni ships are hiding between them. That's why no anti-ship missiles. We'd hit the freighters and create an international incident."

The brash captain protested. "Aren't we already committed to an international incident by attacking the Yemenis?"

After pausing the video, the colonel responded. "The freighters are flagged to Pakistan, supposedly thanks to a relationship between the merchant fleet and military leaders in Karachi. So, unless you want to tangle with a bigger navy and air force than ours, don't so much as scratch the freighters. We'll have enough political fallout to deal with after the navy does its part, but there's a monumental difference between explaining boarding parties and explaining burning hulls. Understood?"

"Yes, sir."

"All of you?"

"Yes, sir!"

"Good. Anyone who puts ordnance on a civilian ship... well, just don't. Now, I trust everyone's content to be armed with bombs instead of missiles." The squadron commander restarted the video.

From the vantage of the task force's drone, Sharifi watched the convoy grow larger as their distance to the camera shrank. Ten seconds elapsed, and the changing direction to the transiting ships revealed a small missile boat behind the lead freighter.

The squadron commander narrated. "On this first *Osa*, note the stains behind the exhaust system. This hull hasn't been cleaned in a long time, and it has a dirtier appearance than the other *Osa*, which we know to have been painted more recently."

Sharifi watched the corvette appear beside the second freighter. Although old and disastrous from a stealth design perspective, the *Tarantul* looked sleek and fast, like its *Osa* companions.

"You'll see that the *Tarantul* has two Styx missiles on each side. On the *Tarantul*, the cannon is also dangerous. Take it out if the Styx launchers are destroyed or–God help the task force–

after the launchers are emptied."

Silent, Sharifi wondered if the fifty-year-old Russian vintage weapons were a threat.

His colonel anticipated the unasked question. "The Styx missile is older than most of your parents, and yes, the task force should be able to shoot them down. But don't let that theory be tested, because a Styx warhead is double that of a Harpoon, and if one gets through a ship's defenses, there won't a ship left to rescue. Also, the Styx flies twenty percent faster than a Harpoon, and Yemeni engineers are notorious for squeezing reliable usage out of ancient weapons. Don't let them get launched!"

Sharifi was engrossed as the video recommenced.

The colonel narrated. "And we almost saw the other *Osa* behind the third freighter. Although we didn't see it, we know something's there, behind it, because of the wake."

Panning from the last freighter, the airborne camera turned back towards the *Tarantul*. Erupting with fire, the corvette's cannon barrel spat out a round, but nothing happened.

"It took them a couple shots to get the range, but that's still good gunnery against a small drone. As you can see, they took it out on the third shot." The video ended after the muzzle's third flare.

Sharifi sighed with relief for sidestepping a dangerous assignment, but then he corrected his attitude. Whatever he had been before the hostilities, he was now a warrior. He craved action and sensed a growing addiction to danger.

The colonel dropped the video controller onto the podium. "Some of you may have heard rumors about the French ambassador to the United Nations being aboard one of these freighters. That was a threat from the mercenaries, but the official position is to ignore it. Personally, I don't care if the ambassador is aboard or not, and neither should any of you. You've got your orders. Follow them. First wheels up in thirty minutes."

Captain Sharifi checked the heads-up display of his F-16

Viper. The icons visible beyond his canopy showed the upcoming clash between maritime vessels converging per his expectations, and they showed an air battle–or lack thereof–unfolding per his desires as his nation's pilots fended off the under-skilled Yemeni fighters.

He also saw the enemy's slow UAV and confirmed its presence visually below him. "Group leader, this is drone team. I see the drone and request permission to strike."

The colonel's voice squawked in the captain's helmet. "You're confirmed, drone team. Strike the UAV."

Sharifi called to his wingman. "Follow me down. Don't waste your rounds unless I miss, and I won't miss." He dived his aircraft and aimed its nosecone at the lumbering robotic helicopter. "Engaging with guns."

His first burst sprinkled the target, and smoke rose under the rotor. The second burst set the Schiebel camcopter on fire, and the engine flamed.

"Group leader, this is drone team. The UAV is disabled, on the way down. We'll circle back and watch it splash."

"Understood, drone team."

Sharifi watched the UAV tumble into the sea.

"Drone team, group leader. Good job on the drone. The task force sees new airborne radar from the Yemeni convoy. They've launched a short-range hovercraft to compensate for their lost drone. The drone is destroyed. Dissolve the drone team. Join the overwatches."

Expecting danger ahead of the convoy to the west, Sharifi wanted the action. "I'll join the west. You join the east, Hamad." The young captain then approached two comrades flying over the convoy's future track. "Major Kashif, I request permission to join your wing."

"Captain Sharifi, take position on my left wing, opposite Captain Noor. Keep your eyes open. The *Xerses* is bound to surface soon."

## CHAPTER 17

Against his expectations, Commander Amir welcomed Captain Damari's presence aboard the *Tarantul*. On the bridge during combat, the senior officer kept out of his way while providing valuable guidance.

Such as shameless guidance to hide behind the convoy's container ships.

The taste of hiding was bitter, and Amir had to share it. "You're sure the freighters will hold course and speed, sir?"

"Where could they hope to run?"

"Good point."

"If the Emiratis wanted to strike them, they already would have."

"Unless they're testing how far we're willing to push ourselves up against them to hide." As Amir had the *Tarantul* steadied thirty meters off a container ship's beam, he feared the larger vessel might swallow his corvette. Ahead, the smaller *Osa* looked like a tiny skiff beside its massive nautical neighbor.

Minutes from being attacked, the captain remained cool. "We'll find out soon. Get ready."

"Right, sir." Amir lifted his voice upward. "Tactical center, bridge, order all machinegun and shoulder-launched missile teams weapons free, all ships. Fire at will at any airborne contact. Don't worry about teams hitting the same target. Just shoot!"

From the ship's central nerve, the executive officer replied over the circuit. "All machinegun and shoulder-launched missile teams are weapons free, just shoot, aye, sir."

Damari's voice was ice. "We may need some luck to survive this."

Amir could muster only a nod before the whine of hostile jet engines filled the bridge. With the captain flanking him, he trotted out the port-side windows and saw seas that were calmer than his stormy innards.

Howling through a wide, slow turn, six single-engine jets

veered beyond range of his shoulder-launched weapons. Despite the hopeless tail chase, a sailor aboard the lead *Osa* sent a missile after the trailing F-16. The guided weapon left a contrail that rose, leveled, and then arced into the water as the flying warhead's small fuel supply gave out.

By hiding against the moving cliffs of the freighters' hulls, Amir had protected his tiny navy from the first hostile pass. But as the Emirati aircraft banked low against the horizon, they created a strafing and bombing opportunity.

Amir yelled and undermined that opportunity. "Tactical center, bridge. To all ships. Fall back."

His officer of the deck ordered the *Tarantul* to a backing bell, the huge freighter slid up the corvette's far side, and the wake behind the lead *Osa* died.

Over the loudspeaker, the executive officer confirmed the maneuvers. "Bridge, tactical center. All ships are falling back."

The *Tarantul* settled in a freighter's wake.

With his naked eyes, Amir watched the aircraft line up on their attack vectors. "To all ships, hold position behind your freighter. Fire when ready–including our cannon at one round per second!"

Representing the longest range of the Yemeni anti-air defenses, the corvette's thumping main gun spat its first shot. Whistling into the distance, the first ten rounds targeted the nearest fighter.

Amir planted binoculars to his face and watched. With laser guidance from an aftermarket sensor mounted atop the corvette's superstructure, the rounds veered towards the flying fuselage, but the adept pilot climbed above the incoming arcs. The *Tarantul's* commander lowered the optics. "Cease fire on the cannon! Wait until the targets are closer."

The deafening echoes subsided.

Against the light blue sky, six aircraft split into three pairs, and as they reached shoulder-launched missile range, the first optimistic sailor tried to bring one down.

A shrill swoosh arose from the *Tarantul's* fantail, and a contrail traced a line of smoke into the humid air. Inspired by their optimistic comrade, the other five teams spaced across the three ships engaged the enemy, placing a half dozen missiles into the sky.

Holding his breath, Amir watched the aircraft pull away in all directions, deploy flares to fool the heat-seeking sensors, and dodge the optical laser-guidance systems the human spotters employed from each team.

The difficulty of shooting down an agile jet with an alerted pilot became obvious.

Six missiles missed.

Six aircraft resumed their attacks.

Amir stuck his head into the bridge. "Have them all reload and try again. And recommence firing with the cannon, one round per second. Keep shooting!"

After the *Tarantul's* main gun fired ten rounds, the aircraft dodged the proximity-fused explosions and then leveled for their strafing runs.

Time stopped for Amir as bullets flew from his ships and as more shoulder-launched weapons climbed into the sky.

Each plane held lethal bombs which grew larger as the flying angels of death carried them closer.

Though terrified, Amir managed to bark an order for his navy to seek shelter on the container ships' far flanks.

Per his order, his officer of the deck turned the corvette towards its freighter's starboard side and accelerated.

As the huge hull became a barricade against danger, Amir wondered who was escorting whom. He checked ahead and behind and noticed the *Osas* shifting to their container ships' far sides. Having hidden, the *Tarantul's* commander had precluded the aircraft from dropping accurate bombs, but he heard chainsaw ripples from their guns as they swooshed by to the convoy's far side.

Concealed behind the container ship from the attack's intended destruction, he voiced his concern. "It feels like cowardice."

Like a defiant statue, Captain Damari remained by Amir's side. "Would you prefer to be gutted like a fish? It's tactics. Get me damage reports from all ships."

Realizing he'd overdone the spectating of other vessels, the *Tarantul's* commander started by sticking his head out the window and looking over his ship's side. Light smoke rose from holes peppered in the hull below the port anti-ship missile launchers. "They were going for the Styxes."

"Understandable. Come up with a plan to use them before you lose them. Quickly."

Amir darted inside his bridge and shouted. "Tactical center, bridge. Get me a damage report for ourselves and for the *Osas*."

Over the loudspeaker, the executive officer replied. "We took about two dozen bullets above the waterline. No casualties, but the port cooling system took some hits and is offline. Engineering has cross-connected cooling, and all diesels are running normally. I'm still gathering information from the *Osas*, but no signs of explosions. They couldn't get their bombs off. Sheltering ourselves with the freighters worked, sir."

With the aircraft circling, Amir examined the nearest tactical display. The Emirati task force was beyond his visual horizon but within view of the small hovercraft programmed to fly above his convoy. Ignoring the unarmed flagship, he counted four surface combatants.

More importantly, he noticed a spread in their positions and thought he could isolate one with weak air defenses. "Very well. I also want you to coordinate with the *Osas* on a saturation Styx attack. Either one of those patrol craft on the outsides of the formation look vulnerable to me."

"Understood, sir. A saturation Styx attack on the vulnerable patrol craft. Also, the *Osas* both report being strafed near their port Styx launchers. *Osa-2* took three rounds in a launcher, but the rounds missed the weapon. We concur that the Styxes are their targets."

The near loss of a missile concerned Amir. "Let me clarify. I want to hold our anti-ship missiles as long as possible. The farther the shot, the more opportunities they'll have to defend themselves. But if the aircraft threaten any launcher again, I want the weapons launched."

"Understood, sir. It looks like we have some time. The aircraft are circling in the distance and appear to be regrouping. One of them is breaking off and heading away from the battle. Apparently, we hit one bad enough to send it home."

"Very well. Use the time to plan for using our anti-ship missiles."

"I'm on it, sir."

As minutes passed, Amir dared to hope the Emiratis would quit, but his lookout standing by the starboard windows called out masts on the horizon. Flanked by the quiet captain, the *Tarantul's* commander marched to the starboard side. "Point to them."

The young sailor obeyed.

Amir stuck his binoculars to his face and studied the masts. The crossbeams and wires gave away the ship's identity. "It's older–not a *Baynunah*-class. It's shorter in mast height, which means it's..."

Damari offered the right guidance. "Don't overthink it. Sink it."

Before he could catch himself, Amir voiced a question. "Do you think three missiles is enough, sir?"

"I think four would be a guaranteed kill. Three... now you have me overthinking it. That's a quarter of your inventory aimed at a quarter of the enemy. Do it!"

Amir announced his desires. "Tactical center, bridge. Do you confirm the identity of the nearest enemy combatant as a *Lursten* patrol craft?"

"It's confirmed as a *Lursten* patrol craft by visual from our hovercraft, sir."

"I want three Styxes, one from each ship, launched at it with waypoints to force a wide arc for the *Lursten's* defense and timed for simultaneous arrival."

"I'll plan it, sir."

"You've got thirty seconds."

The second-in-command sounded uncomfortable. "I... uh... I'm on it, sir."

Amir moved to the nearest display and examined the distance between the enemy ships. Four miles separated the targeted patrol craft from the nearest corvette's air defenses.

"Bridge, tactical center. I've got a plan. We're launching one Styx from each *Osa* followed by one of ours ten seconds later. The *Osas'* weapons will fly immediately to waypoints and then take direct routes, separated by one hundred and sixty degrees of arc. Our weapon will arrive between them. I request permission to–"

Approving the timed geometry, the *Tarantul's* commander shouted. "Launch the salvo!"

"Launching the salvo, sir!"

Amir walked to the starboard windows, opened one, and looked outside. Rising from the leading and trailing *Osas*, plumes of smoke billowed, carved curves in the air, and touched the fiery exhaust of their Styx missiles.

His officer of the deck cried out. "Styx launch. Close all windows! Look down! Styx launch. Close all windows! Look down!"

Amir slammed the window shut, lowered his gaze, and shielded his eyes while the missile roared past the bridge.

Over the loudspeaker, the executive officer announced the obvious. "Styx one is away. Sir, the other *Lursten* is also four miles from the nearest corvette's air cover. Should I–"

Amir took his second-in-command's verbal bait. "Yes. Prepare another three-missile salvo. Thirty seconds."

Half a minute later, the *Osas* sent their Styx missiles into the air, and then the *Tarantul's* officer of the deck called out. "Styx launch. Close all windows! Look down! Styx launch. Close all windows! Look down!"

The corvette's second missile roared by the port bridge windows, and then the executive officer announced it. "Styx two is away."

With his salvos requiring a full minute to reach the *Lurstens*,

Amir turned his attention towards defense. He walked to a display and examined the enemy's aerial status.

Though down one aircraft, the Emiratis had regrouped by pulling one of their overwatch jets onto the attack squad, and they'd repositioned themselves behind the convoy to prepare for an apparent lengthwise run at their targets.

During the next strafing run, Amir and his fleet had nowhere to hide. He muttered to himself. "They adjusted their tactics wisely."

"Indeed, they have."

Startled, the *Tarantul's* commander noticed Damari by his side. "I think it's time to call for help, sir."

"I concur. Call the *Xerses*."

"I am calling the *Xerses*, sir." Amir raised his voice. "Tactical center, bridge. Order the *Xerses* to surface."

"Bridge, tactical center. I'm ordering the *Xerses* to surface."

His ship lacking a sonar system, the *Tarantul's* commander found the deep, pulsating tones reverberating under his feet odd, but he comforted himself knowing the sailor tasked with dropping an acoustic noisemaker over the side of his fantail had succeeded in calling for the mercenary transport ship.

His new concern–the *Xerses* answering.

For a moment of doubt, a nagging voice told him the submerged mercenaries would remain hidden and abandon him.

That doubt grew into fear as the Emirati aircraft leveled low and accelerated towards the rear of his convoy.

He barked his command. "Tactical center, bridge. Have all ships pull forward of their freighters."

Obeying his commander's indirect order, the officer of the deck brought the *Tarantul* to flank speed, slid it in front of the container ship, and slowed.

The drawback of hiding in front of the behemoth was situational awareness as the container ship's hull blinded Amir to the attacking aircraft. "Tactical center, bridge. Get our drone out to the side so that we can see something!"

"I'm already on it, sir."

When the hovercraft slipped aside the freighter, Amir saw the enemy's intent. The Vipers were lined up to buzz the trailing container ship's port side. Assuming they'd dart between gaps in the convoy to attack the combatants, he figured they'd overfly the trailing *Osa* and then pass his container ship to the starboard. He called out. "Officer of the deck, hide us off our freighter's port quarter! Keep us exposed only forward of the cannon."

"I'm hiding us off the port quarter, sir."

As the *Tarantul* repositioned, Amir lifted his voice. "Tactical center, bridge. Have the *Osas* hide off their freighters' starboard quarters."

The Emirati onslaught arrived with howling anger. With the restricted angles of their tight turns ahead of the container ship, the Vipers withheld their bombs, but their twenty-millimeter guns spat anger sideways as they passed in front of the *Tarantul's* exposed bow.

From the weather decks, two shoulder-launched missiles flew, and contrails followed the passing jets. The corvette's three-inch cannon belched rounds at the flying enemy, and Amir watched the exchanges.

As the aircraft veered away to make their passes at the leading *Osa*, the *Tarantul's* commander watched one of them bank and climb from the battle, leaving a trail of smoke, while another jet erupted into ball of flame.

Daring to hope his ship had survived unscathed, Amir noticed his silenced cannon. "Tactical center, bridge. Why aren't we shooting?"

The executive officer sounded somber. "Sir, the turret took severe bullet damage. The gun's jammed. The damage is being assessed now."

"Damn!"

"It gets worse, sir. *Osa-2* took two bombs. It's sinking. The crew is abandoning ship. Commander Gulla says that he desires no assistance until you to win the battle."

Amir inhaled and absorbed the news. "Understood. Keep your

focus on what we can control. Get me an assessment of the damage to our cannon."

"I'm on it, sir."

"And call for the *Xerses* again."

"Sir! No need. Its phased-array radar just lit up off our starboard bow. The mercenaries are here!"

Amir welcomed the news. "Very well, tactical center." He aimed his voice to his officer of the deck. "Slide us to the starboard. I want to see the *Xerses*–and the damage to *Osa-2*."

Moments later, the container ships ahead and behind the *Tarantul* seemed to slip to the left, and *Osa-2's* smoking, listing hulk suggested horrible human carnage.

But ahead and to the right, the well-armed transport ship offered hope.

# CHAPTER 18

Terry Cahill pursed his lips and winced.

Walker called him out. "What's wrong? You okay, Terry?"

Moments before entering a heated battle, Cahill was the least okay he'd been. The count of expended lives weighed on him, grounded in his deepest understanding of all his body's cells by the ache of a lost child. He lied. "Fine, mate. Just trying to decide how to use these MICAs."

"Automated. The system tells you the best targets."

The *Xerses'* commander snapped. "I bloody well know that! But some of these aircraft may be damaged, and we'd be wasting missiles on them..."

"There's no time to get selective. We get only one attack with the element of surprise, and it's now. We need to shoot."

"I know. You're right. Line up to ripple launch the MICAs."

Walker tapped keys. "We're lined up for ripple launch. I've got eight targets with greater-than-fifty-percent chances of successful missile engagement."

Cahill hesitated.

"Terry?"

"Right, mate. I'll do it." The *Xerses'* commander tapped a key and raised his voice to his crew over the open circuit. "Standby for MICA ripple launch." He hovered his finger over the final icon, flushed emotions from his mind, and announced his sentencing of eight Emirati pilots to deadly tail chases. "Launching all MICAs!"

One by one, plumes illuminated above his port hull, and the chorus of burning solid-propellant rocket motors screamed.

As the harsh sounds decayed with distance to the climbing Mach-3 missiles, Walker swore. "Bloody hell."

"What's wrong?"

"Look there." The executive officer pointed at a heavily smoking F-16. "That one's trying to escape the battle, and we just wasted a MICA on it."

His companion's eye for detail above the waves impressed

Cahill, and he avoided the temptation to say he'd predicted the wasted weapon. "Anything we can do about it? I considered the missiles' targets unchangeable, but…"

"It's wasted. No time to redirect it."

"Fine. Find me targets for the cannons."

"Your call, Terry. Surfaced or airborne?"

"Airborne. Attack something that's not targeted by MICAs."

Walker's voice was shrill. "The Emirati combat air patrol just shot down a Yemeni fighter. They're outmatched. We'll need to account for those enemy jets, too."

"That's bad, but you didn't answer the question."

"Right. Finding you a target. They're flying all over the place, but I've got one. Bogey eleven."

Cahill checked the icons of the cannons, which he'd raised as his second action after surfacing, prioritized behind the energizing of his phased-array radar. The system showed bogey eleven as the only UAE fighter that wasn't either engaged in combat against Yemeni jets or dodging a MICA. "Order the gunners to take out bogey eleven."

As the cannons cracked, the first MICA found its target.

Walker's tight voice betrayed his enthusiasm. "MICA six has hit. Splash bogey four!"

"Very well." Cahill appreciated his comrade's excitement in battle, but he wanted a quiet bridge, and his tactical displays, combined with the panorama of chaos flying outside the dome's windows, told him everything. "Belay your announcements of MICAs. I'm watching for meself."

"I'm belaying any further MICA reports."

"Get an update from the Yemeni fleet."

Walker turned to the thirty-something-year-old doctor of languages standing behind them. "What do you hear?"

The interpreter reported the conversations he'd held while the Australians managed the battle. "*Osa-2* is sunk. That's the worst of it, but the *Tarantul's* cannon is also offline. They think they can bring it back with manual loading, but they'll be limited to one round every ten seconds."

"Bloody hell, Terry. This is getting nasty."

Cahill watched his display, which revealed another successful MICA. He then looked through the bridge windows and saw another of his victims die in a fireball. "Nasty, yes. I assume that *Osa-2* went down with two Styx missiles aboard?"

The translator replied. "Yes."

"Then we've got four cannons aboard four UAE ships coming for us, and we've got the railguns and a fraction of the *Tarantul's* main gun capacity, if it comes to a brawl."

Again, Walker's enthusiasm showed. "Make it three cannons! A Styx just hit a *Lursten* patrol craft!"

Cahill refused to believe it. "Seriously?"

Walker stepped backwards, revealing a view through the windows of billowing black smoke rising in the distance. "Have a gander for yourself."

"Alright, then. Three cannons coming for us. And eighteen Exocet missiles."

"The other Styx missiles missed, shot down by close-in defenses and anti-air missiles from the corvettes, but count our blessings that one of them hit the mark."

Cahill considered the carnage. Another three dozen men drowning and burning. "Right. A blessing counted."

Two more MICAs hit their marks, but the Emirati pilots evaded the final four. As the surviving aviators regrouped, the *Xerses'* radar system showed another Yemeni aircraft defeated, two enemy jets remaining distant to fend off the dwindling Yemeni air forces, and two UAE pilots from the combat air patrol joining their four remaining colleagues on the strike team.

The *Xerses'* commander lamented silently. He'd joined the mercenary fleet in part to vindicate himself from the Australian Navy's humiliating treatment, but down deep, he knew he'd counted upon altruism within the expected missions as a means to find his purpose.

The irony of ratcheting up his personal kill count during the fleet's first pure humanitarian mission bothered him like an itch beyond reach, but survival instincts overpowered that annoyance and focused him on reality.

Six aircraft formed on the UAE leader's wing behind the container ship convoy, and Walker alluded to a growing concern. "Do you want to shoot torpedoes, Terry?"

"In case we don't survive the next attack?"

"Yeah."

The *Xerses'* commander recalled the rationale for waiting. "If we were to succeed, the first torpedo to detonate would frighten the remaining ships into unloading their Exocets."

"Possibly. We don't know for sure."

"Doesn't matter. I've got a better idea. Let's force the issue. The aircraft can pick either us or the convoy, but not both. Right full rudder, all ahead flank, steady course zero-one-zero."

"The rudder's right full, accelerating to all-ahead flank, coming to course zero-one-zero."

"Very well. And keep shooting. If they want to get close enough to hurt us, they'll have to do it against splintering rounds."

Walker wanted his answer. "You've forced the issue, but what about the torpedoes if the F-16s decide to come for us?"

"Then we submerge again. No need to shoot torpedoes yet."

As the transport ship distanced itself from the convoy's track, the Emirati jets repeated the tactics of their prior run. But this time, as they buzzed the *Tarantul*, they stayed outside missile range, broke off, and retreated.

Cahill queried his surface warrior. "What's that about?"

"No idea."

"They've got plenty of bombs left, right?"

"Nine hardpoints on each F-16. That's plenty of bombs, mate. And the loose math says they haven't used half of them yet. They're probably down to a third of their bullets, but that's plenty."

The *Xerses'* commander shared his idea. "You think they were testing the *Tarantul's* cannon?"

"Possibly, but for what? They didn't even shoot. Not even at the Styx missiles."

"You're right. That was only a reconnaissance run."

Walker's tone was heavy. "If you do the math on our missiles, they're no longer a threat, with only four remaining. The first salvo hit the one *Lursten* because it was exposed, but the other one's moved between the corvettes for protection. They won't make that mistake again."

"No, they won't."

Over the loudspeaker, the tactical supervisor sounded tense as he announced the Emirati movements. "Sir, we see helicopters on radar. Three of them coming our way from the UAE flagship. And the F-16s appear to be lining up to make a run against us."

Cahill decided the F-16s' prior run by the *Tarantul* was a test of the corvette's main gun. Since the cannon could spew only three rounds, the Emiratis had their answer.

The Yemeni Navy was impotent.

Only the *Xerses* remained as a barrier to boarding the convoy, and six F-16s with bombs supported by three anti-submarine warfare helicopters promised to overwhelm the submersible destroyer.

Walker's enthusiasm was gone. "Damn it. We need to shoot down the helicopters. I'll get the gunners to redirect fire–"

Cahill had a better idea. "No. The F-16s will hammer us if we try that. We need to submerge and hide." He tapped an icon to send his voice throughout his ship. "Prepare to crash dive!"

With the circuit closed for privacy, Walker challenged his commander verbally while his obeying fingers tapped out a sequence to prepare to submerge. "Where can we hide? Three helicopters that know exactly where we are? They'll play sonic ping pong with us as soon as we're under."

"No, they won't."

As Walker finished tapping keys, his tone revealed pessimism. "I hope you know what you're doing."

The *Xerses'* commander watched multiple graphics representing the induction mast, the turbines, the phased array radar system, and the railguns merge into a group of systems to be lowered or turned off upon the touch of a single key. "Me, too. I'll take it from here."

Binoculars to his face, Walker was now facing sternwards. "Those F-16s are making are run, Terry. I can see them coming from behind us."

"Very well. Flooding the forward trim tank and securing the Phalanx close-in weapon system." Cahill tapped an image that ordered huge centrifugal pumps to inhale the sea and drive water towards the forward-most internal tanks. He hit another key and then watched the cylindrical silhouette recede into the port bow. "Placing full rise on the stern planes."

The translator's voice distracted him. "Captain Damari wants to know our intention."

For lack of an encouraging answer, Cahill snapped. "There's no time to explain. We're submerging again. Tell him to keep sending tactical data for our low-bandwidth feed. Helicopter data is the most important. We'll reposition and try to surface and shoot them."

From a display which had been strangely silent, the Frenchman joined the conversation. "I concur with your crash dive. But where will you hide from three helicopters?"

Cahill eyed his boss. "Under a freighter."

Renard raised an eyebrow. "Brilliant. Get under water. Go!"

The *Xerses'* commander tapped another graphic that drove the sterns downward to counterbalance the heaviness of the bows. The added weight lowered the ship in the seas and increased flow friction on the hulls, sapping three knots. He then pressed a button to send his voice throughout the ship. "Prepare to crash dive in five seconds. Four. Three. Two. One. Crash Dive!"

Walker grabbed a railing with white knuckles and turned his head towards the translator. "Hold on. This is our roughest maneuver."

Cahill stabbed his finger against a graphic that ordered the preselected group of systems to shift to their undersea states, and then he walked his hand across the screen to command the stern planes to their opposite extreme, lifting the *Xerses'* rear sections and driving the prows into the waves. Speed pushed the rakish bows under tons of water, and the ship glided through dark liquid.

The sea's opaqueness rushed to the domed bridge and engulfed it in black. The rapid and steep angle tugged the *Xerses* below the waves and created a fulcrum that lifted the propellers above the water. Momentum carried the hulls under.

Walker announced the final state. "The ship's submerged."

Hearing jets roar above the swells, Cahill exhaled and accepted his momentary safety. "Right. Bring us back up to twenty meters. Make us light with a ten-degree down angle." As the ship rose, he balanced against the new decline, and a glance over his shoulder showed the translator as a statue.

The interpreter's knuckles were frozen white over the railing, and in the bright artificial lighting, his skin appeared pasty. The *Xerses'* most violent maneuver had rattled him.

But with seawater preventing the use of voice communications over radio channels, Cahill let the translator recover in silence.

Walker updated the status. "Propulsion is on the MESMA systems. All plants are running normally. We're at sixteen knots, slowing to our maximum sustained submerged speed of thirteen knots."

"Very well, Liam." The *Xerses'* commander spoke towards a microphone above his head. "Sonar supervisor, listen for helicopters."

The response rang from the loudspeaker. "We're listening, sir. Nothing yet. They weren't dipping their sonars yet when we submerged."

"They will soon. Be alert." Then, as Cahill shifted his focus to maneuvering, he felt shame for hiding. Again, he was using other people as shields, and the concept riddled his mind with bitterness. But to complete the mission, get the aid to the mainland, and entertain hopes of reuniting with his wife, he had to accept his behaviors as valid tactics. "Get one man listening to the lead freighter."

"I don't understand, sir?"

"I'm going to park us underneath it. Shallow, so that a torpedo can't tell one ship from another. It's going to be tight."

## CHAPTER 19

Dmitry Volkov thought he'd die of disappointment for being beyond reach of the threatened convoy.

Despite the laws of physics precluding his arrival before the convoy's battle, he refused to give up, and he powered the bobbing and rolling *Wraith* forward while snorkeling. "Time remaining to ninety-percent charge on the battery?"

His grey-bearded veteran at the panel controlling the submarine's critical systems yelled his response. "Twenty-two minutes to ninety-percent charge."

Volkov could only lament the constraints hindering his ship's transit speed. "Very well." Being excluded from the main battle while watching his teammates on the *Xerses* fall was insufferable, but his boss offered him hope.

In the display, Renard's face was stern. "I won't insult your intelligence, my friend. The situation is becoming dire, but we still have several options."

Curious and eager to intervene, Volkov wanted to know those options, but he trusted the Frenchman to share the relevant details. "How can I help?"

"Keep charging forward, making your best sustained speed. There's not much you can do for Terry, but you might be able to keep the situation from getting worse."

Enlivened by purpose, the Russian doubted his English and verified Renard's meaning with his translator. "Did he say it might get worse?"

"Yes, Dmitry. Should I ask him—"

Trumping his translator, Volkov faced the Frenchman and replied in English. "How can it be worse?"

"More enemy ships. Unfortunately, the Houthi-controlled *Tarantul* corvette and its allied Emirati *Baynunah* corvette, *Mezyad*, were seen leaving Aden and heading east."

"Coming to the battle?"

"I'm afraid so."

"Why? The Emiratis have already won, right? Or they are

close to winning."

Renard's eyes narrowed. "They haven't won yet, and like I said, we still have options."

Volkov feared the only remaining alternatives included a ceasefire with a possible surrendering. "Okay."

"I don't know where the *Mezyad* and the Houthi *Tarantul* are, but you can assume they're making the *Mezyad's* best speed towards the battle, and they know you can't reach them. So, expect a direct approach without anti-submarine zigzag legs."

"Okay. I can't reach them?"

"Not before they'd reach the convoy." The Frenchman smirked. "But your torpedoes can, if you shoot them at their lowest transit speeds. I've had the Naval Group engineers here calculate the distance the Black Sharks can cover, and you have a chance to intercede if you manually set them to their lowest twenty-knot run speeds."

The *Wraith's* commander glanced at his translator, who rephrased the Frenchman's advice in Russian. After confirming his hopes, Volkov agreed. "I understand. You want me to blow up the *Mezyad* and the Houthi *Tarantul*."

"No! Actually, I want you to hit them with slow-kill weapons. Depending how the battle fares for Terry, I may be in communication with Abu Dhabi about a possible ceasefire. You would strengthen my position by demonstrating your presence while also demonstrating your restraint."

After awaiting the translation, Volkov replied. "I will load slow-kills and make for the *Mezyad* and the Houthi *Tarantul*."

"Good. I only ask you to trust me and your teammates on the other end of it."

"How can Terry endure much longer?"

"Ah! I have the French ambassador to the United Nations calling the Emirates to back off. I'm not sure how much longer he'll have any clout, but he's forcing the UAE to consider fallout for their actions. I also have several legionnaires aboard each freighter who have shown themselves and their firearms to prying eyes, which will complicate any forced boarding."

After the interpreter conveyed the Frenchman's meaning, Volkov responded. "So, the freighters are still moving towards Nishtun?"

"No. They've turned from the UAE task force to gain time. They're in a tail chase."

"I see."

"And with Terry underneath one of them, he's safe for the time being. The shoulder-launched anti-air missiles aboard the *Tarantul* and the surviving *Osa* are enough to keep helicopters away."

"Then what are the Emiratis waiting for?"

"Their surface combatants must get within a stone's throw of the Yemeni ships. Only then can they guarantee themselves clean shots. Otherwise, they risk hitting the freighters. The Yemenis are being diligent about their repositioning to conceal themselves behind their larger neighbors."

"They will overrun Terry fast. Too much speed."

"But Terry's torpedoes force the Emiratis into anti-submarine zigzag legs, which slows down their speed over ground. Terry's got almost two hours before he and the Yemenis are overrun."

"Oh."

"Things still appear dire for Terry, but as I said, there are options. Do your part to keep those unwanted corvettes from reaching the battle."

Energized with purpose, Volkov agreed. "*Da!*"

Forty minutes later, *Wraith's* commander had his submerged ship cruising at fifteen knots and depleting its battery at a calculated rate. As his concern grew about finding his new targets, good news trickled across his low-bandwidth feed. "Serguei, are you seeing this?"

The quiet executive officer was hunched over the central plotting table. "I was just noticing. It looks like a Yemeni reconnaissance aircraft spotted our targets. We have sufficient targeting data! I'm sending the information to Subtics."

"Very well." The *Wraith's* commander watched two high-speed surface ships appear on his display. "You know what to do next, I assume?"

"I'll calculate an optimum intercept course and speed, sir."

"You can assume these targets are heading straight for the battle. No zigzag legs."

"And a twenty-knot torpedo run, to optimize torpedo range?"

"Yes. And also calculate it for thirty-knot runs. Consider that we may get more than one chance at this, too."

The second-in-command hesitated. "Uh... I'll run a few scenarios. Now that we know their track, I can vary the distance remaining to our launch point with varied torpedo ranges and run speeds."

"Perfect. Then give me your optimum."

Fifteen minutes later, Volkov stood at the central chart beside his executive officer. "These will be long-range shots."

"Longer than the weapons' designed ranges, yes. But we're running them at twenty knots to extend the range, and the wires will be long enough to support guidance. Anatoly has already triple-checked with his technicians."

Accepting his decision, Volkov grunted. "Then we're launching in twelve minutes."

"All tubes, Dmitry?"

"Yes. Three weapons per corvette. All slow-kills."

Twisting in his seat, Anatoly shot his commander an inquisitive glance. "Tubes one, two, and three for the *Mezyad*, tubes four, five, and six for the Houthi *Tarantul*? All set to run at twenty knots, surface targets only?"

Volkov agreed with the sonar ace. "Correct. Make the assignments."

Anatoly stood and hovered over three junior operators at their Subtics consoles and watched them enter the data. When the last sailor finished, he announced their progress. "All tubes are ready."

"Very well. Now we wait. Prepare to launch in four minutes." While watching the *Wraith's* icon move towards those of his targets, Volkov felt a nervous presence.

Beside him had appeared the dolphin trainer, trembling with animation. "Dmitry! I think I figured out how they fooled my babies."

"That's great, Vasily, but now's not the time."

Ignoring his commander's hint, the trainer explained. "My guess? Photodiodes. As soon as the dolphins snapped the photo of the sonobuoy, it sensed the flash. Then it shifted to anti-submarine acoustic transmissions. It probably had other sensors... passive listening for submarine frequencies, obviously. Maybe even pressure sensors in case my babies tried to tamper with it. Or it could've been just a timer and bad timing for us. Whatever it was, I'll make sure we're ready for next time."

"There won't be a next time, at least not in these waters for this mission. Didn't you hear that the Iranians have retreated?"

Vasily gave a blank stare.

"Apparently not. I announced..." Volkov caught himself. "Well, I asked everyone to share the news and assumed it would travel like wildfire. Maybe I should have announced it."

"No. Nobody told me. But it's okay. I've been... reclusive."

Volkov was sarcastic. "You? Reclusive? You gest."

In a huff, the dolphin trainer turned and departed.

Having witnessed the exchange, Serguei chuckled. "At least he's predictable."

Comfortable to have returned to humane, slow-kill weapons, the *Wraith's* commander appreciated his crew's lightened mood. "Indeed, he is."

"One minute to shoot, Dmitry."

Volkov straightened his back and raised his voice. "Attention in the control room. I'm going to shoot all tubes in sequential order. We've never unloaded our full nests in a single salvo. So, everyone pay attention. That's all. Carry on."

Half a minute later, the room was quiet, awaiting the launch.

When ready, Volkov announced it. "In sequential order, shoot tubes one through six!"

The whining pneumatic impulse systems belched weapons

into the sea and popped Volkov's ears.

As the rippled salvo left the ship, the sonar ace announced the targeted corvettes' pending fates. "Tubes one through six are away in impulse mode. We have wire control for all six tubes."

"Very well."

From his seat at the panel controlling the submarine's inner workings, the grey-bearded veteran called out. "Twenty-four percent charge left on the battery."

The *Wraith's* commander moved to his chair on the elevated conning platform. "Very well. Bring us to snorkel depth, slowly." Unwilling to risk announcing his proximity to his targets, Volkov kept his submarine radio-silent while it ingested air through its snorkel mast and information through its antenna.

The high-speed feed presented Renard's face on the screen, but the Frenchman, unsure of his audience's presence, remained quiet.

Volkov joked with the translator. "It's funny to see him with his mouth shut."

"Enjoy it while you can."

The *Wraith's* commander mocked his boss. "Hey, Pierre. *Suka Blyad!* You can't hear me!"

"Now you're just being childish." The translator leaned forward. "And if you don't stop acting so giddy, people will accuse you of being in love."

Volkov frowned. "People, as you say, might be right."

"I'm glad this battle will be over soon. I'm not sure you can keep your focus much longer."

"God willing, I don't even have to think again. The torpedoes should get the job done automatically within ten minutes."

Ten minutes later, Anatoly announced the first weapon's acquisition of a target. "Passive detection, tube three!"

"Very well." Volkov kept his face in his display. "Belay your report of weapons detecting targets. I can see for myself."

"I'll belay my weapon acquisition reports, sir."

After a minute, all six weapons had targets.

The problem–all six weapons had the same target. "Damn! Can I get at least one of these steered to the second target?"

Anatoly was alert. "We're on it, Dmitry. We can hear which target is which through the weapons' hydrophones. All six have targeted the *Mezyad* corvette."

"The quieter ship?"

"The larger, closer ship. We can redirect two weapons to the Houthi *Tarantul*."

"Do it!"

After hovering over two men who furiously tapped keys at their consoles, Anatoly shared the news. "Tubes four and six are steered towards the Houthi *Tarantul*."

"Very well."

The sonar ace's voice rose half an octave. "Influence field detection, tube three! Detonation, tube three, under the *Mezyad*!"

"Count the attaching bomblets and explosions. I know it will get hectic, but count."

Excited, Anatoly risked cynicism. "We won't be able to hear and tally one hundred and forty-four bomblets over the next sixty seconds, Dmitry."

"Do your best."

After another minute, the sonar ace with his team's support gave a rough count. Eighty percent of the bomblets had found their targets and had exploded against their hulls. "We can't hear the corvettes, since they're too far away. You'll need Pierre's damage assessment."

"Very well. Cut the wires and reload all tubes. Give me two heavyweights, two slow-kills, and two Exocets."

"I'll have the torpedo team load two heavyweights, two slow-kills, and two Exocets."

In hopes of good news, the *Wraith's* commander watched his boss' face. After several minutes, something prompted the Frenchman to reach for his screen and tap it.

"I think Pierre sees something."

The translator nodded. "I hope so. You said he's got access to Yemeni reconnaissance aircraft and hovercraft."

Volkov kept his eyes on Renard. "He does."

In a display, the Frenchman became animated. "Ah! Well done, Dmitry! I don't know if you're listening, but well done! You've got the *Mezyad* slowed to fifteen knots and listing to port. The Houthi's *Tarantul* seems to have fared better, but it's riding heavy in the water. I think you hit both targets. I'll play this report in a loop until I have more to say. Here goes." The Frenchman's face froze, and then his report played again. "Well done, Dmitry…"

The *Wraith's* commander muted his boss.

The translator grinned. "Do you want to call him and let him praise you in real time?"

Volkov gave a dismissing wave. "Perhaps in a moment. But for now, I'd like to enjoy success without Pierre's blabbing."

## CHAPTER 20

Hiding underneath a container ship, Terry Cahill watched a gauge showing the *Xerses'* undersized battery discharging itself towards exhaustion. Keeping pace with the convoy as it fled at the slowest freighter's maximum speed, he feared he'd fall behind when his power reserves ran out. "We can't hold twenty-three knots submerged much longer."

Walker was somber. "Do you want to risk porpoising to run the gas turbines?"

"Not really. These Emirati mongrels can't even be sure we're still involved in this battle. I'd like to keep whatever element of surprise we have."

Walker looked at the display showing acoustic data from the *Xerses'* organic hydrophones and its correlation to the low-bandwidth feed from his allies about the locations, courses, and speeds of the Emirati warships. "They're zigzagging like they're afraid of our torpedoes. They're assuming that we're lurking around here somewhere."

"That's because they're smart, conservative, and attentive, which is exactly why I don't want to show them our air intakes."

Walker grunted. "I'm making a mental note to ask Pierre for snorkel mast fairings that can withstand higher speeds."

Cahill guffawed. "The feather those would leave at twenty-plus knots would be visible from outer space. But you have a good point, for next time. For now, I have a decision to make."

"You're not thinking about disobeying Pierre, are you?"

The *Xerses'* commander reread the low-bandwidth feed reiterating his boss' order to hold his torpedoes while giving Cahill continued freedom with his railguns. "Pierre's making this a challenge, but no, I'm not disobeying him. He's right to avoid inviting an Exocet salvo with our torpedoes. I'm deciding whether to stay submerged and fall behind the convoy or to surface and hide beside a freighter."

"Surfacing is the only way we can fight back."

Cahill glanced at the icons showing the Emirati F-16s refueling in flight thirty nautical miles away. "But our hulls span too much breadth. We're so damned wide that those aircraft could easily hit us without risking damage to the freighters."

The executive officer lowered his gaze. "Right. Good point."

"But I'm half tempted to surface just so I can bitch at Pierre."

"About using the torpedoes?"

Cahill folded his arms, shrugged, and gave Walker a harsh look.

"I'll take that as a 'yes'."

"Bloody hell. No, it's still a 'no'. I hate it, but Pierre's right. If I shoot torpedoes, they'll hear it eventually, even if it's hearing the first one explode underneath a keel. Then the other ships would rightfully stop giving a rip about political fallout, and we'd see a swarm of Exocets pummeling every ship in our convoy."

"I'm not arguing it. I want to contradict you, but I can't."

Subconscious forces fought within Cahill's frame for control of his actions. Frustrated, he saw only unpleasant options, but he knew he'd go mad if he continued hiding. "Let's get ready to brawl."

Walker exhaled a whistle. "I hope you're right about this."

"Me, too, mate. Bring us right and get us out from under this freighter. Then steady us back on course."

"I'm bringing us right, sir."

The *Xerses'* commander tapped a key and raised his voice. "This is the captain. As most of you know, our battery's running empty, and we can't sustain our speed. Some of you may be wondering why we aren't launching torpedoes at the incoming Emirati warships, and that's because Pierre ordered me not to, so they don't escalate with their Exocets. And he's right. So, I'm going to surface and deal with whatever happens. Stinger teams, get ready. Gunners, be ready to shoot at surfaced and airborne targets. That's all. Carry on."

"Well said."

"Thanks. Gather reports and let me know when we're ready, including the battery charging lineup and the Stinger teams."

Before Walker could answer, a voice crackled from the overhead speakers. "Bridge, control room. We heard a splash and a shallow explosion in our baffles. Someone's shooting a cannon."

"Understood, control room." His decision to surface into a gunfight affirmed by the first punch, Cahill wanted the action. "Looks like we'll be surfacing into a brawl. Are we ready?"

Walker lowered a sound-powered phone to its cradle. "The battery is lined up to charge. Stinger teams are waiting below their hatches. The ship's ready."

"I'm surfacing the ship." Cahill tapped keys to pump water off the *Xerses* and give it a gentle upward angle. As sunlight danced off sheets of cascading water, he glared rearward through the dome in search of the enemy's combatants.

Though less than halfway to the horizon, the small Emirati ships churned white bow wakes through the seas and looked liked children's toys until muzzle flare flashed from the three-inch gun on the closest corvette's forecastle.

The translator interjected an update. "Freighter three says the rounds are landing by its stern."

Cahill frowned. "You speak Urdu?"

"No. They're speaking English. The Yemeni ships have English translators aboard, but I talk to them in Arabic for speed."

Walker faced his commander. "I believe the lead Emirati ship just reached cannon range of freighter three, and it's targeting the rudder."

Cahill knew what to do. "Then we'll go for its cannon." He tapped a key and raised his voice. "Gunners, take out the cannon on the lead enemy corvette, the one that's shooting at the freighter. Set the rounds to splinter. Commence fire!"

Two cracks snapped from the *Xerses*' sterns. Seconds later, the railguns' rounds landed off-target, one of them driving buckshot across the corvette's hull and the other ripping holes above the waterline. Although missing the cannon, the shots served as spotting rounds for skilled gunners to adjust their aim.

Given the short distance and supersonic rounds, the corvette was vulnerable to simple ballistics. Guidance was unnecessary, and jamming was pointless. The enemy ship veered away, as did its peers in the task force.

The *Xerses'* commander suspected an optical illusion. "They're not running away, are they?"

Walker lowered his binoculars and shrugged. "I can't believe it but yeah, they actually are, after all that sandbag and lattice armor they loaded." The career surface warrior knew to scan the sky. "Damn it. And that's why." He pointed upward. "They're sending in the F-16s."

Cahill's heart sank. "Bloody hell. We can't submerge and hide from the helicopters, we can't shoot down F-16s because they're too agile, and we can't shoot torpedoes at the damned surface ships, even if we wanted to out of spite."

His stern voice rising from a display, Renard interrupted. "If you use torpedoes, I assure you they will retaliate, regardless of your proximity to the freighters. It would ignite escalation."

Seeing hostile aircraft less than two minutes away, Cahill thought of the widow he'd soon make and the children he'd never have. His voice rose half an octave, and his tone became bitter. "Two ships are already destroyed, and an angry swarm of F-16s is coming for mine right now. How much more escalation can there be?"

Renard spat back. "Counting you, ten ships with combined crews of more than three hundred sailors, not to mention the lives to be spared by the cargo aboard the freighters. I know this is difficult, but keep your wits about you, man."

Sighing, Cahill made himself agree. "Damn it. You're right. But I'm thinking that I'm out of options."

The Frenchman smirked. "I'd never leave you without options. Check your MICA fire-control software for an updated status."

Straining to hold his anger in check, the *Xerses'* commander hissed a protest. "I don't have time for games, Pierre."

Staring at a display, Walker interjected. "No, Terry. He's right. We have connectivity to our spare MICA missiles."

Cahill was unimpressed and kept a hard glare facing the

screen. "So what? You've created a long-distance link to weapons over a hundred miles away."

The Frenchman frowned. "Correction. Your weapons are within reach. Look to the south, bearing roughly one-seven-four, and you'll see three fishing trawlers, each of which is carrying a crate of your reloads."

The *Xerses'* commander shot a glance to the south. Masts from fishing vessels represented hope on the horizon. "Whose ships?"

"Family members from the Yemeni *Tarantul.* I had them load your spares and make their best speed after you left for the battle. I trust that you don't mind?"

Recognizing his salvation and reaffirming his trust in the Frenchman, Cahill relaxed. "Not at all. I don't suppose you'll tell me why you didn't inform me of this earlier?"

"Because to be honest, I wasn't sure the weapons would reach you in time."

The *Xerses'* commander realized they wouldn't have reached him without the convoy's southerly turn two hours earlier, but he abandoned doubts and speculation about recent history. "Liam, do we have control of these missiles?"

"It looks like it. I'm connecting and getting positive confirmation from each missile's guidance system now. Yes... I have control of them all." With a look of astonishment, Walker faced his commander. "Just like that... we're ready to fire all twenty-four MICAs."

Renard instructed the Australians. "I believe MICAs nine through sixteen are on the closest ship. I recommend sending one of those towards the leader of the Emirati squadron."

Cahill glanced at his tactical display and envisioned the shot. "Liam, target MICA nine for bogey twelve, the leader."

"With pleasure." The executive officer tapped keys. "MICA nine is targeted for bogey twelve. Ready to launch."

Seeing a red icon appear before him, the *Xerses'* commander stabbed his finger downward. "Launching MICA nine."

Walker called out the status. "The system shows MICA nine away."

Looking off the bridge's port quarter, Cahill saw a flame rise from the horizon and trail a plume of smoke. As the supersonic missile reached speed and altitude, it challenged his eyes in following its rapid movement.

With raw enthusiasm, Walker called out an update. "The F-16s are peeling off! We've scared them away."

Relieved, Cahill replied. "They must've figured out what all those fishing ships are carrying."

"Do you still want to bring down their leader?"

Cahill looked at the Frenchman's face in the display. "Do you have an opinion?"

"Whether you bring him down or not, it won't impede any ceasefire negotiations. I'll trust that you're still charmed and can make the right decision."

The *Xerses'* commander assessed the battle's momentum and reflected upon his purpose within the mercenary fleet.

With his ship surfaced, the Emirati task force distanced itself beyond cannon range from his railguns. With his MICA arsenal arriving, the enemy fighter jets and helicopters retreated. With the freighters still serving as shields, the threat of Exocet anti-ship missiles waned.

A fleet built upon humane naval combat on a humanitarian mission should spare every life. But the irony of the Yemeni theater was the avoidance of hostile escalation through the demonstration of resolve–resolve to kill.

Only heavyweights could have turned back the Iranian fleet.

Only cannon rounds and exploding Styx warheads could have turned back the Emirati task force.

Only MICA impacts could turn back the airborne threat.

He wondered what Jake Slate would do. Would he seek redemption or release his anger in vengeance?

He wondered what Dmitry Volkov would do. Would he weigh the lives spared in further combat against the single life of a pilot?

He even wondered what Danielle Sutton would do, the commander who'd defeated a Turkish submarine without launching a weapon. Surely, like every commander in the fleet, she harbored deep resentment for past transgressions, but she was capable of driving monumental outcomes without releasing any aggression.

But he wasn't Slate, Volkov, or Sutton.

He was a newlywed man trying to find his identity within a fleet and within his private family life.

He was also a commander of the world's most versatile warship, and future deterrence required proof of power in the present.

Walker interrupted his thoughts. "Terry?"

Cahill snapped. "I'm thinking."

"Right. But remember—indecision is a decision to kill. Impact is in ten seconds. You have to decide."

The *Xerses'* commander folded his arms. "Shut up."

"Sorry, mate."

Cahill heard his blood coursing through his veins with each heartbeat, and he left the targeted pilot to his fate. "Let the missile fly."

Walker raised his palms from his console. "Me hands are off the system."

Seconds later, an F-16 was spiraling downward, leaving a helical trail of black smoke.

Cahill held his breath as he scanned the sky for a parachute. When one appeared, he sighed and shifted his thoughts to rescue. He looked at his boss. "Pierre, are you sending a ship for *Osa-2's* survivors?"

"Of course. Another fisherman from the Yemeni Navy's family."

Cahill looked to his translator. "Does the Yemeni Navy know about this? Are we in communication with the *Osa-2* survivors?"

"The Yemeni Navy is aware of and expecting a fishing ship to rescue the *Osa-2* survivors. It's expected to arrive in four hours."

"That's not good enough. Those are traumatized men at risk of being rescued by their enemy, if we don't get someone to them sooner." Cahill's comments spurred his next thought. "We don't need *Osa-1* anymore. Ask it turn back and assist with the rescue."

Renard interjected his commentary. "Good thinking. I agree."

Moments after the translator relayed the message and announced the Yemeni Navy's agreement, the remaining *Osa* rolled through a tight turn behind the domed bridge and accelerated northward.

Cahill was ready to shift his focus from killing to sparing lives. "While you're at it, have the fishing trawler stop and pick up that pilot I just shot down."

The translator relayed the message and the Yemeni Navy's confirmation.

Accepting the battle's end and completeness of the rescue operations, Cahill reorganized the convoy. "Let's regroup with the fishing ships and get this humanitarian aid back on course for Nishtun."

## CHAPTER 21

Commander Amir walked across the girded brow from the *Tarantul* onto the Nishtun pier. Relieved to place his feet on the safety of solid concrete, he counted the cost.

Twelve sailors aboard his countrymen's *Osa* missile boat had perished, and his Emirati enemies had likely lost twice that many lives aboard the *Lursten* patrol craft. Counting the Iranian *Ghadir*-class submarine crews, the sunken Yemeni transport ships, and all the downed aviators pushed the death toll above two hundred.

Then he questioned the benefits as he watched a crane lift an orange crate from a moored freighter over the pier. He wondered if the container held medical supplies, food, clothing, or other goods that people in the nation's eastern region needed.

A voice from a quiet companion startled him. "You think it was all worth it?"

Amir shot his inquisitor a glance and recognized his boss, the commodore. "Hard to say, sir."

Captain Damari remained a hard, unreadable stone. "I'll tell you my opinion, Amir. We must convince ourselves it was worth it, or else we'll go mad."

The *Tarantul's* commander scanned the waterfront. Overloaded by the convoy's arrival, the wharf's staff operated one of two cranes and tended to berthing areas which they'd limited to four ships.

Balancing the lengths of vessels to fit against the available mooring space, the waterfront staff had guided the *Xerses* behind the *Tarantul* on one side and a fishing ship and a freighter on the other. The other ships remained at anchor. After lifting the MICA missiles off the fisher, they'd sent off the small ship's lines and then let the *Osa* dock in its place.

After loading the MICAs into the *Xerses'* vertical launch cells, the staff had redirected the crane to the humanitarian goods aboard the first docked container ship.

Amir risked candor. "We overthrew our corrupt admiralty,

we ran from our home, we invaded an island, we lost a dozen sailors, and we partnered with shady mercenaries. Now, we're depositing only three freighters' worth of aid into the least ravaged section of our country, we haven't brought relief to the worst regions, and we've done nothing to help our ground troops. After all this, we're lucky if we're not already mad."

Damari issued the first laugh the *Tarantul's* commander had seen from the stoic commodore. "Maybe we are mad and don't know it. But what comes next will prove it or not."

"What comes next, sir?"

The smile fell from Damari's face. "Diplomacy. If we don't come out of our upcoming meeting feeling like pawns in a chess match, then we're already mad, and it's too late for us."

"Meeting with whom?"

"Politicians. Talking heads and smiling faces that will jockey for position in front of cameras to thank us and to take credit for whatever they can."

Exhausted from his post-battle adrenaline ebbing, the *Tarantul's* commander lacked the patience for the empty talk of statesmen. He appreciated being able to share the burden with Damari and his navy's other commanding officer.

From across the wharf, the surviving *Osa's* commander approached. Commander Gulla stopped and saluted Damari.

Damari returned the salute and then extended his hand. "Well done, commander."

Gulla accepted the shake. "Thank you, sir." He turned towards his friend, the *Tarantul's* commander, and reached for him.

Before having time to think, Amir accepted the tight hug. Seeking words of greeting, he found none and instead concentrated on keeping his fluctuating emotions in check.

The *Osa's* commander backed off. "Sorry, Andi. I still don't believe what we just did. We beat the Emiratis!"

Captain Damari rendered judgment. "You handled your ships and crews well. Everything I'm about to say in your public praise is heartfelt. You've both earned my admiration."

Amir shared a blank stare with Gulla.

Damari turned and stepped away. "Come with me, gentlemen, and take some credit."

Nishtun's waterfront office was comparable to that of Socotra–undersized for multiple parties with posses of minions fighting for visibility.

Appearing overwhelmed and overeager, a portly man in a tailored suit stood out as the tiny town's mayor. Flanking his forced smiles were his junior council members seeking to grab face time with the photographers accompanying a small media team.

As Amir scanned other occupants, his interest grew.

He recognized the outspoken governor of the al-Mahra district, a puppet the Saudis had installed two and a half years earlier to help rule the region on their behalf. Before Amir could ask about the man's presence, his commodore answered his unspoken question.

Damari leaned into Amir and Gulla. "The governor will be taking credit with the people of al-Mahra for the aid we brought and will make promises of continued aid to Nisthun. He'll also take credit with his Saudi puppet masters for our efforts in pushing back the Emirati influence."

Amir scowled. "Just like that? He does nothing, risks nothing, but takes credit?"

Damari countered. "He did something. He allied himself with her." The commodore pointed at the final leader in the room.

Socotra's loyalist resistance leader, Nuha Shaman, was standing with her entourage of fellow supporters of Yemen's proper president. Wearing her purple hijab, she looked regal under her flowing fabric as she faced the region's governor and offered a slight bow.

From the gaggle of media people, flashbulbs flared as the two diplomats greeted one another.

The showmanship unsettled the *Tarantul's* commander. "So, what did she do to earn credit for any of this?"

Keeping his voice low, Damari was cynical. "She's protecting our families and letting us use her island, in case you've forgotten."

"That's just the humane thing to do. She shouldn't be boasting about it."

"Careful, Amir. Without her, we wouldn't have a navy at all."

Amir vented his frustration. "A two-ship navy, maybe four if we can convince the other *Osa* commanders to join us. Plus a few transport ships. Maybe this wasn't all worth it. What do we have left to show?"

The commodore spun around and exchanged glances with the talkative *Tarantul's* commander and the quiet *Osa's* commander. "Keep this secret for now, but ever since the mercenary submarine slowed the Houthi-occupied *Tarantul*, I've been working a plan to get that ship back."

The news encouraged and confused Amir. "What? How?"

"Colonel Mohamed was hesitant at first, but with pressure from Miss Shaman, he'll have no choice but to dedicate a strike team to the task. He needs to gain some credibility for his ground troops in the wake of our naval successes."

"He's going retake *Tarantul* hull two back from the Houthis?"

"Correct. And we're going to keep one *Tarantul* here to provide naval gunfire support to our ground troops and one in Socotra."

Amir's mind raced. "You're sure he'll risk it?"

"Our victory over the Emiratis in this political show gives me the clout I need to ask Miss Shaman. Since she's allying herself with the governor, she'll have to agree."

Assessing the political alignments, Amir saw a flaw in the logic. "But the governor is pro-Saudi. Why would he want a loyalist ship in his most important harbor?"

"Concessions. Who do you think he was on the phone with when we entered the building?"

The *Tarantul's* commander recalled the region's top diplomat frowning while speaking into a phone during a short conversation. "Someone on President Hadi's staff?"

Damari smirked. "It was President Hadi himself. I called his chief of staff as we docked, and he told me that Hadi would be negotiating with the governor ways to slow the Saudi advance into his region in exchange for keeping the flow of goods into the land. We're now at the center of a complex political balancing act."

"And you think you can get support to retake the other *Tarantul*? You'd be doubling our navy's firepower. With two cannons, we could make a difference for our army's coastal defenses."

"I'm sure of it. The ship is slowed by the damage from the humane torpedoes, and it's been abandoned by its Emirati escort. It's limping back to Aden, and it's vulnerable."

Amir sensed hope with the potential growth of his navy.

The commodore clarified his intent. "When you get back to Socotra, you'll gather the survivors of *Osa-2*. You'll take them aboard your ship and train them in operating a *Tarantul*. When we recapture the one the Houthis stole, we'll need a crew for it. I've got calls out for recruiting some former sailors."

The *Tarantul's* commander risked optimism. "You think the news of our victory will help recruitment?"

"Yes. That, and offering reliable paychecks to hungry veterans."

As if an invisible maestro had willed the concise timing of the group's movement, the governor and his entourage marched towards the naval officers. One of the man's staff directed the reporters and photographers towards the officers' flanks.

Damari stiffened his back and whispered as the politician approached. "Pull your brims low and keep your heads down. The photographs are going to highlight the governor and will identify us as naval leadership, but we don't want our faces exposed."

As the governor reached the commodore and greeted him, the men exchanged inaudible words as camera bulbs flashed.

Seeming to have captured the desired image, the media personnel darted away, seeking something else to chronicle. One of them, an apparent supervisor, shouted above the room's din. "We need to capture a video of the mercenary transport ship pulling away from the pier, then one of the next freighter pulling in, and footage of containers landing on the pier and pulling away on the trucks."

The governor nodded and waived the media away. "Wait for me so that I'm in the shots. I'll be there shortly." He sent two staff members ahead of him to oversee the photographers, and then he shook Commander Gulla's hand. Next, he stepped to the *Tarantul's* commander.

Amir accepted the salutation. "It's an honor to meet you, sir."

Unable or unwilling to look the naval officer in the eye, the politician hurried through the un-photographed meeting. "Uh... good job, sailor. Good job." Then he snapped back his hand and darted away.

The three naval officers stood in silence as the next politician escorted her posse towards them. But instead of racing through a photo opportunity, Nuha Shaman said with her calm and slow movements that she was interested in holding real dialogue. "You've done well, Captain Damari."

The commodore's response contradicted his terse demeanor and seemed like a rehearsed greeting coached by President Hadi's staff. "Thank you, ma'am, but the credit must be shared with my commanders and their crews. They proved their skill and bravery in battle and demonstrated President Hadi's resolve to stand against our common enemies, to protect our people, and to provide for the needs of those who have been suffering too long."

Behind her, a staff member lowered the phone he'd been using to record the meeting. "Got it."

Shaman nodded to her underling and then replied to the commodore. "I'll be sure to thank the president personally when I next speak to him."

"I assume that will be soon?"

"Quite soon."

One of her staff members tapped her shoulder, whispered in her ear, and then extended a phone.

"How about now?" Lifting the phone to her ear, she spoke

in a reverent but strong tone. "President Hadi, I'm honored to hear from you... of course. One moment." The Socotran leader lowered the device and tapped the speaker key. "He wants to address all of us."

The president's voice rose from the phone. "Captain Damari, Commander Amir, and Commander Gulla, I congratulate you all on a truly magnificent display of your professionalism and courage. You've placed the nation and my presidency in the strongest position I've enjoyed in months."

Amir recognized his leader's voice and let his boss answer.

Captain Damari handled the salutation. "The pleasure is ours, President Hadi. We're honored and proud to serve our nation's rightful leader. My commanders and their crews were skillful and courageous."

The president's tone became grave. "I'm sorry that you had to suffer loses. Each casualty aboard *Osa-2* is a hero to the nation, as are our two pilots who sacrificed their lives today."

"Agreed, President Hadi. Commander Sharki sends his regrets for being unable to receive your call, but I've ordered him to stay in Socotra with the survivors of his ship."

"Understood, captain. A grateful nation thanks you all."

Shaman withdrew the phone to her ear, finished her private conversation, and then handed the device back to her minion. "As you can tell, the president's in a very good mood. He's had little to cheer about recently, and this is a huge victory. Now's the time to ask for what we need."

"Did his staff mention anything to you about our plans to retake the *Tarantul* corvette the Houthi's stole?"

She nodded. "What can I do to help?"

"I would appreciate your backing when I approach the army for taking part in the assault. If Colonel Mohamed balks, which he might, I'll need your people's support. Let him know secretly how difficult life can be for an occupying force that fails to meet the will of the people."

She smirked. "I'll do more than that. I'll make it known publicly. You'll have your assault force."

For the first time during the diplomatic exchange, the commodore sounded surprised. "How can that happen?"

Her smile spread wide. "An ousting of the pro-Emirati regime on the island followed by President Hadi appointing me as the governor of Socotra."

"I would have expected an election."

"There will be, after I'm in power and the outcome is known."

Damari jumped on the glaring disconnect. "A female in such power? That's bold."

"It is, but President Hadi needs to show boldness. He needs as many headlines as he can get in the international press. Placing me in charge of Socotra only helps him."

"And with the continuation of the support you've already given our navy, it only helps us as well. I hope my congratulations aren't premature for the election I trust you'll win."

"Thank you, captain." She frowned. "But I know your heart isn't with Socotra. It's not your home. I trust you won't take it as an insult that I'll be planning to defend my island without your navy, after you leave. Your home is Aden."

Damari nodded. "Indeed, it is. And eventually, we'll return there."

Asking the tough question, she folded her arms. "Will the mercenaries join you in that?"

Eager to know if his new comrades in arms would remain friend, turn into a foe, or slip into indifference about the Yemeni plight, Amir listened in hopes of bringing his family back to the home they'd abandoned.

Damari was neutral. "It's difficult to say. The mercenaries have shown great courage and virtue, but they work for pay. President Hadi will only keep the money flowing as long as we keep winning. So, let's keep winning, as we turn our attention towards the Houthi and the Saudis."

"I believe we'll keep winning, Captain Damari. But I also think that you're underestimating the mercenaries. Something about them makes me think they're getting some benefit from helping us... something that transcends money."

## CHAPTER 22

Dmitry Volkov sat in his stateroom in search of quiet moments. Having scheduled a conference call with Danielle Sutton for later in the day, he replayed in his mind the questions he'd ask her and the information he'd share.

So much was happening to him and between them, and it was happening quickly–at least for his experience.

With his religious conviction and past dedication to the Russian Navy, he'd dated sparingly. Now, with Danielle always in his thoughts, the adage of absence making the heart grow fonder played out within his body.

He felt nervous and giddy. "You're like a schoolgirl, you silly fool. I suppose that means it's true love?"

As his question to himself lingered unanswered, he saw a chime on his laptop indicating an incoming call. He accepted it, and Cahill's face appeared in the screen. "Hello, Terry!"

Cahill used simple English. "Hello, mate. Do you have time to talk?"

"Yes. Where are you?"

"I'm aboard that big transport ship that just anchored in the spot next to yours. It's called the *Xerses*. Perhaps you noticed?"

Volkov waved his fingers dismissively. "Sergeui is on the bridge. I am having time off now."

The Australian nodded. "You earned it."

"Thank you. You, too."

Cahill's tone became serious. "Look, Dmitry. That secret I shared with you about Ariella and the lost baby, let's keep that a secret. Okay?"

Volkov repeated the sentiment in his own words. "You want me to keep the secret about lost baby. Of course. I tell nobody."

"Thanks, mate. I don't know why, but it's bothering me."

"Bothering?"

"Troubling me."

"Oh, yes. It is trouble. You lost a real child. In my religion, we believe life begins when... how do you say it?"

"Uh… when the sperm penetrates the egg?"

Volkov wondered why the Australian mentioned an egg during a conversation in which food was irrelevant. "Sorry. I don't understand. There's a specific word for it. I look now." He reached for his phone and the English dictionary it held.

"I think you mean 'conception'."

"*Da*. Yes. Conception."

"Well, whether or not it's true, I just know it's a terrible feeling."

"Terrible. Yes, Terry. I prayed for you and Ariella. I still do."

"I know that won't hurt. So, thanks, I guess."

"It's what I must do. I believe God hears."

Cahill glanced down from the screen, frowned in thought, and then looked up again. "We've seen enough death recently."

"Yes, much death. You and me are killers, Terry. I fear we become bad men."

His Australian friend looked away in contemplation. At least he was no longer thinking about his lost child. "I think we're going through something like what Jake went through when he joined Pierre's fleet."

Volkov caught most of the meaning. "Jake. You mean angry. Maybe getting angrier as he killed people."

"Possibly. I have no desire to look inside his head, mate. It's a nasty place."

"Inside his head? You want to cut open his brain?"

"Ha! No… I mean to examine his mind."

"Oh, that. Ugly place, I'm sure."

"Yeah. No kidding." The Australian stared back in uncomfortable silence. "Well, we should probably get ready for our team meeting. You'll need your translator."

Volkov checked the time on his phone. "You're right. It's almost time. Thanks for telling me."

"Thanks for listening, mate. I owe you one."

In the *Wraith's* control room, Volkov sat next to his translator.

"Can I open the line, Dmitry?"

"Yes, yes. Please. I don't want to be late."

"We've got a couple minutes." The translator tapped keys on a console, and four faces appeared, one each taking a quarter of a split screen. Clockwise from the upper left, Renard, Slate, Cahill, and then Danielle each wore the starched white collared shirt of the fleet's uniform.

Volkov's heart fluttered when he saw the female commander, and he noticed her face flushing as she recognized him. He hoped the bond wasn't obvious and distracting for the team.

Renard addressed his staff. "I see we've got the last person. Welcome, Dmitry. Right on time. Even a minute early. I like punctuality in my commanders."

The translator looked to the *Wraith's* commander with a silent request to interpret the Frenchman's words, but having understood, Volkov shook his head. "I'm happy to see everyone."

The Frenchman smiled at his own success. "Congratulations are in order. The mission's first phase is complete and successful. Our clients suffered losses, but the net gain is more than enough to declare victory. We control Socotra, we control Nishtun, and we will continue to escort aid to Nishtun. I'm happy to report that word of our success has reached benefactors who are now willing to subsidize additional deliveries of humanitarian goods."

Jake answered. "That was the intent of phase one, right?"

"Indeed. Well, one of several desired outcomes. There are political maneuvers taking place behind closed doors that would require a doctorate degree to understand, but we won't worry about them just yet."

Jake interrupted again. "Good job guys. I'm jealous. While Danielle and I are enjoying an all-expenses paid trip around the flipping world, you two morons are taking all the credit."

Volkov looked to his translator. "Flipping? Morons?"

His companion explained the meaning.

"*Blyad*! Why call us morons?"

"He meant it as sarcasm. I'm sure it was a complement."

"Oh. Okay, good." Volkov was encouraged to joke. "If I am a moron, you must bite me, Jake."

Cahill piled on. "And kiss his bare hairy arse. In fact, you can kiss mine, too, mate. You flipping Yankee."

Jake folded his arms. "I'm just upset that I've missed all the action. Danielle is, too, I'm sure. We didn't join this fleet to watch the action from far away."

Danielle raised her palms. "Speak for yourself. If you guys want to vent your testosterone at each other, keep me out of it."

Renard quelled the goofiness. "She's right, and that's enough. I'm sure we all want to get on with our evenings."

Anticipating a private talk with Danielle, Volkov agreed. "*Da*! Let's do our briefing please."

The Frenchman continued. "The Emiratis have agreed to an indefinite ceasefire with President Hadi's loyal forces. For what it's worth, the Iranians sent informal word through backdoor channels that they also agree, even though they were never publicly part of the hostilities."

Having killed more Persians than he cared to count, Volkov asked a question. "Will we face the Iranians again?"

"They may come back to challenge the Saudis. They have both economic and cultural reasons to stand against their neighbors across the Persian Gulf. You'll need to be aware of their presence, even if they remain neutral. They'll be tempted to watch us."

After his translator clarified the detail, Volkov continued his questioning. "Which way will the Saudis go? For or against Yemen?"

"That remains to be seen. They despise the Houthi and will help us attack them, but they're also the power-hungry gorilla in the neighborhood, so to speak, who have already moved to control portions of Yemen. By knocking the Emirates down a notch in credibility, we've created a bit of a power vacuum."

"So, what we do next?"

"You and Terry will escort freighters from a pickup point

north of Socotra and take them to Nishtun. The next run is with six ships, and there's an even larger one taking shape as benefactors arrange their resources."

"Who will challenge us?"

"God willing, nobody. Your presence going forward will be a deterrence until we prepare our next strike, which will be when Jake and Danielle arrive. At that point, we'll target Houthi and possibly Southern Separatist assets at sea and on land. Captain Damari has shared with me his plan to take back the Houthi *Tarantul*. We'll see if that's successful before we make any further plans."

With the other commanders remaining silent while the translator addressed him, the *Wraith's* commander kept his lead role in interrogating their boss. "When we go into battle against the Houthi and Southern Separatists, will the Saudis join us or watch us?"

"Excellent question. I've approached Riyadh for negotiations, but it's too soon to tell if the effort will bear fruit. Either way, our first target is the port of Aden. We'll help our Yemeni clients find their way home. Beyond that is a matter of speculation, but tasking could include challenging the Houthi stronghold in Al Hudaydah, which would break open the flow of humanitarian aid to those who need it most."

"I thought we already helped those who need it."

"Of course, we have. But with respect to the humanitarian impact, Nishtun is but a toehold. Aden would reach those who've seen war longer, and Al Hudaydah would be a dream. If we could take and hold all three harbor cities, we could help Yemeni air and ground forces retake and control major areas they've lost."

Volkov waited for his interpreter to finish. Believing he'd learned as much as the Frenchman knew, he retreated from his line of questions. "That's all my questions."

With the opening, Jake interjected. "Does this make financial sense, Pierre? I mean, you said this was essentially out of the kindness of your heart, but you can't be paying for this all by yourself."

"I was at first, but I did set up revenue streams for myself. In fact, I broke even when the thirteenth crate from the second freighter landed on the pier in Nishtun."

After some silence, the American protested. "Seriously? You track your profits at that level of detail?"

With a mocking smile, the Frenchman chortled. "No, you moron! I wanted to see if you'd believe me. And now that you realize you'll never believe anything I say about my finances, I trust you to stop asking."

Red with embarrassment, Jake salvaged some dignity. "I see your point, but I make no promises."

"Alright then. That's all I had. I'll send preliminary battle plans when I have them. If nobody has any more questions, I suggest we sign off and get some rest."

After everyone said their goodbyes, Volkov remained seated, staring at Danielle's face in the lower right quadrant of his screen. "You want to talk in private now?"

She nodded. "Of course. Give me five minutes."

In his stateroom, Volkov sat before his computer and hailed Danielle.

A minute later, she appeared. "I think we're alone."

"I hope so. I miss you a lot."

"I miss you, too, Dmitry. I've been worried."

"Oh, no. Not that. We said no worrying, dangerous jobs or not."

"I know I said that, but I do worry about you. I can't help it."

"I would worry more, but I have faith. No matter what, something good will happen, if only to our souls."

Her voice took on an admissive tone. "You know when I said I'm Anglican, I'm not really Anglican. You know what I mean?"

"I think so. Weak faith."

She grunted. "No faith. You've got a long argument to convince me otherwise, but I'll let you try, like I promised."

"Thank you. I appreciate that."

"Uh... *pozhaluysta*."

"Did you say '*pozhaluysta*'?"

"I think so. I hope so. Was it that bad?"

"No, it was fine. I understood. No problem. But when did you start to learn Russian?"

She paused, looked downward, and confessed. "When I realized I was in love with one."

Volkov's heart jumped from his chest. "Love? Do you believe that we are in love?"

As she looked up, her blush turned her cheeks beet-red. "Yes."

"That's good. That's very good. I was afraid I was getting sick. But now I know that my only disease is loving you, and I feel much better."

Though her face filled the screen, a man's voice rang from the laptop, revealing an invisible eavesdropper. "I heard you two lovebirds, and I think it's adorable!"

Danielle shouted. "Damn it, Jake! Hang up!"

Volkov yelled. "*Suka Blyad*, Jake!"

The American's laughter was mischievous. "Sorry! I never signed off, and I just overheard you in my stateroom. Don't worry. I don't think anyone else is on the line."

Frowning, Danielle raised her voice. "I don't believe you!"

"Oh, get over it. If you kids think this is a secret, you're fools. Everyone's aware of it. Come on, everyone's rooting for you two."

Volkov regained some composure. "I call you tomorrow, Danielle. Same time, without Jake."

"Yes. Without Jake, please!"

"I won't eavesdrop again. I promise. It was just too good an opportunity to ignore."

Volkov's tone was stern. "And Jake?"

Between laughs, the *Specter's* commander replied. "Yeah?"

"Bite me, you moron!

THE END

# EPILOGUE

A crest lifted Captain Sharifi, and using his height above sea level, he scanned his horizon. After drifting for hours, he saw a ship's masts and waved his arms. Uncertain if he'd been seen, he risked hoping for extraction from the water.

Until now, no aircraft had overflown him in a search and rescue effort, and no ships had arrived.

He reflected upon his predicament.

After his superior officers had been shot down, a chorus of captains had called for him to lead their attack formation.

Hungry to take out the *Xerses*, he'd accepted the lead position. Then, as he'd leveled and accelerated into his run, an alarm had sounded in his cockpit alerting him of the incoming MICA.

He'd had no chance.

The last missile of the final battle's last encounter had been his to absorb. It had struck behind his engine, crippling his F-16, but he'd bailed out.

During the slow drift to the water's surface, he'd noticed each limb still attached to his body and working. Hopeful of his rescue, he remained in high spirits.

Another crest lifted him, and he studied the seas in the direction of the masts. They were moving closer.

Rescuers were arriving.

Realizing he was at the mercy of whoever found him, he analyzed the worst-case scenario.

If the Yemenis took him, he'd become a detainee, although he recalled his leaders referring to his captured countrymen as prisoners of war, which theoretically entitled them to rights.

More importantly, Sharifi decided that being a prisoner of war would boost his career and free him from his father's influence.

Having been the only pilot–the only Emirati–to escape the ambush of Socotra and having prevented his F-16 from landing in enemy hands, he'd created a name for himself within the UAE Air Force. Then he'd returned into battle three more times, placing one of two laser-guided bombs on the doomed Yemeni *Osa* missile boat, shooting down an enemy drone, and leading the final charge against the mercenary transport ship.

His courage was giving him credibility, and he was certain that a nation hungry for heroes in the wake of a defeat would focus on the aviator who'd risked himself the most times.

Being a prisoner of war would assure it, he hoped.

After half an hour, the fishing trawler slowed beside him and lowered a ladder. Men above him leaned over the railing and yelled in his native language for him to climb.

Waterlogged, he felt his arms and legs becoming burdens, but his zeal to stand upon something solid fueled him upward. As he reached stanchions rising from the ship's deck, he grabbed them and felt hands tugging the back of his flight suit. "Who are you?"

A gruff voice carried the reply. "We'll ask the questions, pilot. Who are you?"

Unwilling to anger his newfound colleagues, the captain told the truth. "Captain Ali Sharifi, United Arab Emirates Air Force."

Surrounded by men carrying fishing spears, the man addressing him looked older than the rest. "We found him. Radio it in."

"Yes, sir." A younger sailor darted away.

The older man looked down at his captive. "Captain Sharifi, this is a Yemeni fishing vessel, and I'm its captain. I'll be taking you into custody and bringing you to the Yemeni military. Rise to your knees and place your hands behind your back."

Moving as ordered, Sharifi felt a zip-tie clamp around his wrists.

Then two men clasped him under his armpits.

"Get up, Captain Sharifi. We'll transport you to our wardroom, where you'll remain under guard until we reach Socotra."

As his fate came full circle to the small island, Sharifi chuckled.

The fisherman's captain scowled. "What's so funny?"

"You said you're taking me to Socotra."

"That's right. It's the closest landfall, and we have a group of Emirati detainees there already. Our military is giving your countrymen humane treatment, and you can expect the same, starting here. Nobody on this ship will hurt you."

"I appreciate it, since our nations are at war."

The captain grunted. "Not anymore. There's been a ceasefire between Yemeni and Emirati forces for more than two hours. If it endures, you may be home sooner than you think."

For the first time, Sharifi looked forward to getting back to work, and he hoped his next assignment would be a desk job.

## About the Author

*After graduating from the Naval Academy in 1991, John Monteith served on a nuclear ballistic missile submarine and as a top-rated instructor of combat tactics at the U.S. Naval Submarine School. He now works as an engineer when not writing.*

Join the Rogue Submarine fleet to get news, freebies, discounts, and your FREE Rogue Avenger bonus content!

# Rogue Submarine Series:

# Wraith Hunter Chronicles:

*WRATH OF THE ANGEL (2016)*
*PROPHECY OF ASHES (2018)*
*PROPHECY OF BLOOD (2018)*
*PROPHECY OF CHAOS (2018)*
*PROPHECY OF DUST (2018)*
*PROPHECY OF EDEN (2019)*

<u>John Monteith recommends:</u>

Graham Brown, author of The Gods of War.

Jeff Edwards, author of Sword of Shiva.

Thomas Mays, author of A Sword into Darkness.

Kevin Miller, author of Raven One.

Ted Nulty, author of Gone Feral.

# ROGUE NAVY

Copyright © 2020, 2021 by John R. Monteith

## Braveship Books

www.braveshipbooks.com

The tactics described in this book do not represent actual U.S. Navy or NATO tactics past or present. Also, many of the code words and some of the equipment have been altered to prevent unauthorized disclosure of classified material.

ISBN-13: 978-1-64062-106-0
Published in the United States of America

Made in the USA
Columbia, SC
04 February 2021

32225880R00129